Love and Hope

Love and Hope

Oby Cherian

apk publishers
BY WRITERS. FOR WRITERS.
www.apkpublishers.com

Copyright © Oby Cherian 2021

First edition: March 2021

Published by:
APK Publishers
5/301 Ved Vihar, Near Chandni Chowk,
Paud Road, Pune 411038
Mobile: +91-9822796490
Email: info@apkpublishers.com
URL: http://www.apkpublishers.com

Cover Design
Vinay Kuruvilla

ISBN-13: 9798739555403

Contents

Chapter 1

Leech Valley

"Shall we go to the Leech Valley, Amma?" It was the third time that Jasmine had asked the same question.

It was a sunny afternoon. The kind of day that tempted you to celebrate, even when you didn't feel like it. Usha relented. "Okay, Thangam," she said. "Put on your sandals and we will be on our way."

Leech Forest lay about a kilometre and a half further up into the mountains. It occupied a narrow valley beyond the Pachalur village across from where they were. You had to go through the village and up the next hill. An indistinct path by the side of the road took them through a crowd of cottonwood trees, and on to a wide expanse of grass interspaced with rocks. Standing here, it felt like you were on a shore, with the woods a vast green sea stretched out below you. At the further end of the meadow, rough steps hewn into the rock led them down into the jungle. Slowly, they descended into it and left the world behind.

At the bottom of the wide gully ran a playful stream of crystal clear water. It skipped across the rocks and leaped over a boulder into a bubbling pool of delight. It was so small, an adult could hardly have done much with it, but it was just right for Jasmine—her favourite spot. She sat chest deep in water and let the stream cascade over her head and shoulders. Tall trees spread a leafy canopy high above them. The stream and forest bed got no direct sunlight, but it was bright; the very air was suffused with a mystic green radiance.

As the afternoon wore on, things changed. Unknown to them, fickle weather had turned face. It had become darker, as though someone had dimmed the lights. "It's enough, Jasmine, you'll catch a cold; come out," shouted Usha.

Cocooned in her watery nest, Jasmine pretended not to hear. Soon, her mother's strong arms reached into her retreat and pulled her out. She felt smothered as a bath towel descended over her head; her scalp and hair were given a good rub. The distant rumble of thunder made her mother stop momentarily.

"There is rain coming, we must hurry, Jasmine," said Usha as she helped Jasmine into her clothes. They went up the forest slope briskly. It somehow began to become bright again. When they had almost reached the open meadow, Jasmine ran ahead; something had caught her attention. Sunlight had burst in through a rent in clouds and bathed the clearing with gold. From below where her mother stood, it was as though Jasmine had walked onto a floodlit stage. She was chasing a red and black swallow-tailed butterfly. She reached for the sky as it winged its way out of reach.

She glanced at her mother before taking off again around a clump of rocks. This time, it was a pair of much smaller butterflies. Their wings were lilac around the centre, melding into a lemon yellow border. They cavorted in wild circles around each other, like a pair of binary stars. They did not let up one bit on their whirling dance as they gracefully swung away from gleeful hands that reached out to them. They disappeared over a clump of thick bushes at the edge of the meadow, leaving Jasmine staring after them in awe and wonder.

By this time, Usha had come up behind her.

"Don't chase the butterflies away, Thangam."

"Do you think they were friends, Amma? Why did they go around each other?"

"Maybe they love each other, Thangam."

Then, after a thoughtful gap, and almost to herself, Usha said, "Love makes you do silly things, but it's what keeps the world going around."

Jasmine did not know what made the world go around, but she threw her arms around her mother's waist and said, "I love you, Amma!"

The rain caught up with them just as they reached the gates of the campus. Jasmine had to be wiped dry all over again. But she did not seem to mind as she smiled up at her mother and gave her another hug.

Later that night, Usha sat by herself at her desk. They had returned from Leech Valley three hours ago. It was now three weeks since Suresh had gone, and two years since their wedding day. In her thoughts, the dates and hours had ceased to exist, except as memorials to the life they had shared.

Usha sat, hunched and immobile. A small lamp lit up a circle of light within which her delicate hands held a letter. And now, as she straightened and stared vacantly into space, her silhouette rose above the array of dim shadows that lined the opposite wall. If anybody had seen her outline at that moment, it would have been hard to forget. This face seemed to tell a thousand tales of timeless sadness, and yet, with high cheeks and pinched nose held up, it had a defiant beauty that whispered 'hope'.

Jasmine had gone to sleep and all was quiet. Outside, beyond the fence, night sounds drifted in from the dark—the chirping of crickets, the occasional croak of a toad. Far away, a dog barked in fits and starts. Usha had not moved; her eyes were still not focussed on anything in particular, but those gateways to the mind bore witness to the grief inside, and filled up with tears. When she looked down at the letter, it overflowed like molten wax and dropped down on the page, adding yet another smudge.

My dearest Usha,

If Dr Ravikumar has given you this letter and you are reading these words, it means that I am well on my way.

In time, she folded the letter, returned it to its place in the drawer, switched off the light and climbed into bed. She lay awake in the darkness for a long time, and finally tossed and turned her way into fitful sleep.

Many hours later, that familiar dream came knocking.

They formed the apices of a triangle, the three stars that looked down at her from the southern sky. One of them was smaller than the rest and very faint. The smell of the sea was everywhere. Salt spray peppered her cheeks and mingled with her tears, and both of them tasted the same when they came down over her lips. Suddenly, the boat hit a swell and took a jolt that jarred her spine; the next moment, she was in the water. Now going down, she could still see the triangle of stars through the blue water, which soon turned aquamarine, deep green and inky grey. She felt her heart sink within her and find depths that her body could never reach. *I will never see him again,* was what she thought.

But this time, it was not her father's face that came floating up into her subconscious, it was Suresh's. She could see him clearly, and then it faded away and all was dark once more.

The sun came in through the eastern window and draped itself in wavy rectangles over the table and across the floor. But it was not the sun that awoke Usha the next morning. Grubby little hands caressed her face.

"Amma, I am hungry," whined Jasmine.

Like most children whose natural rhythms have not been tampered by the trappings of civilisation, Jasmine had woken up with the dawn. She slid out of bed and walked into a new day. She had curly black locks hanging over both ears and dark brown shining eyes. Her crème and chocolate skin was not as dark as her mother's, but not as light as her father's (her biological father, whom the child could hardly remember). Most times, she was a vivacious little creature who could charm the scowl off the most unfriendly face. She made them smile, every one of them.

She went looking for her doll and found him face down on the steel trunk that stood in a corner of the living room. She picked him up on the way to the sofa, climbed on and knelt beside the window. She placed him on the sill, looked out blankly and said, "Will you also die one day, Tinto? Will you become thin like Suresh Appa?

"My Appa died before I knew him. Grandmother says it's my bad luck because I was born on a Saturday. Is that true, Tinto? Am I unlucky? Is it unlucky to be born on a Saturday? When were you born, Tinto?"

Strange and weighty thoughts for a four-year-old, but have them she did. Outside, the deep resonant call of a coucal made her smile, and then the jolly face of Sindhu her friend came to mind. She forgot all about death and dying. She stretched both her arms high above her. *Why does it feel so good to stretch?* she wondered. Soon, her stomach stirred inside her, reminding her that she was hungry. She gently laid Tinto on the sofa and went trudging into the next room to wake up her mother.

Usha stirred, opened her eyes and looked into her daughter's face.

"Oh, Thangam! Have you been awake for long? I am sorry. Amma slept late today," she said apologetically as she sat up, raised her hands and tied up her loose hair into a rough knot. She got up and walked to the bathroom. She splashed some water on her gaunt face and looked in the mirror. She looked a sight! *I will have to hurry*, thought Usha. She had a long day ahead—breakfast for both of them and then she would have to start packing. This was a large residence meant for doctors, but now that Suresh was not there, she was not entitled to occupy it any longer. Already, they had been kind to allow her to stay three weeks. She would have to shift house today, to one of the nurse's quarters, about 200 metres away.

Perhaps it is just as well I am moving, she thought to herself. It would have been difficult to be here in this place she had shared with Suresh. It would be easier to start afresh in a new house.

After breakfast, Jasmine went out into the garden with her dolls and Usha was left alone. She went around from room to room, not knowing where to begin. Memories beckoned to her from every corner.

Yes, she would start with the kitchen—where there would be little to remind her of Suresh—that would be the easiest. So she set to work; the pots and pans would go into an old carton and the bottles into another. In half an hour, she was almost done with the kitchen, only the tidying-up to do. This she would leave to the men. Veeran, the ward aide, had promised to take half a day's leave to help her shift.

She took a break, went out and sat on the porch. She heard the nine-thirty bus labouring up the road. Murali, her brother, would be on it. He lived in Kariyampatti, a small village on the plains, and was now on his way up to help his sister shift house. The road started from Oddanchatram, the market town at the foot of the mountains. It slithered up the lower range of hills before levelling off across the Parapalar valley at 1,000 feet. Having crossed the basin, it skirted the lake and climbed, taking nine hairpin bends to the high ranges. Pachalur at 4,000 feet was the first large village on this mountain road that reached further into the Western Ghats of southern India.

The morning sun seemed to give everything an extra dose of life. The leaves reflected a vibrant green, the bees buzzed around with added zest. Usha looked to her left to see a sunbird flit across to a patch of garden, where it settled on a stem and deftly dipped its long beak into one of the red trumpet-shaped flowers. Behind this patch of coral flowers was the pine tree, and towering above it in the distance was the peak of the Boar Mountain. Wild boars had been sighted there in the past. How often she had sat here with Suresh.

The Hill People's Cooperative Hospital and its campus was spread across five acres of gently sloping woods. It overlooked the Pachalur village on its southern side and reached up north to a broad ridge where the land fell away gradually into the Reserve Forests below. The hospital occupied the lower ground and the staff quarters took up the higher end of the campus. The doctors' residences stood towards the eastern edge of the ridge, where the drop beyond was precipitous and therefore, the view was incomparable. This was where Usha now sat. The whole of the Parapalar valley was set out before you. Her eyes settled on the silvery blue surface of the lake far below.

A river had once meandered through this vast valley, disappearing over its north-western edge, running through a narrow gorge before plummeting over a two-hundred-feet waterfall to the flatlands below. Forty years ago, they had thrown a gravity dam across this running water at the narrow mouth of the gorge, piling back the water to form the swollen Y-shaped lake that now shimmered in the distance. The valley held this body of water in its hollow, as a cupped hand would hold a bit of precious oil.

I am going to miss this view, thought Usha as she went back into the house. She got a couple of suitcases down from the ledge in the storeroom and carried them to the bedroom. She opened the cupboard and arranged her clothes into one of the suitcases. Then there were Jasmine's dresses and finally, in the topmost shelf, Suresh's pile. She held a couple of his underclothes close to her and thought a faint whisper of his scent still lingered there. What would she do with his clothes? She would allow Murali to choose the best of them and leave the rest for Veeran.

After the cupboard, she shifted to the table. Piled on the floor to one side were Suresh's papers. Copies of review articles, notes on various topics, some letters, a few papers he had helped publish, important memos. All of them were important, not just the memos. Important: until a few weeks ago. All very precious: until a few months ago. Papers that would never have been treated so carelessly now lay in an untidy heap, waiting for the fire or rubbish dump. *How meaningless it all seemed*, thought Usha. How irrelevant things became with the passing of time. In a few weeks, everything was forgotten as though someone never was, except in the minds of a few dear ones, where remembrances were treasured in bits and pieces for another few years.

There was the trunk full of medical books, which she would donate to the hospital library. The stethoscope she would keep. The other diagnostic tools she would give to Dr Ravikumar.

Soon, Murali and Veeran arrived and things moved faster. A trolley was used to shift the boxes, four or five at a time to her new home. By 4 pm, the house was empty, except for the bare furniture that belonged to it.

I have spent some of the best days of my life here, Usha thought as she went from room to room for one last time.

She felt cramped in the new house. After shifting the cartons and boxes to their appropriate places, Veeran departed. She unpacked a few essentials and then made some tea. They sat on the small portico, sipping the tea and watching the sun go down.

"Do you have to go today, Anna?" Usha asked Murali.

"I have to catch the seven-thirty bus. I promised Shanthi I would be back tonight."

Poor Murali, thought Usha. Shanthi had him on a line, but she was efficient and hard-working and looked after their parents and his children well. What more could one ask for?

With a thin, weather-beaten face and balding hair going grey in patches, Murali looked every one of his 39 years, and perhaps a few more. He had a pointed moustache, sharp intense eyes and a long scar on his left forearm.

He saw her now looking steadily at that same scar, but knew her mind was far away. She had probably drifted back to the time when there was no scar and their lives had lay unblemished before them. To a time, when there were no wounds to remember and their spirits were free.

"What are you thinking about, Thankachi?" he asked.

"Oh, nothing," lied Usha.

"Come on, you know that is not true."

"Yes, that's not true. I was daydreaming. I was once again playing 'Kokan', the game you taught me."

"Did I teach you that, Usha?"

"You did, Annan. You would have much rather been with your friends, but you suffered being away from them to play with me."

By this time, Usha's eyes were full. Murali wanted to reach out his hand to her, but for a second, the thought went through his mind, *Was it safe to touch her?*

But the next moment, his heart had overruled his mind; his hand went out to hold hers.

"It will be alright, Usha; I just have not come prepared to stay today. Another day, we will all come: Shanthi, the children, mother and father as well."

Usha wiped her wet cheeks with the back of her hands and then they both sat, steeped in thought, watching the last glow of pink fade from the sky behind the hills. "Perhaps the game will be forgotten," she said suddenly. "We must teach the children to play 'Kokan'."

Chapter 2

Paradise Lost

A smooth stone rose into the air, while nimble fingers quickly reached for a few more from the sand. Each stone had to be snatched from the ground without disturbing any of the others.

Eight-year-old Usha was playing Kokan, and she was playing it solitaire.

Usha lived with her parents and an elder brother. They lived on an island. An 'island' makes you think you are never far from sandy beaches and pounding surf. But this was no ordinary island. At its broadest, it was almost 300 kilometres across. Usha and her family lived in a large inland village in north-western Sri Lanka. The population was predominantly Tamil in this part of the country. The sea was far away. In fact, she had seen it only twice during her entire life.

This island nation had almost been paradise once; 'Ceylon' was what it was called then and it rested like an emerald pendant around the neck of the vast subcontinent.

Things were different now; the British had left decades ago. Today was 12 August 1977. Marauding mobs of Sinhalese youth were at this moment running amok on the streets of its capital, Colombo. They attacked Tamil houses and chased down those who managed to escape. They broke, pillaged and set on fire what was left. This riot and others that followed left at least a few thousands dead, and a hundred times that number homeless and destitute. Another band of exiles was born. Another refugee people, left to roam the earth in search of a place to lay their heads.

The smouldering animosity between the two communities was soon to ignite into widespread armed conflict. This island would no more be the paradise it was. It would slip deeper into civil war and hang like another teardrop on the face of an aching world.

Oblivious to all this, Usha continued to play. One more stone rose into the air; by the time it came down again, she had picked the rest of the stones off the ground and her hand was ready to catch the one coming down.

Usha was getting good at it. Soon, she would be able to manage a whole hand (all eleven) in three throws. When Murali annan came, she would show him. How proud that would make him.

Later that evening, Murali came back from school and she showed him her prowess at the game he had taught her more than a year ago. Then together, they went into their house.

It was a small home with wooden rafters and a tiled roof. A ten-by-eight feet room for her parents, a similar one for the two children on the opposite side. A bigger room connecting the two served as the dining room, drawing room or whatever other room you wanted to call it.

A tiny wood-burning kitchen jutted out like an appendage at the back. You could see that it had not been built along with the rest. With a tin roof and the floor at a lower level, it was an obvious add-on. There was a little more than an acre of land around the house, most of it taken up with coconut palms except for an open bit at the back, away from the road, next to the fence. This was where they grew yam and lentils.

With the smell of fish wafting in from the kitchen, Usha could hardly wait for dinner. They sat around cross-legged on mats with stainless steel plates before them. Mother served the rice and Sodhi—a fish curry made with coconut milk and saffron. It would have been difficult for any of them to imagine life without fish and coconuts. After the meal, a few chores had to be done and then she said her prayers to the family deity before retiring to her room.

The mats they slept on were rolled up in a corner; another corner held her brother's possessions—a two-foot steel box and a large board that served as his desk. She went to her corner where a wooden shelf held their clothes, her slate and a cardboard box. She sat down and wrote a few pages from her textbook. Then she watched a gecko as it stealthily stalked an earwig on the wall. Then she daydreamed. Then she opened the box and took out her pencils with a contented smile. She had her family, her Kokan stones, her rag doll with the coconut shell face; she even had her precious box of six colour pencils that had come on her last birthday. *Yes*, she thought to herself, *she had everything.*

Usha's father, Muthiah, was a driver in a private transport company and her mother a teacher. They were not rich, but they were happy. Her father augmented the family income by the bit of agriculture he undertook in their plot of land. They could not afford hired labour and so, the whole family pitched in for the work. Usha, being the smallest, was kept busy as an errand person. Her little legs would run willingly to fetch water, some rope and a box of nails or a jute gunny sack.

The coconut palms were their main source of income. In one ingenious way or another, every part of the palm came into use. Even the leaves could be woven into flat sheets, which could serve to make thatched roofs and rough enclosures. Weaving the palm leaves was something that Usha could do, along with the others, and just as well as them.

Four years went by.

Usha no longer played Kokan, but she still had her raggedy doll and her pencils. But there was one thing she missed. She missed Murali, who had gone off to join the rebel forces almost six months ago. They seldom heard from him.

Ever since Murali had left, a pall of sadness had descended on the household. Her parents did not talk much anymore. Each carried their own secret fears for him and their faces betrayed the burdens that their minds carried inside them. Her mother would occasionally give her a weak smile and then quickly draw her close so she would not see it fade away.

Every morning saw their mother with flowers at the temple, praying for her son, and today, 17 June 1980, was no different. She had two lessons to take for her primary school class before she came for lunch. She had taken leave for the rest of the day to catch up with some work around the house.

Usha came in from school at half-past three. It was too hot to visit her friend two houses away, so she stayed inside and finished her homework. As the hot sultry afternoon wore on, dark pregnant clouds gathered overhead. Supper that night was accompanied by the steady rhythm of rain.

After the cleaning, washing and putting away was done, she went and sat on the window sill and stared into the dark wetness outside. A bolt of lightning gave her the fleeting silvery images of waving branches and little rivulets.

Her father was not religious and had little use for prayer, so she felt it was up to her to augment the petitions that her mother made to the powers above. She went to the little alcove in the wall that held the family deity. Her mother had lit the small earthen oil lamp at sundown before any other lights were put on. Nobody had noticed it go out. Usha carefully trimmed the wick again over its spout and lit it. The flame sprang up and then swayed with the draught from the window, catching her intense face in a wavering glow of gentle light. Her palms were pressed together in supplication, as she marshalled all the concentration that her young mind could generate.

Bring my brother back, she prayed silently.

Little did they know that tonight, they would have him back, but not in the way that they would have liked.

Chapter 3

War

The 'diving board' was the perfect place from which to launch an ambush. Yes, that was what it was called, but this one was not poised over a swimming pool. Hinged from the trunk of a palm, it hung suspended twenty feet above the green undergrowth of the monsoon forest.

The palm was carefully chosen from a host of its neighbours. It lay about 10 feet to one side of a path that led out into a sun-drenched clearing hundred feet further south. The ground between the palm and the bright area was densely wooded with tall trees, thickets of bamboo and a web of vines that leaped from branch to branch. Further on, a huge lichen-covered mahogany stood like a sentinel guarding the way. All these seemed to conspire together to complete the camouflage and hide the diving board from anyone using the path. Anybody walking in from the brightness would have to get adjusted to the muted light.

And at this moment, three soldiers were about to do just that. It was a little after 3 pm on the 16th of June. The soldiers were part of a company coming in from the south. This campaign was codenamed 'Operation Green Thumb' and it was designed to reclaim the forests from rebel hands.

This bunch had broken with the rest of their platoon that morning, as they fanned out in smaller groups. They had not encountered any resistance all morning, but half an hour ago, they had heard gunfire a few miles to their left. From then on, they wore their caution on their sleeves; they had their fingers on the triggers with the rifles held upright in readiness.

They were not the only ones who had heard the shots. Murali and his senior comrade, Mohan, were on the diving board, and they had heard too. These two had seen the soldiers as they emerged on the farther side of the clearing; they now stood alert and waiting, Mohan in front and Murali behind and to his left.

As the soldiers came nearer, a knot of fear began to tighten somewhere between Murali's chest and abdomen. Everything had been agreed upon and they each knew what to do. Murali would aim for the last one and Mohan would go for the other two. They would start firing simultaneously when the first soldier crossed the thin rubber tree on the other side of the road, about fifty feet away.

As the first volley came in, the soldiers hardly knew what had hit them and where it came from. The first one crumbled to the ground almost instantly, the second let out a cry of pain and lay writhing on the ground.

By this time, the last man had taken cover behind some bushes and the trunk of the rubber tree, from where he returned fire with deadly accuracy.

Just before he let out the first shot, Mohan had instinctively gone into a semi-crouch to maintain his balance and aim.

On the other hand, Murali stood almost upright. The AK47 shuddered in his hand. The palm shook and swayed with the recoil. Murali lost his balance and the bullets splayed out harmlessly into space. As he stumbled back, the return fire came at him fast and furious. They came at hundred rounds a minute, for that was how furiously an assault rifle let go of its ammunition. One ricocheted off the frame of the platform with a metallic 'ping' that jarred his ears. Searing pain shot through his left forearm as another grazed his skin, leaving behind a two-inch lacerated wound. Another centimetre or two, and it would have found and shattered his bone.

"Down," cried Mohan. The warning was taken, but rather involuntarily. Murali fell back against the trunk of the palm, slid down and came to rest on his haunches. There he sat in a daze.

The diving board provided a vantage point, from which it was not difficult to see the last soldier behind the thin rubber tree; most of his body covered only by bushes. Mohan was almost fully prone now; he raised himself on one elbow, lifted his rifle, fired and found his mark.

A strange mixture of burning cordite and blood reached Murali's nose as an uneasy silence descended around him.

After a while, a soft groan sounded somewhere near. Very near. Slowly, his eyes focussed on the motionless body sprawled out in front of him. Mohan's left arm hung flaccidly over the side of the platform.

Murali crawled up and knelt beside Mohan, cradled his head and turned him gently on his side. Underneath was a spreading pool of dark blood that startled Murali. He turned him further onto his lap and bent down to hug him.

"Anna!" he cried in quiet anguish. "Anna, don't leave me." At this, the dying man seemed to stir a little.

He opened his hazy eyes, "Murali," he whispered, "it is finished for me. You must continue. We must have a land of our own."

Everything was silent again. Slowly, Mohan's eyelids drooped and closed; his head dropped back and his body went limp in Murali's arms.

The boy sat there, dazed and pale. After a while, his lips started quivering and his body shivered uncontrollably. His eyes looked around wildly in panic. With an effort, he took in great gulps of air, which gradually calmed him down. Slowly, he raised himself up, ripped off a piece from the bottom of his shirt and tied it crudely around his bleeding forearm with the help of his good arm and his teeth. Then he shinned his way down the palm.

Murali gazed around at the dead soldiers, their well-fed bodies, helmets, uniform and shining boots—and then, sadly down at his own threadbare sandals. He could not help noticing the contrast. A piece of tape, which held up his patched-up trousers, was all he had for a belt around his scrawny middle. Nothing on his head, except a mop of untidy hair. There he stood for a while, his back stooped and eyes staring vacantly into space. Suddenly, he straightened up, as though something had abruptly cleared in his mind. By all conventions, he should have proceeded north down the path and regrouped with fellow rebels at their rendezvous point two kilometres away, but Murali had other plans.

He quickly walked over to one of the soldiers, undid the knapsack on his back and swung it over his own shoulder. He tried on one, and then another, pair of enemy boots for fit, but his own sandals he carefully stowed away in the knapsack. He took a couple of long hungry gulps from the aluminium water can found on one of the soldiers, and then struck out away from the path into the jungle in a north-westerly direction. There was now only one thought that filled his entire being—home.

Ten kilometres to the west lay the A2 highway. It ran through shifting battlefronts and then all the way to Trincomalee. He knew he should not get on to it this far south, for there was no saying whose territory you would land on. He would keep going northwest until he could hear the sound of distant traffic, and then he would head north, staying parallel to the road. He stumbled on around trees, over thorn bushes and vines. At last, he heard the whine of a distant truck.

By this time, the sun was setting somewhere in the west. He foraged around and found a long stick that would help him travel at night. Now he needed a rest. Fifty feet to the right was a large patch of bamboo. He squeezed between the long stems and found a rather cosy space just large enough for him to sit in. He settled down on the floor, leaned his back against the trunks and looked up; high above was a bit of sky. It felt like he was in a deep well, but it also felt secure as though he was in a cradle. He explored the contents of the knapsack and came up with some biscuits, which he wolfed down eagerly. He took another drink from the canteen, which was now almost empty. He looked up at the pink sky that was rapidly turning grey even while he watched.

He had turned eighteen two weeks ago. If he were at home, he would have had a party, or at least some sweets for his friends. These and other such thoughts swam lazily through his mind.

He must have fallen asleep, for when he awoke, it was dark. From the opening above, a single star looked down on him. The night about him was alive with sounds—chirping crickets, whining beetles. The bamboo stems swayed intermittently and creaked against each other. It was difficult to say how long he had slept, or what time it was.

Could have rescued a handsome watch from one of the soldiers, he thought to himself. But it was too late for that.

His bottom and legs felt numb; he slowly shook them awake and gingerly stood up. He would have to keep moving. He gathered up his things, squeezed between the bamboo trunks and out into the open. He looked around, orienting himself. There were the three Palmyra palms he remembered crossing; that would be south. He adjusted his backpack and rifle, all the while listening. Soon, he heard engines, quite a distance to the left of him. Satisfied with his bearings, he set out in the direction that he thought was north. He would have to keep the sounds of traffic on the left.

He travelled cautiously and noiselessly. In places where there was a lot of grass, he would poke around with the long stick in front of him as he went. Often, a rustle in the grass would make him stop. He kept on for hours and stopped when he felt he could not go on any longer. He was thirsty, but the aluminium canteen was now empty; more than this, he was tired to the bone. He stepped aside into some tall grass and stomped around until he had made himself a bed of sorts. He lay down wearily and was soon overtaken by sleep.

He awoke to the sound of birds—a flock of mynas squealed at one another as they flew by, some playful babblers foraged among the dry leaves and hopped around a tall cactus. He stood on his knees and peered over the top of the grass. It was just light enough for him to see a grove of mango trees some distance away. Murali reckoned he had travelled sufficiently north to be out of the government-held territory. Now he would go west, hit the road and try to hitch a ride.

He turned to his left and made his way through dense vegetation; tall hardwoods ruled the roost here, with vines and creepers making up the floor. After half an hour, the forest thinned out into grasslands. He crossed a dry ditch and up onto a ridge. He looked for some signs of a stagnant pool of water. As far as his eyes could see, there was none. Thirst was now his dominant craving, although a tinge of anxiety was creeping up inside him. He kept trudging along, listening carefully as he went.

He passed a paddy field, but the grain was almost ripe and there was no water in it. He went through a forest of teak, and then down into a gully at the bottom of which lay a dry streambed. By this time, his thirst was unbearable. He frantically followed it for a distance and then retraced his steps, beyond the point where he had first met it. He must have gone about a hundred feet when he saw, between a sand bar and a great big rock, a tiny pool of dirty green water. Normally, he would not have washed his clothes in it. But now, he did not think twice before he bent down and slowly dipped his canteen sidewards into the water, keeping the nozzle just below the surface, to get the cleanest top layer. When the can was about half full, he took it up, looked at it apprehensively and then quickly put it to his lips. It tasted muddy and smelt like rotten cabbage, and by the time he stopped drinking, he had a fair amount of grit and algae in his mouth. Yet, it was water and he felt a relief that was difficult to describe. He spat out the dirt in his mouth and went back down the stream. He decided to follow it, for it would probably bring him to the road. In this he was not wrong, for presently he heard the welcome roar of a motorcycle. It did not seem far away. The streambed took a sharp right and joined a small river. He turned to see it disappear under a brick arch bridge. Over this bridge ran A2— the road to Trincomalee.

Snaking along one edge of the river was a tiny stream of clear water. Murali washed out his canteen, filled it up, rinsed his mouth and drank to his heart's content. He walked up to the bridge, lowered his head and got under it; there he sat and waited.

The sun was up by now and beat down on the asphalt, but where he was, it was still cool. He stayed there comfortably, till the shadows began to lengthen again. Then he decided it was time to move. There was something coming down the road, but it was coming from the north. Murali sat still and as it came nearer, he swallowed hard and felt his heart beat faster. The truck, or whatever it was, rumbled overhead and then passed on, its sound slowly fading away into the stillness of the afternoon.

Another 15 minutes passed before he heard the distant moan of an engine. This time, going in the right direction. He got himself ready. He took off his boots and put his own sandals back on his feet. He shoved the knapsack, canteen and the boots into a hollow between two boulders and covered it over with sand and brushwood. He got out from under the bridge and calmly walked up the bank of the river onto the road. He turned and walked north, as though he had been on the road for a while. He glanced back and saw that it was a bus.

He passed a milestone that said Trincomalee 52 kilometres. So Wagera would be only 37 kilometres from where he was. If all went well, he would be there by the time it was dark. Three kilometres, on a small road heading west from Wagera, was Dibara and all that he held dear.

He turned around and waved his rifle. By now, the vehicle was near enough to see more details. The old pug-nosed bus was packed to its seams with passengers; in the front, next to the driver, sat two rebel soldiers. The bus slowed down with a screech of brakes and rattled to a stop.

The rebel fighters jumped down from the bus and approached him. Murali held out his arm to reveal a tiny tattoo with his number. They took it down and asked him, "What is the business?"

"Have a message for Colonel Anton from segment 16."

"OK," they said suspiciously, after looking at each other for a moment.

They waved him to the back door of the bus. He got on and squeezed himself up the crowded stairway to the top step. There he stood, hemmed in by a perspiring mass of humanity. A few looked at him with admiration, but most ignored him. Murali relaxed when he saw there was nobody he could recognise, but not entirely, because every once in a while, one of the rebel soldiers would look back to see where he was. No doubt they were going to keep a close watch on him.

The bus slowly shook and swayed its way to Wagera with an endless number of stops in-between. It stopped longer at Wagera, where he and most of the passengers got down to stretch themselves or have a snack. This would be the time to make his getaway, but there was no way he could pull it off. All the time they were on the ground, one of the armed men was always watching him like a hawk. When finally the bus horn blared to beckon its own back, he thought he would cry. With an effort, he blinked back his tears and nonchalantly climbed on with the rest of them. But he was careful to keep to the stairs. Not the last one though, for that would attract too much attention from the hawks. *Now, what would he do?* he wondered, as he worried and waited.

The evening sun made him feel hot and sticky, especially when the bus stopped to exchange passengers. Three kilometres beyond Wagera, the bus came to a grinding halt; ahead was a line of vehicles, whose end he could not see; there seemed to be smoke rising into the sky some distance ahead. The two rebel soldiers jumped down from the bus and went forwards briskly, skirting around vehicles, rifles held up in readiness.

Murali knew his time had come. He took a deep breath and pushed out of the bus as though he were following the other two soldiers. Once on the ground, he took three quick steps, stopped, turned and broke for the bushes by the side of the road. With one bound, he was over them. He ran across a dry field, while behind him, someone on the bus raised an alarm.

Murali climbed over a barbed-wire fence around a haystack and into a large cowshed. He ran between two rows of startled cows, out through the back door and made for a large field of tall maize that stood above his head. He plunged in just as, in the distance, a commotion started from the road towards him. He waded furiously through the maize for about fifty feet, then he backtracked a dozen steps before deftly parting the tall stalks on his left without breaking them. He lifted his left leg high through the gap and leapt sidewards, leaving an unbroken stretch of maize behind him. He pushed on at right angles to his original path until he heard his pursuers spill out of the cowshed. Then he stood motionless, hardly daring to breathe; if his heartbeat was as loud as it seemed to him, they could have heard it a furlong away.

The lead soldier ran to the spot in the maize field where he saw the stalks were slightly parted and plunged in, following the trail of ruffled grain. By the time he emerged on the farther side, others had come around the field, hoping to cut Murali off. Some way ahead, the mooing of a cow caught their attention. The animal looked restless, as it strained at its rope and stood away from the coconut palm to which it was tied. Next to the palm was a farmhouse. Most of the crowd and the soldiers ran to the farmhouse and went in by a gap into a walled-off courtyard. An old lady sat there on the veranda steps, winnowing a 'morum' of paddy. She looked up in fright. The 'morum' loosened from her hands and slid to the floor as she stood up shakily and moved back to lean her spine against the pillars that held the roof up.

"Don't be afraid," said the soldier. "Did you see a young man with a gun come by?"

"No," she replied, "I have been here for the last 15 minutes and saw nothing."

This seemed to satisfy them, as they backed out and went around the house. Across a mud fence was a field of sugarcane big enough for a man to hide in. "He could have gone into that," said one passenger. The soldier leapt across the fence and looked up and down the first line of cane. Nothing was out of place. After a few minutes of searching around, they turned back.

Meanwhile, some of the others had gone gingerly around the cornfields; none dared enter. Looking for a man in a two-acre maize field was tiresome any way, but this one being armed and desperate, it would have been a perilous affair. By this time, they could hear the blaring of horns and the rumbling of engines from the highway. The traffic had resumed and the others were waiting.

After talking to one another, the soldiers decided to abandon the search. In frustration, one of them turned and sprayed a hail of gunfire into the standing grain, taking in about one-sixth of a circle. Had Murali been in its arc, he would probably have taken a bullet.

"We will get him in a day or two," they said aloud as the crowd trickled back to the bus.

Murali was now alone, but he did not allow himself to relax until the last of the vehicles had lumbered away and silence reigned around him. Then he collapsed and fell back, taking a swath of maize with him. He closed his eyes and lay there, breathing heavily and trembling through every limb. It was a quarter of an hour before he looked around him.

Even though the evening was getting on, there was still too much light and too many houses and farms around. He would have to wait for darkness again. He reached out for a cob of maize presenting itself just inches from his face, peeled away its coverings roughly and bit down on its lily-white kernels. The maize was not ripe and as he chewed, it tasted like raw milk and flour, but he knew it would nourish him.

He lay on his side, waiting, half asleep yet watchful. Clouds were gathering above him, but not enough to hide the sunlight that poured in from the west. Somewhere, there must be silver-lined clouds and a glorious sunset. But he could not see it from where he lay; all he saw right above him was a black mass of clouds that seemed to grow darker and angrier by the minute. A flock of egrets flew by effortlessly, in perfect formation. In a few minutes came a disorderly horde of crows, cawing and flapping along. *What a difference!* he thought. The egrets took the long fluid strokes of a master swimmer, while what the crows achieved looked like the dog-paddle of novices. Somebody had come to untie the cow, for he could hear her bells tinkle.

The night had settled in firmly, when Murali finally crept out from his hideout. The farmhouse lights were going off one by one. Going to the highway would be dangerous. He would head south along the farmlands and come on to the small road that led west from Wagera. Had he been able to get off at Wagera, this was the road he would have taken.

He went quietly, keeping clear of the houses, across paddy fields, over fences and walls. Once in a while, Murali heard a dog bark hesitantly, but none came close to sight.

The next brick wall was higher than usual. He climbed it and just as he was dropping down on the other side, the beast came upon him from his left side. Murali did not want to shoot, for this would attract too much attention. Instinctively, he crouched, thrust his hands forwards with fingers held out like claws bared his teeth and snarled menacingly. This somehow stopped the dog short. It locked its eyes on him and continued a low guttural growl. They must have stood there face to face for almost a minute, trying to stare each other down. Ultimately, the canine looked down and backed away. As Murali rose to his full height, the animal turned around and loped off into the darkness, barking defiantly even as he went.

Lights came on in a house about a hundred and fifty yards away, but by this time, Murali was on to the next property and running as fast as he could make it. He crossed yet another compound before he slowed down. Another hour, and many dog barks later, he finally came to the familiar road. He climbed up to it, knelt down on its gravelled surface and sobbed like a child. It was like finding a long-lost friend. It would be only two kilometres to Dibara. But he did not want to reach the village. He would turn off onto the side road just before reaching the village and then down the alley between Kumar's house and the tailor's shop. He would pass by the godown and a couple of neighbours; then he would climb over the last fence and into his own backyard.

The first raindrops, like tiny beads, gently stung his arms and face. Then as he trudged along, curtains of water fell around him, but he did not notice it one bit for he was almost home now.

Chapter 4

Flight

It was well past 11 o'clock and they had all gone to sleep. It was dark everywhere, except for a box of light in the wall, where stood the little lamp that Usha had lit. It flickered dimly now, drawing on the last bit of oil, defying the darkness and keeping a lonely vigil for all of them.

Above the sound of the rain, Usha's mother thought she heard a faint knocking on the back door. She lay still; she thought it may be the dog rubbing himself on the raised edge of the door. But no, it came again and this time more distinctly. Two clear sharp raps. She nudged her husband awake.

"There is someone at the back door," she said.

"What!" he snapped, annoyed at having been woken up. "It must be the dog," he muttered.

"No!" she replied. "Listen." They sat up. It came once more. Two unmistakable taps on the door.

They got up, switched on the lights and went into the middle room.

"Who is that?" Muthiah asked loudly. His voice displaying more confidence than he actually had.

The reply surprised them.

"It is me, Appa," said a tired voice that they would have recognised anywhere, any time. How often they had longed to hear it.

Muthiah rushed to the kitchen door, pulled back the bolt and threw the door open. A wet dishevelled figure ambled in from the dark. His wiry frame was smattered with dirt and leaves. He wore a rough bandage on his left forearm.

As they fell into each other's arms, the Kalashnikov that Murali was holding clattered to the floor between them. By this time, Usha was awake. She opened the door a crack and peeked through. Father and son were held together in an embrace. Subdued sobs punctuated their breath; their chests heaved against each other. Usha saw the rifle on the floor at their feet, with its barrel at an angle, pointing menacingly in her direction.

Their mother stood a few feet behind, leaning on the wall. She had bunched up the hem of her sari and held it against her mouth, in an effort to smother the weeping that lay waiting inside.

It was quite a while before the commotion died down, and with it the rain. The ladies went back into their rooms, while Murali and his father sat and discussed his predicament. Soon, they seemed to have come to some agreement and Muthiah went into his room.

Usha heard their hushed voices and bits and pieces of the conversation before she drifted back to sleep. The only thing she could remember was Murali's anguished tone telling his father, "I can't go back, Papa, I can't; you don't know what they will do to me."

While Usha slept on, various things happened that night. It was only many years later that Murali told her.

When Muthiah emerged from his room, his face was set, as though some definite plan had consolidated in his mind.

Meanwhile, Murali had taken off his clothes and wore an old shirt and 'sarong'.

"Let's get to work," his father said urgently. "Bundle the clothes you came in and bring them with the gun."

They went out through the back door. Grabbing a spade from the yard, they wound their way back through the coconut grove and stopped short of the vegetable patch.

They went to work in the faint light of a half moon. Taking turns, they dug a 3-foot trench.

"Put them in," his father ordered.

The metal stock and magazine shimmered dully as Murali held the weapon close to his chest. He closed his eyes for a moment, before lowering it into its grave. The clothes went in next and then they shovelled back the loose earth and stamped down on it a few times to make it firm.

They walked to the cowshed and removed the plastic sheet that covered a large mound of coconut husks. They filled two sacks with it. They didn't bother to replace the plastic sheet. As they turned to go, Muthiah stopped and took a penknife from his belt. He walked over to Budhi the cow, who looked up serenely at him. He cut her rope close to the halter; at least, this way, a long leash would not tangle and catch on something and Budhi would be free to search for grass.

They lugged the sacks back and emptied its contents over the freshly settled earth. Now they only had to sprinkle a bucket of water over the pile and it would be done.

The rest of the night was spent in packing their most precious possessions. At the end of it, they had two airbags, a plastic suitcase, a metal box and an assortment of cloth bags. In the morning, Usha found these gathered in a corner of the middle room.

Murali and his father had gone to get the most essential things done. There was one small hospital, fifteen kilometres away, where they could get his wound attended to.

"What happened?" asked the doctor suspiciously, looking at the wound and then at his face. Murali looked down, while his father spoke for him.

"He was husking coconuts, doctor, and you know the rain makes them slippery, doctor. One of the big ones was wet and it slipped from his hand. He lost his balance and hurt his arm on the husking spear, doctor."

"Hmmm," said the doctor as he wrote on a card. He looked up with a hint of a smile, which made them wonder if he had swallowed the lie.

"The wound is at least a day old," he asked them. "Why didn't you come earlier?"

"I was away from home, doctor, and this boy will not do anything for himself."

"Hmm," the doctor said again, as he gave the orders to prepare a set of instruments for the suturing.

"Thank you very much, doctor," his father said. Then with his eyes pleading and his hands held up in supplication, he added, "Doctor, please could you give us a certificate for his school?"

There was a long silence, before the doctor shook his head to himself and agreed. "Meet me again after half an hour."

Murali, who had sat there with a sullen impassive face, was led to the next room, as his father almost prostrated himself before the doctor with a profusion of grateful words.

The next thing to be done was to meet their temple priest and get the letter that he had promised them earlier that morning.

They were planning to travel to Mynnar on the coast, about sixty kilometres away. This was the closest point to the Indian mainland.

It was indeed a strange arrangement.

A Catholic padre in Mynnar and the temple priest in Dibara had known each other before, but now they were in active collaboration, helping their people. The temple priest had a few letterhead papers signed and sealed by the padre. The only thing to be done was to type in the details, saying that Mr Muthiah, the bearer of this letter, and his family belonged to his church.

Deep in the innards of his steel trunk, wrapped in multiples layers of plastic, Muthiah had another set of very different papers. Their land documents, land tax receipts, family card, salary slips, the children's school marksheets and a few others.

As soon as they reached back, Murali changed into a loose, full-sleeved shirt that would hide the bandage on his forearm.

By twelve noon, they reluctantly set out, each carrying what they could. As they came to the small wooden gate, Usha's mother stood for a moment and looked back at their home. As though on cue, everybody turned and flung their arms around everybody else and wept in a chorus of muffled sobs.

Their father was the first to recover.

"Don't worry," he said reassuringly, "the fighting will soon be over and before you know it, we will be back here again."

After a while, they gathered up their things and set out again. This time, no one looked back.

Mr Muthiah had on his khaki uniform. He had made arrangements with another driver, a friend who drove on the route to Mynnar. This friend would make place for them on his bus. He would even let Mr Muthiah drive. After all, who would suspect that a driver on duty was taking his whole family away into exile?

Everything had gone according to plan. It was 4 pm now and they were on the bus from Dibara and headed for Mynnar.

Back in Dibara, the house they had left behind lay silent. Budhi the cow grazed peacefully, but Ravia the dog seemed to sense that something was amiss.

He sat on the front steps all through the hot afternoon, waiting for someone to return. Finally, as the shadows lengthened around him, he threw his head back and howled mournfully. This he did from time to time, well into the night. If he were a cat, it probably would not have mattered, he might have settled in comfortably, happy to have the house all to himself. But not Ravia. The dog in him would never allow him to do that.

But even Ravia gave up his vigil by the next evening. Before darkness came, he was off looking for a new master and, if he was lucky, perhaps even a new home. He had also become a refugee, a vagabond, looking for a place where he could safely curl up and lay his body down.

Mynnar was a coastal town that catered to the needs of its farmers inland and its fishermen along the coast. A few shops lay scattered around a dilapidated old concrete bus stop. It was the last stop and everyone got down. They checked on each other and the luggage before they asked a passer-by the way to St Anthony's church.

"You go on that big street," he said, pointing his hand in its direction. "Almost at its end, you will see another side road that runs by the shore. The church is half a kilometre down that way on the right side."

"Thanks," said Mr Muthiah.

They walked the road, weighed down by the luggage; all the while inviting knowing sympathetic glances from doorways and windows along the way.

The houses became fewer and soon, the road met the beach. Usha put down the cloth bag that she was lugging and just stood there staring anxiously into the endless expanse of blue-black water. The sun had gone down a little while ago, yet a last tinge of grey faintly lit the western horizon. Behind her, another light was beginning to make its presence felt. The moon, with half its face veiled, hung above the tiled roofs like a shy bride. But Usha was too full of anxious feelings to notice. *Would they really have to cross all that water?* she wondered.

The others had turned down the narrow gravel and sand road that ran beside the shore, and now her mother was calling out for her.

"Usha, come along. What's the matter? Are you tired? Is the bag too heavy?"

Usha let out a long breath, heaved the bag to her shoulders and turned towards her mother who was waiting impatiently.

Sand got in-between the soles of her feet and the plastic slippers she wore, making it uncomfortable to walk. She had to shake it off every so often. Finally, they arrived at the small church and went through a narrow V-shaped gap in the wall. The large church door was locked.

"Sir! Hello sir!" Mr Muthiah called out. After a moment or two, a tall white-robed figure emerged from a low-roofed building behind the church. He walked up to them. Mr Muthiah promptly gave him the letter his priest had given.

"Ah," he said, looking them over with kind but worried eyes. "I thought as much," he said, half to himself.

"Come," he said as he went towards a side door. He opened a padlock, flung open one half of the door and invited them in. Once inside, he waved his hands towards the back of the church.

"You can stay here at the church tonight. Tomorrow, I will try and arrange passage for you. I hope you have got money. The fishermen are very reluctant nowadays. The navy has stepped up its patrolling."

"Please help us, Father," Mr Muthiah begged. "As you can see, we are not rich."

"Yes, I know. All of them who come to me are poor. Otherwise, why would they take the risk? They would have travelled to the south and flown out from Colombo long ago."

There was an awkward silence while the padre opened a window.

"They usually charge 5,000 rupees per head. I will try and talk them into accepting the whole lot of you for about twelve or fifteen thousand," he continued. "But I cannot promise anything," he quickly added. With that, he was gone and they were left to themselves.

They looked at each other and for some time no one moved; then they began arranging things for the night.

Soon, the padre was back. He put his head around the door and held out something.

"Here is a matchbox and some candles. Lock the door from the inside," he said before he disappeared again. They did not see him until the next morning.

That night, Usha lay awake for a long time and listened to the disquieting sound of the sea. Each wave broke with a roaring sigh that faded quickly and echoed in the distance along the shore. Then, like the pause between breaths, a brief moment of stillness before the next one came crashing in. Eventually, this timeless rhythm of the ocean lulled her asleep.

The next morning, Usha heard it dimly in her mind before she was fully awake and thought she was dreaming. This notion was dispelled quickly as she opened her eyes and saw the rafters and then the walls of the church. The others were already up and about.

Mr Muthiah and Murali were nowhere to be seen. Her mother was sorting out some luggage. By afternoon, their plans were more concrete.

They would set out a little after midnight and walk along the shore for two and a half kilometres. There, in the dead of night, they would board the boat that would take them across to India. The nearest point on the Indian side was Dhanushkodi, which was only a little more than thirty kilometres across the Strait.

In the afternoon, Murali and his father went out to the town to get some last-minute things. Two loaves of bread, an extra plastic bottle for water, some peanut candy and a few other things. After this was done, there was nothing to do except wait. The padre came around and advised them gently.

"Take an early meal. Don't eat anything after this. Get some sleep if you can. I will wake you when it's time."

True to his word, he came around at eleven and found them all awake. He walked them to the beach and stood watching as they walked away across the sand. His eyes misted over and he tightened his lower lip between his teeth, something he did when his emotions moved him, as they did now. Would he ever see them again? He wondered. He bowed his head and breathed a silent prayer for them. When the figures had almost disappeared, he turned back to his little church.

Meanwhile, the family walked on. A ghostly company moving across the shore. The sand crunched softly under their feet. The palm leaves swayed a little in the breeze that blew in from the sea. There was not enough moonlight to throw any shadows, too many clouds lay overhead. They could just about make out each other's form, the white surf and then vast darkness beyond. After almost forty-five minutes, they heard two low whistles and then one more.

Mr Muthiah returned with two short ones and then two more. That was the signal.

Soon, dark shapes and scurrying figures came into dim view. Two thirty-foot boats lay along the shore. The one nearer to them was drawn up; its prow tethered to the beach with a stout rope that ran to a stake in the sand. The front end of its keel was loosely embedded in the sand beneath the surf and stayed steady. The boat's stern bobbed gently in the waves and hanging over its side was a 90HP Yamaha outboard. A tall sinewy fisherman, stripped to his waist, stood in the surf beside the bow with one hand on the gunwale; with the other, he helped passengers over the side of the boat. His mate was at the outboard tiller, urging the passengers to sit steady and still.

Meanwhile, Usha and her family had been directed to join a group of fellow travellers gathered further along the shore and destined for the other boat. There was another family, with an infant and a three-year-old. There was an older couple with a grown-up daughter, and two young men. There was one other man, middle-aged, educated and of some social standing, who quickly assumed a leader's role.

The last passenger was on board the first boat and it was ready to leave. The fisherman untied the rope from the stake and tossed it into the boat. Another friend had come alongside to help him. They bent forwards, steadied their hand on the bow of the boat and pushed with all their might. Slowly, the keel disengaged from the sand and the craft slid into the sea.

They kept up the pressure, their feet clawing the sand then pumping powerfully under water. They were almost waist-deep now; while his friend stopped short, the fisherman reached for the gunwale, lifted himself out of the water and vaulted over the side. Once inside, he sprung up and took hold of a long oar; facing sternwards, he lowered it over the port side of the bow and dug into the water. A few powerful strokes swung the bow sidewards and further out into the deep.

At that moment, the outboard motor sprang to life, its loud roar breaking the stillness of the night. The boat jerked forwards, ran parallel to the shore for a few metres and then turned ninety degrees to face the open sea. They could now see its stern moving away gradually, leaving in its wake a swath of white frothing water. The fishermen in the other boat were calling out to them now.

"Come on, come on, it's time," barked the fishermen.

The second vessel was now ready to board. First went the middle-aged man, who then helped the family with the infant. The two young men followed. Finally, it was Usha's turn. She waded out gingerly, holding on to the side of the boat that seemed to tower over her. When she could go no further, strong arms lifted her up and waiting hands reached out and pulled her into the boat. She stood for a moment and then stumbled towards the stern and sat next to her mother on a cross board one-third of the way from the rear end. All this time, she had her cloth bag clasped to her side.

When the last passenger was in, the same routine was repeated. The engine was started and their vessel wheeled out to sea. The shore was falling away behind them. The little land that they could see dissolved into the murky darkness, and then there was only the rumble of the motor and the dull beat of waves against the hull of their boat.

Perhaps it was the steady drone of the motor that put her to sleep, but its absence definitely woke her up. It was about two hours since they had started out. There was a general stirring and the boat people were gathering their things together. Carried by its momentum, the boat was sliding gently towards a thin strip of surf some distance away.

"Are you sure this is the place?" asked the middle-aged man.

"This is where we usually let them off," said the tall fisherman.

"Why are there no shore lights?" retorted the middle-aged man.

"Because of the navy patrols, nobody stays on the shore. Can you see those lights? They are only one kilometre away. Half an hour's walk should get you there. Other places where there are more people are not safe."

This seemed to satisfy everybody. For sure, in the distance, there were rows of lights out to the west.

The outboard started up and purred gently for a few seconds and was cut again, giving them enough impetus to gently crunch the forward keel into the sand. The sea was rougher than when they had started.

The tall one was out of the boat in a flash. Thigh deep in water, he waded ashore with rope in tow; finding nothing to which it could be hitched, he gave it two strong tugs and left it trailing in the sand. He meant to ask the young men to hold on to it but never did. The middle-aged man went first, and then the family with the small child. Usha's father went and came back for more luggage and now stood in the water, helping her mother off the boat. Having gotten her safely ashore, he came for Usha.

After considerable coaxing, Usha put one leg over the gunwale, fixed her toes in the crevice between the planks on the side of the boat and gingerly reached down towards her father with one hand. Of course, the other hand held her precious cloth bag with her coconut shell-face doll and her colour pencils.

The next instant, before their hands could meet, a big swell lifted the boat and carried it back into the water. Usha screamed, felt her foot loosen its grip and then went tumbling into the water. She made an effort to stand but there was nothing but water under her feet. She spluttered and lashed out with her arms as she went under. She drew a breath that brought stinging brine into her nose and throat. She coughed instinctively, but the next breath brought more of it. She felt her chest burn as it had never done before.

The tall fisherman had gotten hold of the collar of her dress and was now pulling her ashore, then her father gripped her by her arm. She came out, spitting water out of her mouth, her eyelids blinking in panic and her cloth bag wet and streaming, still clutched in her left hand.

Her father carried her crying and coughing onto the shore. Her mother quickly threw a towel around her. Usha sat motionless for a while in the dry sand, nestled against her mother. She shivered a little, retched and then puked onto the sand. While her brother hovered over them, her father gently rubbed her back. And told her, "You will be fine, you will be alright."

Whether it was her father's reassurance or the vomiting, she did not know but surprisingly, she felt much better thereafter.

By now, the fishermen were hurrying their last passenger onto the shore. That achieved, they quickly put out to sea. Without the additional drag and with their motor at full throttle, they moved away swiftly.

The passengers watched wistfully after the boat until it was almost out of sight. Soon, even the familiar noise of its engine was lost to them. In spite of the ceaseless sound of the waves, they felt a great silence descend on them.

One of them showed no interest in the departing boat; instead, the middle-aged man had turned the other way and was now looking suspiciously at the faraway lights. It was he who got them on their feet.

"Come on," he urged them, "we must reach those lights by daybreak." They clambered to their feet, reached for their burdens and followed their leader slowly. The sand seemed to ascend a little before long and then started dipping down again. They had not gone five minutes before a cry of alarm arose from those in front.

"There is water here," exclaimed the leader. "We have been tricked!"

"Perhaps there is a way to one side," suggested someone.

"We will see," said the middle-aged man. "Let us split. You go to the right," he told the two young men. "You go to the left," he instructed Murali and his father.

It did not take long for them to discover that they were on a small islet hardly two hundred feet across, separated from the faraway lights by who knew how many kilometres of water.

They gathered their things together and slumped down wearily onto the sand. Usha looked up at her mother and asked, "Will another boat come to pick us up?"

"Yes, Usha," her mother reassured her.

As they sat, there was grumbling all around.

"I knew those fishermen were crooks," someone said.

"I hope they will discover us in the morning," said someone else.

In time, all conversation ceased. Usha stared steadily at the lapping waves and the vast ocean, and then she saw them, low in the western sky. Three stars that formed a triangle. The sight of them brought warmth to her spirit. Even though everything was strange and new around her, at least these three little lights were familiar. She had seen these same ones from her garden on many an evening. How was it that she could see them just as clearly, so far away from home? Had they moved alongside to keep her company? She was not left to think about the stars for too long, for there was fresh jeopardy at hand.

The tide was rising.

Muttering and murmuring, they got to their feet and moved inwards a little, but within half an hour, the waves were at their feet again. This time, they moved further till they were huddled in the centre of a mound of sand about hundred feet across. A tiny speck in an immense, dark, restless sea. Some of them wondered if they would have to stand with their luggage held aloft over their heads.

But it did not come to that. The waves paused and then very slowly receded. There was a palpable sense of relief as tense muscles relaxed all around. The gloom lifted further when grey light filtered in from the east and the sun gently kissed the dawn awake with orange and pink. As its first molten rays gleamed across to them over the shimmering waves, hope began to rise within them.

Soon, mothers were rummaging through their bags for breakfast. The baby was being fed. Light-hearted chatter was doing its rounds.

The mainland appeared a long distance to the west. They could see other islands dotting the coastal waters. Some as bald as theirs, others much bigger with rows of palm trees on them.

The day wore on to noontime. The sun that had been such a comfort to them that morning was becoming a menace. Its hot rays beat down on the defenceless lot. Families were bunched together under bedsheets that were held up by aching hands. Some lay with their bags leaning over their heads. The white sand reflected the harsh light into their eyes, making them squint. The last of the water was soon gone and thirst was on every lip. Despair set in once again. Had they escaped drowning, only to now die of thirst!

Usha was sitting between her mother and brother, their father sat opposite them; between them, they had a piece of linen spread over their heads. But the heat of the sun bore through this feeble cover offering them little protection. As the minutes ticked by, they slowly began to feel dull and drowsy. Not very far away from them, the baby in her mother's arms whimpered incessantly.

"Where is the boat that you said would come?" Usha demanded suddenly.

"It will come," replied her father with all the confidence he could muster.

Usha looked slantingly up at her brother and saw tears on his cheeks.

"What the matter?" she asked as she gave him a nudge with her elbow.

"Oh, nothing," he replied.

"Tell us," persisted Usha.

"I wish I had died with Mohan in the war. Then you would not have been put to all this trouble."

Usha put her arms around his neck and gave him a tired hug.

"Don't think that way, son," his father said gently as his own eyes misted over. "We are all together now. Isn't that what matters?"

Except for the lapping of the waves, everything was quiet; even the baby had fallen silent. A light breeze blew in from the east, giving them some respite.

The sun was well on its way down when, through the haze of their weariness, they thought they heard voices in the distance. A fishing boat was approaching them from the north and as it came closer, they could see that its tall triangular sails were made of white plastic gunny sacks stitched together. They were all on their feet now, waving and shouting as best as they could through their parched lips.

"We are from Elangai. Help us."

As the boat came closer, they saw there were two fishermen in it. The craft was slowing down now, as they furled the sails in and heeled in the boat almost to a stop, perhaps twenty feet from the shoreline. The fishermen threw two plastic bottles of water that landed on the beach with a thud. While a couple of them retrieved the bottles, the rest pleaded with the fishermen to rescue them. But their pleas seemed to have fallen on deaf ears, as the fishermen trimmed their sails, skirted around their island and headed towards the mainland.

The coming of fresh water was welcome. It was decided that the baby could have as much as she could drink. The rest was rationed out equitably and carefully. Each got only enough to wet their mouth and have a gulp or two. It was better than nothing. But the change that came over the baby was remarkable. Her face brightened up; soon, she was smiling, gurgling and reaching for her mother's ears.

"Why didn't they pick us up?" asked Murali with disappointment writ all over his face.

"I don't know," his father replied, shaking his head.

When it came to refugees, every fisherman in Rameshwaram and Mandapam knew what not to do.

If caught carrying aliens, the very best they could expect would be a sound and proper grilling by the coastguards or the police. Apart from this, everyone had heard of what had happened to Ramanathan about a year ago. This kind fisherman had brought his boat to shore to let on a bunch of stranded exiles. Even as he tried to explain that he would come back for the rest, they crowded into his boat, swamping it completely. He lost his catch, valuable fishing gear and his mast lay broken. The stricken boat had to be towed in the next day. None of them would take such risks again.

Most would make an anonymous call to the coastguards as soon as they could, but in a few instances, the rescue had come too late. Children and a few old people had died on the sands before help could reach them.

Thankfully, the little company that sat huddled on the shore had no knowledge of these happenings. But as the sun set on fire the western horizon, some of them wondered if they would ever live to see it rise again. The quiet splendour of the tropical sunset with its chorus of colours passed them by. Indeed, beauty could have held little meaning for those in such desperate straits. For most of them, the waning sun was only a harbinger of dread and gloom. The short twilight was wearing away fast, the colours gave way to shades of grey and soon even this was swallowed up in a shroud of darkness that rose from the east. Soon, the tide was on the rise again and the ocean began to close in on them once more like the iris of an eye. They wearily made for higher ground. There was nothing to do but wait. Someone was weeping softly; the murmur of conversations rose and fell and then, only the whisper of the sea remained.

Two hours into the darkness, they heard a rumble in the distance that grew louder and louder. It was definitely a big vessel. They wondered if it would pass them by. All at once, a few kilometres to the east, a white finger of light stabbed through the darkness; it swept the sea as if looking for something and then settled on another island like their own, but only further eastwards. It hung there for some time before slowly swinging out in their direction. It wandered over the water for a few minutes before it came on them. All of them were already on their feet, and now they were jumping up and down, waving sheets and towels. At first, the light barely caught their outlines, but as it came closer, the frantic figures could not be mistaken.

The rumble that had now become a roar suddenly ceased, but the lights were still on them. A loudspeaker crackled to life and they heard a strange Tamil voice telling them that this was the Indian coastguard; it told them to remain calm and that boats would soon be sent to rescue them. Soon afterwards, the light was gone and they felt it was as dark as ever.

After a few minutes, their eyes grew sensitive and they saw it, parked about a kilometre to the south, a huge craft, its decks alive with flickering lights.

Usha and her family hugged each other, while others variously knelt on the sand or stood immobile. Even though their parched tongues grated on their palates, many of them had tears in their eyes. In time, two twenty-foot boats were on their way. As they came closer, they saw smart officers with white uniforms, one in each boat along with a couple of sailors. Their crafts beached and they jumped ashore and secured the boats. Sachets of water were passed around and before they did anything else, each of them drank their fill; never had it tasted so good.

The boats carried them to the coastguard vessel, which towered over them. A short steel ladder took them onto its deck. There, they were asked to sit on the floor, while their luggage was searched with flashlights. The vessel vibrated under them as its huge engines rumbled to life and they headed for the mainland.

They spent the rest of the night on the wharf and the next morning, a white government van carried them to the Mandapam refugee camp.

The camp was a ten-acre affair; old school buildings stood at one end of it. This was where they were held now. Behind these buildings lay an open space. Two steel posts with hooks on them indicated that it might have been a volleyball court at one time. Further back stood rows of bamboo and thatched booths. Each row had three sets of four stalls each, and they could see at least five rows one behind another.

Breakfast of rice gruel and lentils was dished out in one of the classrooms. At about ten in the morning, officials came in jeeps and set up tables out in the open. The newcomers were made to stand in a queue and enrolled in big registers with as many particulars as they could furnish. After this, they were told to go and find a stall for themselves.

They wandered among the rows. The front rows were better maintained but were all occupied. They wandered to the back rows and the further they went, stronger was the stench from the makeshift toilets at the furthermost corner of the compound. They walked down the last but one row and found an empty booth that looked reasonably intact. All these temporary shelters were of similar design. Stout bamboo poles driven into the ground formed the framework, cross beams made of the thin trunks of casuarinas held up the thatched roof. The flimsy walls—if at all they could be called that—were made of woven coconut leaves providing partitions between the booths, but they stopped well below the roof so that a moderate leap could provide one with a peep into the next enclosure. The back, front and outer sides of the quadruple complex were made of sterner stuff. Thin, worn-out tarpaulin sheets were stretched across the bamboo poles and held there by ropes that went through grommets along their margins. A dark blue plastic sheet across the entrance endeavoured to provide some sort of a door for each enclosure. A single naked bulb dangled precariously above the partition between two booths.

Ventilation there was plenty; draughts that came and went through the many gaps had a free run of the place. The sun glinted in through the many holes in the thatch above and made patterns on the floor. The floor itself was made of a large sheet of plastic-backed jute cloth, held down at its corners by the weight of four rough-hewn granite blocks. It might not have been 'The Taj', but for Usha and her family, it provided a welcome respite from the elements they had battled with only a short while ago. They looked around and laid down their stuff. Usha's mother brought out a sheet and spread it in a corner.

"Come, Usha," she said, "lie down for a while." Usha obeyed without a fuss and within a few minutes was fast asleep.

By the time Usha woke, the evening was far gone. She had rolled around a little and the sheet had crumpled up under her. Her head lay partly on the sand that showed through a large rent in the plastic underneath. She lay half-awake a few moments and thought to herself, *I must have gone to sleep in the garden. Why did I do that anyway?*

Slowly, she looked around and took in things as they were. She had woken into a bad dream. Here she was in a strange land, and the faint bad odour that came to her nose was something she would get used to in a few days. Her father and brother were nowhere to be seen. Her rising fear was quelled when she saw her mother sleeping nearby.

The next week or two went by. The adults went around with woebegone faces, sharing the experiences of some who had come earlier and morosely discussing their own plight. But the children soon had happy faces, a game to play, a smile for a new-found friend, and very often, some little miracle brightened every day. A spider's web in the morning sun, the flitting flight of a palm swift, a pretty pebble or a snail's shell; any of these was enough to make them stare in wonder. Usha did not have any family known to them, but she made a bosom friend with whom she played Kokan. Her prowess at the game soon made her quite popular with her compatriots.

A little more than two weeks had gone; they would soon have to travel to more permanent settlements. One day, they were told to pack their things and go with an official. They boarded a bus for Madurai. After four hours, they reached this big city. They had seen nothing like this. The crowded streets, the blare of horns, the rush of traffic and the mammoth bus station with hundreds of buses; all this was new to them. They were particularly fascinated by the autorickshaws that zipped in and out of traffic like scurrying insects.

Here, they boarded another bus that took them further northwest. As they went, the vegetation became sparser; the parched grass could scarcely hide the dry, dark-orange soil that stretched for barren miles on either side of the road. Even though huge tamarinds lined the sides of the road, not many other trees could be seen. At least, nothing they would have called trees. The straggly, pale tan-coloured, thorny acacia trees seemed to be natives of the land and dotted the countryside, but they could hardly be called trees. Their bare outlines looked more like skeletons from which all the flesh had been stripped. Most of them thought of their own country and the lush land they had left behind. How different it was going to be.

After about a hundred kilometres, they finally arrived at Virupatchi, a little hamlet at the foot of the Palani hills. The bus dropped them off on the main road, from where they had to walk two kilometres into the flatlands that stretched endlessly before them. This refugee camp had been set up a few years ago and built on the left side of the mud road they were on. They went in between two granite posts that marked the entrance to the settlement. The initial path branched into five more paths, like the symmetrical limbs of a candlestand. On the sides of each path stood small houses. The initial few roofs were asbestos, then there were some with tiles, then some more with asbestos. The first building on the right of the middle street was the camp office, where they now stood in a circle, as the camp officer explained the rules to them.

They would be allotted houses.

Each family would receive three hundred rupees in the first week of every month. They could come the next morning to collect their first instalment.

They were free to go to the surrounding villages for work, but they would have to be back by 6:45 pm, when a roll call would be taken.

Anyone missing from the camp without valid reasons for more than a week, ran the danger of being struck off the rolls and losing their privileges as refugees.

New arrivals would be given packed meals from the camp office for three weeks.

So on and so forth went the long list, most of which they could not remember.

The light was fading in the west when, at last, they were led to their allotted house, number B9 in the second row. Mr Muthu, who had come here during the initial years of the camp, was their guide. They found out he was from Sengai, a town not far from Dibara. Mr Muthu unlocked the rough-hewn wooden door that had no latch, but only a rusted steel ring that aligned with another set into the doorpost.

"This lock I have to return to the camp office," said Mr Muthu. "But here is another one I have," he continued as he reached for it in his pocket. "You can use it and return it to me once you get one for yourselves."

This would be the first of many favours they would receive at his hands.

The adults had to bend low to get into the ramshackle tenement. The torch that Mr Muthu held sent its beam into its recesses. The floor was bare, but tidy.

"I live in B3," said Mr Muthu. "If you need anything, come over. You better go soon and collect your food packets and some candles from the office before they close."

Later, by candlelight, they looked over their new dwelling. It was a single room, with a U-shaped earthen wood-burning stove in one corner from which an asbestos pipe led up through the roof. Roof tiles were supported by thin tarred rafters and beams, which in turn rested on stout Y-shaped wooden pillars incorporated into the mud wall. The rough cement floor was broken and potholed. *Anyway*, they thought to themselves, *it was better than bamboo and thatch*. It would be their home for many years.

Over the next few weeks, they settled into camp life. Every morning, while the men went in search of work, Usha helped her mother around the house. They did up their home as best as they could. From their neighbours, they learned how to make the floor better. They filled up the gaps and fissures with clay and then scrounged around the farms nearby for hay and cow dung, which they worked into a thick paste. This paste was then applied evenly over the floor. When dry, it provided a warm cardboard-like surface.

They dusted off the mud trails of termites from the woodwork and dabbed it with lime. In time, the walls also received a thin coat of lime. A lot of time was spent in looking for firewood—twigs, wood chips, brushwood and even plastic—anything that would burn. Here, dry cow dung came to their rescue. The farmers had their own use for cow dung, so the refugee children had to often find their own. So you might have seen many of them hanging around cowherds and their grazing cattle, and as the dung dropped to the ground, the youngsters would zoom in on the steaming pile and scoop it up into the bamboo baskets that they held on their hips. Another source of cow dung was the main road, where droves of cattle were sometimes herded along westwards to Kerala, on the other side of the mountains. But here, you had to get them before the fast-moving traffic smeared them all over the tarmac.

When their baskets were full, they trudged back to camp, where the children deftly slapped handfuls of the stuff onto the outer walls of their houses and then patted them down into flat discs. After a few days, they could be peeled off and again dried in direct sunlight before they were ready for the stove. These cow dung cakes often bore, on one face, the marks of the fingers that had made them. And as they went into the fire, those little handprints brought tears to many a mother's eyes.

In a month's time, her father got a job driving an old Leyland truck in a quarry about six kilometres away. Murali joined a group of men who climbed coconut trees. Here, his training as a rebel soldier stood him in good stead. They climbed the tall swaying trunks to put down the coconuts and dress the top of the palms. Soon, the insides of his palms were calloused hard from the work, but it was good money. Each tree climbed fetched them eight rupees.

Unlike the children in the Mandapam camp, the kids here were not so friendly and Usha spent a lot of time playing alone. There were not many girls of her age. In time, she learned to play with the boys. It was too late to enrol in a school that year. So she spent her days careless and free. She waited for Saturday when the other children in the camp would be on holiday and she could have some company. This was how she spent a hot Saturday morning in late March.

Usha spent the first part of the morning following the boys as they wandered about, near a low hill about a kilometre to the north of the campsite. Their activities were centred around a lonely mango tree, in the no man's land between the hill and road, which skirted it on its south-eastern side. They would allow her to join in some of their games, but not this one they were playing now. 'Gilli and Dhandu' was deemed too dangerous for a girl.

Guru was the one with the Dhandu. He struck the Gilli and it sprang to life, spinning up into the air. On its descent, he tapped it deftly up again, slowing its rotation, and then gave it a wicked crack that sent it whistling past the fielders who had instinctively turned their back to the danger they knew was coming. It landed a good forty feet away. No doubt Guru was the best, but even for him, this would be a rich haul. The others stood around him as he measured off the points.

This traditional village sport had no teams. It was each man for himself, with the others trying to get him out. Once in a while, the Gilli would tear into somebody's arm or leg, bringing on blood and pain, and later on, at least a mouthful when they got home. A long stick called the Dhandu served as a sort of bat. This crude instrument was used to hit the short stick on the ground. The short stick, called the Gilli, was tapered to a point on both ends. So when it was struck at its end, it rose up into the air whirling around on its central axis. The striker was then required to hit the Gilli again with the Dhandu, as hard as he could while it was in the air. If he got it right in the middle, it would travel the most distance. Further the Gilli went, more the points. The points were usually measured off in Dhandu lengths from the Gilli's final position to the point where the Gilli lay at first before the innings began.

I suppose we should know how the game begins.

At the start, the short stick or the Gilli was placed across a small groove dug into the ground, and the bigger stick was placed vertically behind the first one with its end at the bottom of the groove. The open palm of the left hand of the batsman— or rather, the stick man, in this case—would rest lightly on top of the long stick, steadying it. With his right hand, he would strike the long stick as low down as he deemed best, thereby levering the Gilli and sending it flying through the air. At any stage of the game, if the Gilli was caught while it was airborne, the striker was out.

The next stage of the game began where the Gilli landed. The focus would shift there. The other players waited in a new circle to catch the Gilli. This time, there was no groove to help the incumbent. The striker would have to deliver his blow onto one end of the Gilli; only then would it take to the air. If the stick man was able to tap the Gilli up once, before the final stroke, he could count the points in Gilli length, as Guru had done. If, in the rare instance, a player was able to keep the Gilli afloat with two taps, he could count off the points in half Gilli lengths.

While the children played, they kept a casual watch on the half-dozen goats in their care. This was easy, because they were feeding at various levels on the hillside and could be seen easily.

As the morning wore on, Usha got bored watching 'Gilli and Dhandu' and the boys showed no sign of wanting to shift to a gentler game. So, Usha retired to the shade of an acacia tree, about a third of the way up the hillside. She sat on a large boulder rolled up against its base and leaned back comfortably against the trunk, worn smooth by others who had sat there before her.

She gazed lazily into the distance. The plains that stretched before her changed from dun to bluish green in the distance. White cumulus clouds drifted by slowly, driven along by the wind that steadily carried them eastwards. *That cloud looked like a dragon's head*, she thought, *and that other one like an old man with a beard*. She watched as the beard gradually grew shorter by the minute. Then she heard it. The high-pitched cry came from above her and far to the right. She followed the sound, wondering what it was. She was then treated to a most unusual spectacle.

A fully grown Brahminy Kite was about twenty feet off the ground. Usha had seen these creatures way up in the sky, but seldom so low. She was struck by how big the bird was. She wondered why it had come so low. *Maybe to pick up a rat or a chicken*, she reasoned.

Whatever the cause, the big fellow had not a morsel in its beak; instead, he had a problem on his hands. He was being heckled by a gang of crows. One of the assailants came at him from the rear. A flick of his wing was enough to take the kite out of harm's way and send the attacker tumbling past in a chaotic mass of wings and feathers. Another concerted approach from both flanks was met by a few strong strokes of his huge wings that brushed them aside and took him a few steps higher.

The smaller birds came on again and again; some of them ruffled his outer feathers, but nothing more. His nimbleness was more than a match for their persistence. He stalled at a foot's notice and then banked gracefully, sweeping around the lot of them swiftly, leaving them confused. Although the incursions broke his rhythm frequently, the raptor was steadily flying in ever-widening circles that took him higher and higher at every turn.

One by one, the crows fell away. But not all of them. There was one–just one—who clung on doggedly. This brave-heart stuck with the kite, flapping his wings frantically to keep up with the bigger bird. He did more than just keep up; he was making life difficult for his foe.

Getting in a peck here on the tail and there on the wing. Up and up went the pair, 200, 400 and finally, what must have been almost 700 feet. Then suddenly, the smaller bird could take it no longer. He tucked in his wings and dived steeply for the ground, streaking in like a dark missile closing in for the kill. He levelled off at about 200 feet and disappeared around the slope of the hill, and that was the last Usha saw of him. Meanwhile, the Brahminy Kite had become a fuzzy dot behind the fringes of the lowest clouds.

Usha stood there for some time, staring into the vacant sky, lost in a world quite apart from hers. She returned soon enough as the hot sun reminded her that she was hungry and thirsty, and the time must be well past noon. The boys and goats were nowhere in sight, and so she made her way home alone. On the whole, she deemed her life happy, but soon her wild and carefree days would come to an end.

Her mother found a local school she could go to and she was enrolled in the fourth grade. The first few months were almost intolerable. Her mother knew that she was miserable in school, for she often came back crying and at times refused to go, but she was determined that Usha must somehow finish school. Her classmates were a mean lot. They teased her no end for her quaint accent.

"Do you have only these two sets of clothes?" they taunted her.

After a week or so, it didn't hurt her anymore. Not because it didn't reach her, but because she had withdrawn into a stone-walled citadel, from where she looked out at the world in sullen silence. Her body continued to move by rote, fulfilling the demands that each day thrust on her.

Chapter 5

A Nurse and a Mother

The chapel bell tolled gently and patiently. It could be heard from any place on the campus and when you heard it, you knew it was 7:30 am. Monday morning had begun at the Community Health Centre, Chatrapatti. Soon, a bunch of student nurses in starched white saris spilt out of their hostel like a flock of egrets disturbed from their roost. They headed for the hospital and split up to reach their assigned wards.

Usha was posted to the medical ward today. As she dispensed tablets, filled up records and did her other chores, she thought of her family. She wondered how she would break the news to them.

It was eight years since they had come to India, and much had happened since then. A year and a half into their sojourn, Murali was discovered by Karuthappa Gounder, who first noticed him one day when Murali had come with his compatriots to climb the palms and put down the coconuts. The man took an immediate liking to Murali. This association grew to such an extent that Murali found that, for most of the week, he was working on Karuthappa Gounder's family estate in Kariyampatti.

Kariyampatti was a village about 9 kilometres north of Virupatchi, and Karuthappa Gounder was its panchayat president—as had been his father and his grandfather before him. This influential clan of landlords ruled the roost in this village and its surroundings.

Nine kilometres was a considerable distance to travel; it meant he had to leave early and change two buses to get to the camp in time for roll call. More than once, Mr Karuthappa Gounder had suggested he come and live in Kariyampatti. Murali mulled over the suggestion for months before he took a decision. Murali stopped reporting to the camp and stayed on in an outhouse in Karuthappa Gounder's fields. One week passed, then two and then three. By the end of the month, the die was cast; Murali had severed his last ties with the past. He would visit his parents from time to time, but most of his days were spent looking after the affairs of his employer.

Camp rules were strict; anybody missing from camp for more than a few weeks was liable to get his name struck off the rolls. He would lose the monthly allowance and all the benefits that the refugees were entitled to. He would be considered a fugitive, an alien, and if apprehended, he could face deportation. Even though he knew all this, Murali, like many others, had opted to leave and slowly merge with the teeming millions that churned to and fro across the face of this vast land.

Two years further on, his parents arranged a match for him. The girl, Shanthi, was from a refugee camp in Viralimali near Trichy, a city about 110 kilometres away. Karuthappa Gounder bore a good part of the wedding expenses. After a few months spent in the small outhouse, the couple moved into their own tile-roofed cottage in the village. Karuthappa Gounder had the documents to the house registered in Murali's name, on the condition that he allow a monthly deduction from his salary to pay for it.

Karuthappa Gounder even helped him get a ration card, which would give them all the privileges of citizenship, except perhaps a passport. What would Murali do with a passport anyway; he was happy where he was and unlike his parents, he harboured no hope of going back to Sri Lanka. The scar on his left arm was now the only thing that sometimes made him think about the land of his birth.

Usha's parents still lived in Virupatchi, even though not in the same camp. The government had moved them to a more permanent settlement. In this new site, they had a much better house with a thin concrete roof.

As for Usha, in spite of the stormy start, she did finish her school final exam. She had long since come out of her shell and was now a vivacious young lady. In fact, there were many who thought her too sociable for her own good. She was an average student and it was decided that she should study nursing; something that she herself was not averse to.

So her father went to see the nuns that ran the hospital in Chatrapatti, a small town on the main road ten kilometres away.

"You have come too late for this year's admissions," they told him.

"Please, let her join as a nurse's aide," he begged them. "If she can prove herself, then please consider her for the two-year certificate course next year. I am leaving her here as your child."

Usha had joined this hospital three years ago. She had worked as a nurse's aide for a year and was now entering her second and final year as a student nurse.

Murali would visit her every three months or so, and last time he came, Shanthi had come along with their one-year-old on her hips. Her parents visited her every month without fail, lugging along a canvas bag full of the things she loved—coconut sweets, rice flour balls and sometimes even a little plastic box of 'dried fish' curry.

She had finished her work in the medical ward this morning and should have headed back to the hostel. But what was she now doing, walking towards the surgical block?

The answer lay in room number eight.

The hospital buildings were arranged in the shape of an 'L', with the medical wards at the end of the short arm. The surgical wards, on the other hand, were at the end of the long arm of the 'L'. Usha now found herself walking down the long covered corridors that linked the wards.

It was at the beginning of her last semester that life had taken a curious turn for Usha. She still remembered that time a month ago; it was a cool and pleasant January day—a week into her posting in the surgical wards.

She had given a few patients their sponge bath and changed the linen, imparted health education to a few more, written up her records…then there was that patient in the single room—bed number 8. This patient had been allotted to her for the first time this morning and his injection was due at 11 am.

She carefully arranged the injection tray with its sterile syringe, a spirit-soaked cotton swab and the vial of antibiotic, which she double-checked against the doctor's orders. With the tray carefully balanced in her hands, she walked briskly down the corridor and then turned left into a blind-end extension that had the six private rooms. Number 8 was the last room on the right side; it had windows with a view to the garden outside.

She found the door slightly open, put her left foot into the crack and swung it out just wide enough for her to move in sidewards, all the time watching the tray she held.

She looked up into the dark handsome face of her patient. She looked away shyly almost immediately, but not before a twinge of something stirred within her. Anandhan was a tall policeman with a burly moustache, sharp nose and steely eyes that looked out at her confidently from beneath thick eyebrows.

"What is your name, Sister?" he asked.

"Is that any business of yours?" she replied with a smirk.

"Oh, I just asked," he said apologetically.

His right leg was elevated on pillows, supported posteriorly with a plaster of Paris slab and swathed in white gauze bandage.

She set down her tray and told him matter-of-factly, "I have got to give you an injection. Where would you like to have it— on the arm or here?" she enquired, indicating the buttock.

"Wherever you choose, Sister," he answered meekly.

"It will be less painful here," she said, pointing towards her own buttocks.

"Sure," he said as he turned over on his side, pulled down his striped lungi and underwear and offered her one half of his bare buttock.

She carefully loaded the syringe, uncapped the needle and reached for his iliac bone and spine with her thumb and then drew her index finger downwards and outwards to find the bulk of the gluteal muscle. She dabbed the spot with some spirit.

"It's going to hurt a little," she said as she plunged the needle in and aspirated for blood to make sure she was not in a blood vessel. She emptied the syringe into him and withdrew the needle, giving the site a good rub.

"It did not hurt at all," he exclaimed, his eyes shining. "Nobody has given me this good an injection. My name is Anandhan," he added as he sat up in bed.

"I know!" said Usha curtly. "I can read the chart."

She recapped the needle, looked into his medicine box, took out a few tablets, checked it against her card and laid it on the bedside table.

"Make sure you take these, because I am going to tick it off on your chart."

As Anandhan reached for the tablets, Usha turned and walked out abruptly, but she could feel his eyes following her. She was sure that if he could stare around a bend, that was what he would be doing.

The next day, care for their patients included a sponge bath, which she and her partner Manjula had to administer. It was the rule that nurses were never allowed to give a male patient a sponge bath on their own. You had to have a female relative standing by, or there had to be two people to a patient. So this time, she found herself in room number 8 with Manjula. While they were wiping him down, Manjula left, saying she would be back in a minute. Anandhan waited just long enough to have Manjula out of earshot before he announced triumphantly, "I found out your name—Usha."

"So what?" Usha replied with little emotion. But Anandhan noticed an almost imperceptible smile spread across her face. By this time, Manjula was back and they finished their assignment without further conversations with Anandhan. That evening, to her surprise, Usha found that more than once, her thoughts had wandered to that man in room number 8.

Manjula was allotted room number 8 for the next two days; at the end of the first day, Manjula had a message for Usha.

"Hey, Usha," she said while walking back to the hostel, "that policeman wants to see you again. If you want, I will exchange places with you tomorrow."

"OK," she agreed readily, while another part of her tugged at her sleeves, whispering, *Should you really be doing this?*

The next day, as she walked towards room number 8, her breathing came faster and a tinge of excitement rippled through her person.

You could see that Anandhan was waiting for her, for he was smiling even before she came in. He had on a freshly pressed shirt. His meticulously shaven face was topped by a well-arranged mop of hair, which even had a stylish puff, upfront over his forehead.

As she walked in, his smile broadened. "How are you, Sister?" he gushed enthusiastically. "I did not see you the whole of yesterday."

While she loaded her syringe, he told her that he was from Keesavapatti, a nearby village. He had an older sister who had married and moved away to Palani, a temple town about thirty kilometres to the west. Then he asked, "Where are you from, Sister?"

As she briefly narrated her story, he listened with rapt attention.

"How did your leg get injured?" she asked in turn.

"I slipped in the bathroom and my leg hit the side of a bucket."

What he said was partially true, but there was plenty he did not tell her and plenty she would have known had she bothered to read the admission notes on his outpatient chart. This was what it said: '27-year-old policeman, alleged to have fallen in the bathroom and injured his foot on the sharp ceramic edge of the toilet, which had broken with the impact of his fall.'

After a few more 'time and place' details, the doctor's notes had his findings on examination: 'Patient in an inebriated state, breath: a strong smell of alcohol ++.'

After a few lines: 'Lacerated wound over the Tendo-Achilles. The tendon is severed with no strand of continuity.'

The same night he came in, Anandhan had been taken up for emergency surgery and his tendon repaired.

Fifteen minutes had elapsed—a long time for an injection and some tablets. Usha decided to say goodbye and leave before somebody looked in on them.

From that day onwards, a course was set that neither of them seemed to have the power to alter.

They met often and somehow managed to evade the surveillance that the nuns had in place. Her postings changed to another ward, but she would go to see her friends in the surgical ward on some pretext or the other. Her records had to be completed, she had to put up a poster—there would be a dozen other reasons. These were excuses, but what actually drew her was the tall patient in room number 8. *He was not a just a 'patient' anymore*, thought Usha, as she walked on down the corridor, each step taking her closer to the surgical ward, room number 8 and Anandhan. They met in the physiotherapy department towards the end of his stay. Once, they even held hands for a timeless moment.

His sutures were removed, physiotherapy had been taught and Anandhan was ready for discharge. By this time, they had shared addresses and various other particulars, and in their own minds, things were pretty much made up.

After his discharge, she did not hear from him for about a week, but hardly an hour went by that she did not think of him.

Then one day, Muthusamy, the ward aide, came up to her. He looked around cautiously before discreetly handing over an inland mail. She quickly put it into the pocket of her white coat.

Later, in the confines of her room, she had a good look at it. Her roommates had gone for supper. She pretended that she was not hungry—a farce that concealed a greater hunger. She took out the familiar sky-blue inland, but what was unusual about it was that it had not been opened. All the students were used to having their letters opened and read by the hostel warden before it reached their hands. A smile spread across her face as she saw her name scrawled in tiny letters on the upper left-hand corner of the address box. The rest of the box contained Muthusamy's address in bold.

Anandhan had befriended the ward aide and confided in him; there might even have been some exchange of money. Anyway, Muthusamy became a regular conduit for his letters.

Months rolled by and it was June—time for her final examinations. The first thing Usha did after the last paper had been handed in was to go out to the booth and phone him.

She breathlessly dialled the number that Anandhan had given her. On the other end, a rough voice replied, "Chatrapatti police station, speak on."

"I want to speak to PC (police constable) Anandhan," she said after a moment's hesitation.

"Be on the line," the gruff voice replied. Then she heard him call out, "Hey Anandhan, come, it's her, your girl."

He has told his friends at work, she thought. She felt irritation rise within her, but the next moment, it was smothered by a warm feeling of belonging.

At last, Anandhan's crisp voice came over. "It's me, Usha," he said.

"My exams are over," she replied.

"How did they go?" Anandhan enquired. "And what about your parents? Did you tell them?"

"No," replied Usha. "I will tell them today or tomorrow. How is your leg?"

"It's alright," said Anandhan. "I have got some urgent work. I must be going."

"Alright," said Usha reluctantly. *Couldn't he have talked for a little longer?* thought Usha, as the click on the other end signalled the end of the call. *Ah*, she consoled herself, *there will be time for that.*

Anandhan had already told his parents and the news at first was not warmly received. "Some refugee from Elangai (Lanka)!" said the old man. However, they slowly came around because there was much in Usha's favour as well.

The fact that she was a nurse certainly helped. The other was the age-old system and the coloured threads that held society together—caste.

When finally the parents met, Usha's father proudly presented their family details. They were not untouchables; they belonged to a middle-order land-owning community very much at par with, if not a notch above, Anandhan's family.

Then there was her horoscope, which again her father managed to extract from the corner of some old diary. It matched Anandhan's perfectly.

While these discussions progressed, from week to week, the lovers found places where they could meet. In the Oddanchatram town market, and often under what they soon called 'our tree'—a huge banyan by the side of the river that ran down from the mountains and through Virupatchi village. It was walking distance from the road, yet hidden from it by a bend in the river. They spent many an afternoon sheltered between the huge roots that spread down from its branches.

The wedding was held in Sundaram Pillai's hall in Chatrapatti village. It was mainly financed by Anandhan's parents; Usha's parents chipped in with some expenses. There was the question of how many sovereigns of gold the bride would bring. Usha's father mentioned a modest eight sovereigns, even though they had only six with them. A few weeks before the wedding, they made a trip to Madurai, the nearest big city, to complete the promised eight sovereigns of jewellery. They also had to buy the expensive wedding sari, with a broad gold-embroidered border. They chose a dark green colour for the saree, which was what the elders recommended.

The wedding day and the previous evening saw bright lights and blaring loudspeaker music, which could be heard across the village. The circle inspector was there and so was Karuthappa Gounder, Murali's boss, and then there were a few of her friends. Her friends stood around the bride in an inner room as she dressed and then waited. They giggled and poked fun at each other, but soon it was time for goodbyes, time for the bride to be led out onto the stage. Her mother clutched her close to her body, heaving with waves of suppressed weeping. Together, they tasted that sugary sadness that came with all weddings. Till now, they had travelled a common path and now they were at a parting of ways. Usha was starting down another road, where they could not follow. They could only stand and wave.

The honeymoon was just as it should have been. Anandhan had a week's leave; they went on a trip to Palani, the temple town nearby, and came back to settle into Anandhan's house with his parents. They spent time around their banyan tree. Those happy days hardly prepared her for times ahead.

The first month was perfect bliss; Anandhan was as loving as ever, her mother-in-law was kind and mindful of her every need. But soon, boredom set in as she had nothing to do after Anandhan was gone. One day, her mother-in-law suggested that a job would bring in some much-needed income. So she decided to look for a job.

By this time, her escapades had come to the knowledge of the nuns in the hospital and they were not likely to give her a job. There was a nursing home in the nearby town but she had heard from friends that the atmosphere was cramped and degrading. Finally, when the urge within her proved too strong, she timidly made her way to the nuns. She was not surprised at the frosty welcome, but her words of remorse and her disarming manner soon softened their hearts. The nuns knew that Usha was very good with her ward work. It was as though in nursing, Usha had found her niche. All these worked in her favour and before long, they relented. A job was given and gratefully accepted.

Four months went by and her life had fallen into a happy routine, when her monthly periods failed to arrive and then came the nausea. Something had begun, which was slowly stretching her from within, growing and kicking its way into her life.

Jasmine was born on Saturday, 21 November. With her flat, smudgy face, she looked as nondescript as any just-born child and at 2.9 kgs, she was as healthy and active as the best of them. By the end of the first month, Jasmine's face took on some of the sharp features that she had inherited from her parents.

Her maternity leave over, Usha was back to work again, leaving Jasmine to be taken care of by her mother-in-law during the times when she was in the hospital.

Anandhan was not the same; there were fits of rage that he quickly tried to hide, but not before Usha noticed the change. The façade was slipping and before long, there was nothing to hide. On many a day, he would come home drunk; if there was an altercation, it would often end with him landing a blow on her chest or head. There was also talk of another woman whom Anandhan had been seen with, in another village. Her mother-in-law was vaguely supportive, but there was little else she could do.

They had sex alright, but they did not make love any more. Rather, these brief encounters resembled the way of a rooster with his hens—just the act, with nothing before and nothing after. At first, she resisted when she really did not feel like it, and then the whole thing would become unpleasant. In time, she learned that it was easier to get it over with. Usha was always glad when it was done and she could get back to her life, which more and more centred around Jasmine, who was almost a year old now. Over the next many months, the physical abuse did not let up. To make matters worse, her mother-in-law somehow was now on her son's side. She would often make snide remarks that seemed to blame Usha as the cause of her son's problems. There seemed no escape from this unhappy situation, until suddenly, a door seemed to open for her. The nun, who was the medical superintendent, called her into her office one day.

"You see, Usha," she said, "there is this hospital for tribals—the Hill People's Hospital—in Pachalur up in the hills. They need good nurses. Would you be willing to go?"

"I will think about it, Sister," she said mechanically while her mind raced ahead with thoughts falling one on top of the other. *How far was it? Would she be able to manage the child on her own?*

She mulled over the offer for the next couple of days. The more she thought about it, the more she liked it. Jasmine was a little over an year old and she could be left with a neighbour, or perhaps there would be a playschool. This could be her chance to get away from everything, but how would she broach the topic with Anandhan? Heaven knows what he would do.

After a few days of deliberation, she found him in a good mood one morning. They had had one of their brief encounters the previous night and she had actually kissed him.

"The nuns talked to me the other day," she opened gingerly. "They are not very happy with me here and they might not renew my contract," she lied. "There is a vacancy in Pachalur, with a better salary, which would be a good opportunity for me."

"What!" he shot back loudly as his face grew grim and sparks leapt into his eyes. Then just as suddenly, he lowered his head and said, "OK, we will think about it."

Usha concealed her joy as she went about her tasks. Her mother-in-law reacted with an outburst of grief.

"You are deserting me? And now what will I do?"

But this spell was so short-lived and pretentious that it hardly touched Usha. Her mother-in-law's mind was on other things. Had she not the custody of much of Usha's jewellery?

Who wanted to look after a girl child anyway, and the new job would pay more.

So they kept to their different ways for the rest of the time they spent under the same roof.

The next few weeks were spent sorting out things. Anandhan was cooperative but Usha could feel an animosity that lay smouldering beneath the surface. Anandhan would come up with her and help her settle down. They would then visit each other as often as they could.

Anandhan had travelled up to Pachalur once, with the luggage on the back of a jeep he shared with others. Now he was going up with Jasmine and Usha who had to join work the next day.

On a crisp February morning, the bus wound up the ghat road with its 14 hairpin bends. The sun reached into the windows in a clear stream; now on one side, from behind, and then it came straight at them through the large front windows as the bus swung into its path.

The first set of hairpin bends took them onto a plateau, where the road ran flat, skirting the Parapalar dam and its large lake. Now, they were traversing the higher set of bends.

The cool breeze offset the warmth of the sun on their arms, the strong green of the forest turned turquoise among the distant peaks. The faint smell of cut wood and grass wafted in and out. There was something in those hills that sharpened the senses that tethered you to life.

The silence between them grew until they both felt it; even Jasmine was unusually quiet. They reached about 11 am and trudged up into the campus. Leaving the hospital on the left, they came behind it to a row of houses. The third one on the left was the one allotted to her.

She looked around the house and put things in place while Jasmine tagged along after her.

"Shall I put some rice to boil for lunch?" asked Usha.

"I have got to go," said Anandhan, abruptly getting up from the only chair that the house had.

"So soon?" Usha asked.

"Yes, there is some urgent work." So saying, he took up Jasmine in his arms and smiled at both of them.

"Now I must go," he said as he handed over the child to her. "Look after her well," he added, "and you must come down home, at least once in two weeks." The next moment, he was out of the door and walking down the path. As Usha leaned against the doorway and looked after him, her eyes overflowed and a tear fell on Jasmine, who looked up at her questioningly.

Anandhan turned back once and waved before the hospital buildings hid him from view.

Chapter 6

The Hill People's Hospital

The Hill People's Hospital was built on a hillside that overlooked the Pachalur village. The road to the campus led steeply up from the village, past the forest guesthouse and took a sharp bend to reach the gates of the hospital. About twenty yards from the gate, broad stone steps brought you up to the OPD lobby. As Dr Ravikumar had humorously observed from time to time, "Any patient who can take those steps need have no fear about his cardiac fitness."

A further forty yards away, as the road reached the level of the hospital buildings, a short branch to the left allowed vehicles to bring sick patients directly to the wards. To the right of the stone steps, a small terraced garden sported some zinnias and a few rose bushes. From the top of the steps, you could look down south onto the Pachalur village, its dark brown roofs arranged close together like biscuits in a tray.

In its northern extent, the campus spread all the way up the slope, spilt over the ridge and occupied a flat acre and a half that accommodated most of the staff quarters. After this, the land fell away steeply into the Parapalar valley. Most of the buildings had tin roofs and whitewashed brick walls, except the two doctors' quarters in the eastern corner of this small plateau. These had granite walls, because they had been on the property even before the Hill Tribe Society had acquired it. Dr Suresh was happy to be staying in one of them, the one further out. It had such a beautiful view over the Parapalar valley, the lake and out onto the vast plains beyond.

Dr Suresh had joined the staff of the hospital five months ago and now was very much a part of the team. People did not know much about him, but they guessed he must have been about 31 or 32. Their guess was right, for Dr Suresh had his 31st birthday soon after he joined the hospital and now he was running 32. His skin was fair, the colour of light sandalwood. His scalp held a full complement of lush thick black hair, which made him look younger than he was. Slim without being thin, his face was sincere, yet the Roman nose, square jaws and piercing light brown eyes gave it great strength. Almost 5'9" tall, Suresh carried himself well.

Before the hospital came up on this five-acre piece of property, it had been sparsely wooded. Silk cotton trees grew in plenty, interspaced with lime trees and patches of coffee. In fact, two of the coffee plants had survived the change and could still be seen just after you passed the main gate of the hospital, one on each side. There they stood like sentries, their fat sinuous trunks corkscrewed and gnarled with age. When he saw them, Suresh had more than once caught himself thinking that they would have made such wonderful lampstands. The property had belonged to Ratanavadivel, a wealthy contractor. There was a story behind how the Hill People's Hospital came to own the land; a story that Suresh did not know as yet.

Suresh glanced across the chicken-wire partition that separated the OPD from the small foyer of the hospital and the medical records department. Judging by the queue at the counter, it would be a busy Monday.

He had to finish the first lot of patients waiting for him. This done, he got up to go to the wards for rounds. As he left his table and turned into the corridor, a cheery voice called after him.

"Sar, Sar!"

He stopped and spun around to see who was calling. The man hurried up to him and now stood respectfully before him with a beaming face. With both his hands, Marimuthu caught hold of his doctor's right hand and shook it.

"How are you, Sar? How is everything? You will come back to the OPD, won't you?"

"Yes, I will," Suresh answered him reassuringly.

As he walked back down the corridor, Suresh recalled that Wednesday morning about a month back when he had first set eyes on Marimuthu.

Early one cold November morning, at a call from casualty, Suresh had reluctantly gotten into his clothes, put on a jerkin and trudged his way to the hospital. Marimuthu had been brought in at 5:45 am.

He was stretched out on one of the two beds in the room. His breathing was laboured, his anxious eyes were barely visible under drooping lids. He could hardly speak. The relatives informed Suresh that about half an hour ago, he had told them that he was bitten by a snake on his left foot.

Suresh walked to the end of the bed and bent down over his foot to locate the tell-tale twin fang marks that characterised a venomous bite. He had just located it when he realised that something was wrong.

Marimuthu had stopped breathing at least a minute ago, and now his eyes rolled up ominously; his oxygen-starved brain fired away at random, sending his limbs into decerebrate rigidity. Suresh berated himself for not having acted earlier. Surely, this was a cobra bite—the difficulty in breathing, the drooping eyelids, lack of local swelling—it was all there in plain sight. The neurotoxin was well on its way. He should have gotten ready for assisted breathing earlier, instead of taking a slow history and searching for bite marks.

"Mask and Ambu!" he shouted as he ran to the head end of the patient. He bent the neck back and supported the patient's jaw, pulling it forwards.

The single nurse on duty was taking too many precious moments to find the mask and Suresh shouted again, this time for a laryngoscope. He thought of mouth to mouth resuscitation, but he knew he could not because of his problem. But even if he could, he probably would not have put his lips to Marimuthu's dirty foul-smelling, frothing mouth.

At last, the mask and Ambu-Bag arrived; the mask was a little big but it would have to do. He clamped it over the patient's nose and mouth, supported the jaw with his little fingers and tilted the head back a little, asking a bystander to press the bag. Meanwhile, two other nurses from the wards had come on the scene. Suresh told one to hook up an IV line and the other to attach an ECG monitor.

Suresh again called out for an endotracheal tube and a laryngoscope. It finally arrived. *Hope the batteries are alive and the light working*, he thought as he removed the mask.

"Ready for intubation?" he bawled over the clatter of running feet and wailing relatives.

With his left hand, he introduced the blade of the instrument, clicked it in place behind the tongue and lifted the epiglottis forwards. *The lights worked fine*, he noted with relief.

He could see the posterior end of the vocal cords. With his other hand, he grabbed the tube but without a stylet, it was pliable and could not be directed adequately.

"Stylet, stylet!" he yelled. "Will anybody offer an endotracheal tube without a stylet?" he added angrily.

He clamped the mask back onto the patient's face and prayed as the nurse frantically searched for the stylet. The bystander was faithfully pumping the bag. The doctor noticed that the chest was moving, but only slightly; clearly the ventilation was not adequate. Air was leaking around the ill-fitting mask and a good part of it seemed to be going into the stomach, which was bloating up dangerously. If the contents of the stomach should decide to come up into the larynx, the game would have been as good as lost. The vomit would have drowned him, and if he escaped that fate, the acid stomach content would have ruined his lungs.

Finally, the endotracheal tube with the stylet was handed to him; with difficulty, he manoeuvred the tube between the cords. Straightening himself slightly, he removed the stylet and connected the Ambu-Bag to the tube and asked the bystander to resume bagging. Suresh noted with satisfaction that the chest was heaving up nicely with each volley of air. Meanwhile, the steady beep of the ECG machine that somebody had hooked up showed him that the heart was still ticking away, but at a dangerously slow rate. He called for an ampoule of atropine and some sodabicarb. All this time, the doctor's left hand securely held the tube to the patient's mouth. He asked a nurse—now there were quite a few of them around—to connect the earpieces of a stethoscope to his ears; his right hand held the chest piece to the ribs first on the left side, then on the other. At each stroke of the Ambu-Bag, he was glad to hear the whoosh of air equally well on both sides.

He fastened the tube to the patient's face with tape before he finally let go of it. At long last, both his hands were free. He straightened up fully, took a deep breath and stretched his shoulders back a few times.

Now to assess the damage, he thought, as he bent down once again. This time, he used the laryngoscope like a torch, shining it into the patient's eyes. The pupils constricted reflexively as the light hit the eye. *The brain was not too badly damaged*, he reckoned. *But we would never know until the patient started talking*. The brain was always the worry, the one with the least tolerance to anoxia. Shut off its oxygen for more than five minutes and it could be damaged forever; on the other hand, the limbs could go without oxygen for half an hour and still bounce back with nothing to show for the insult. He looked at the ECG; the rhythm had picked up and his blood pressure seemed to be holding.

Now it was only a question of maintaining ventilation till his own breathing revived. They had no ventilator machine so the nurses would have to take it in turns to bag him for however long it took to get him out.

The cobra venom acted like the paralysing poison, curare. Therefore, in addition to a bolus dose of anti-venom, they gave the patient titrated doses of Neostigmine, which would hopefully antagonise the curare-like action on the neuromuscular junctions and shorten the period of respiratory paralysis.

By this time, somebody had carried the news to Dr Ravikumar who arrived to find casualty turned into a sort of ICU. He was happy at this, because they had no regular ICU. *This is how it would have to be*, he thought to himself, *at least for now*. Dr Ravikumar was a few years his senior in college, and he was the one who had started the work and founded the hospital.

"Cobra," Suresh said, looking down at the patient.

"Umm," replied Ravikumar. "Cobras are rare. Usually, it's a viper. You see, cobras are fast, they usually get out of the way before an unknowing foot steps on them. Good job, Suresh!" he added.

The patient suddenly became restless, his heart rate shot up, he was fighting the tube. It was clear that he would not tolerate the tube without sedation. In went an ampoule of morphine and another of diazepam via the IV line that was already in place. The drugs would hit the brain in five seconds. Within half a minute, Marimuthu had become quiet, his heart rate settled down to a steady 76. A roster was drawn up, which helped the nurses take turns at keeping his ventilation going.

Later that evening, he had started breathing on his own. The Ambu-Bag was disconnected but the tube stayed until the next morning. The next morning, even the tube was removed and he was now being seen on rounds.

Marimuthu was drifting back to consciousness one more time; he saw the face of Dr Suresh and his team looking down at him. He knew he was in hospital but did not know how long he had been there. His thoughts went back to the day when he had gone out to relieve himself in the dim light of early dawn. He had stepped on something and immediately jerked his foot back involuntarily as a stab of pain shot up through his leg.

Must be a nasty big thorn, he thought to himself as he grimaced, stood on one leg and pulled up the other. He looked down to see what it was and it was then that he spied the creature out of the corner of his eye. The four-foot cobra slithered noiselessly over the grass and disappeared into the undergrowth.

As things turned out, Marimuthu walked out of the hospital three days later. He was a coolie and much of the bill that stood against him was written off. After having come so close to the brink, he had a full life ahead of him. All he had to show for his ordeal was a tiny scar on his leg and the memory of a good deal of kindness received from Dr Ravikumar and his team.

This whole episode ran through Suresh's mind by the time he reached the surgical ward. He examined the young woman on whom he had done an appendicectomy over the weekend. She had done well and was tolerating fluids; her IV line could now be taken off.

The lunch break was short that day. Usually, OPD finished by about 5 pm but today, it was past 6 pm when the last patient was seen. Suresh took the small path behind the hospital that led him to the dirt road. This road came in at the main gate of the hospital, lay in front of it and then skirted it around its eastern border. The small path that Suresh was now taking would join the road at this bend. On the other side of the road was a grove of eucalyptus trees, beyond which lay the fence. Dr Ravikumar's residence could be seen about a hundred yards away to the left as Suresh was now walking past the driveway that led to it. Just before the ridge, another branch turned left and lead to a row of staff houses. Beyond the ridge, the road lay flat, narrowed considerably and came to an end at the base of a huge old pine tree on one side of which was the path that led to a wicket gate, and then the doctors' quarters, which was Suresh's residence.

Suresh's accommodation was luxurious, compared to what Dr Ravikumar had gotten when he first came to Pachalur 6 years ago. A social worker had told the young medical graduate about how backward the place was. He also heard about the exploitation of the tribals at the hands of the plains people.

Dr Ravikumar had come on a reconnaissance tour and knew that this was the place that needed him. He looked around for accommodation for a whole day with little success. Most of the houses in the poor (untouchable) part of the village were little more than hovels with mud walls and thatched roofs. The portions where the caste people lived had better houses. But even they were small, one or two-room structures with tiny doorways through which you had to bend to get in. Windows were non-existent or wee-sized pigeon-hole like structures set high on the walls. Most of them had native tile roofs. None of the houses had toilets except a few—the previous headman's house being one of them. Of course, they had no headmen now that democracy had reached even this remote area. The chief now was an elected representative of the people—the panchayat president. The present president's house had a toilet; he even had a concrete roof. As for the rest of the people, they used the fields around, any public land, forest land or the side of roads.

On the second day of his search, Dr Ravikumar located a two-room house with some land around. It had brick walls. The roof was made up of row after row of crude half-barrel-shaped native tiles. These, with their convexity facing up, interlocked with another row of tiles that you could not see that had their concavities facing upwards. There was no toilet. Nobody had lived in it for years because it was thought to be haunted. The owners told Ravikumar that he could use the house, rent-free. Dr Ravikumar had no qualms about accepting the offer. Ghosts were the least of his problems. But a toilet would have to be built. He entrusted this work to a mason, who promised to have it ready by the time he arrived with his things two weeks later. As he spent the next day cleaning up the place and having it whitewashed, he often thought to himself, *I wonder how Malathi will like it.*

He had yet to hear Malathi complain about anything. But what would prepare her for this? From the beginning, Malathi had known she would not have the comfortable life of a typical 'doctor's wife'.

It had been an arranged marriage. Ravikumar had seen two other prospective brides before Malathi came along. One was a doctor and the other a physiotherapist. Ravikumar had told them in no uncertain terms at the very first meeting, "I am planning to work among poor people in remote villages. Are you willing for this?"

The doctor and would-be bride looked for a moment as though someone had struck her, but she regained her composure almost immediately.

"I want to do paediatrics and work in a teaching hospital," she replied resolutely.

"That is a good idea and paediatrics is a good subject," Ravikumar said. They continued with idle talk but it was clear that the meeting was over.

The physio, on the other hand, broke into a frivolous grin, fiddled with the end of her sari and seemed to lose interest in any further conversation.

As for Malathi, her pleasant face wore a mixture of apprehension and excitement as she thought through this over a long interval of silence. "Yes," she then said, slowly and deliberately.

The first six months of their married life were spent in a big secondary-level hospital in Chinalapatti, a town about 70 kilometres away, where Ravikumar had come to learn all-round skills that would help him serve in a smaller place. This hospital was started and run by a charitable trust along Gandhian ideals. Indeed, he was still working there when he made this exploratory trip up the Palani hills and to Pachalur. Malathi was a high school teacher in Chennai before their marriage. She had to resign from her job to join her husband. She was content to keep house, cook and wait for Ravikumar to return from work. Her sincere love, her simple and winsome ways softened Ravikumar's business-like outlook on life. This subtle change happened ever so naturally that even he did not know it. He smiled more often and laughed more frequently. Difficult as it would be, Malathi would not grumble or pout, this Ravikumar was sure about.

Two weeks later, Ravikumar came up the hill in a jeep with their things—a couple of suitcases, some foldable furniture, a cardboard box of medicines, another with books, yet another with aluminium pots and pans. This last box also held a pressure cooker, a humble utensil that would, in the days to come, play a stellar role in their work among the hill people. Their small bureau, which now doubled as a steel trunk, was stuffed with clothes and other articles. To his disappointment, he found that the toilet was not yet ready. The mason had some silly excuse. Now that he was on the scene, Ravikumar was constantly on his back and it was finished within a few days.

They put the small foldable steel bed in the inner room, the other became the kitchen, dining and sitting room all rolled into one; its door opened to the outside where a few steps took you down to an open space between the house and road. *This open area would be their 'hospital'*, thought Ravikumar wryly, smiling to himself. On the third day, workers came to put it up. Bamboo poles were erected on its four corners. The roof— woven palm leaves quilted onto a framework of casuarina poles—was first put together at waist level so that they could stand on the ground and work on it. Once it was finished, the whole structure was raised and fastened securely in its final location, eight feet from the ground. The thatched walls reaching up to a man's height were worked in and before sunset, their hospital was in place.

True, it would not keep out the rain but it would shield them from the sun, provide some privacy and regulate the flow of patients. A corner next to the house was walled off from the rest of the space with a double layer of thatch; this would serve as the examination room. The patient would lie on a plastic mat spread out on the sand and the physician would kneel beside him. The space next to it towards the road would be the consultation room, with a foldable steel chair and a stool. With time, the doctor hoped a table would join them. The rest of the space would be the waiting area. The pharmacy was a wooden wall-mounted shelf just inside the front door of the house. *It would do*, thought Ravikumar as he looked around at it all. *There would have to be a grand opening*, decided the doctor.

So one evening, a few days later, the hospital wore a festive look with its façade festooned with tube lights wrapped around with red and blue cellophane paper. Excited children ran around in circles and two blaring loudspeakers presided over everything. These last symbols of civilisation were a nuisance if you were a neighbour, but they had come to stay and had taken the place of the tom-tom drums that announced major events in bygone days. Everyone within a radius of two kilometres would know that some event was going on. Each would ask next door and soon everyone would know what was happening. The number of loudspeakers in action was a measure of the grandeur of the affair.

A bright pink tape ran across the gap in the thatched wall, which was the entrance to the 'hospital'. Just outside this was set up the foldable table with a microphone and its stand. If you had asked Dr Ravikumar when the function would start, he would have shrugged his shoulders and said, "Sometime around six. It could be six-thirty, seven? Whenever the panchayat president turns up."

And turn up he did, with a crowd of his sycophants and cronies. 'Vanakams' with folded hands were exchanged all around and then the speeches. Mr Sundaram Chettiar said that he hoped that soon the hospital would grow to such an extent that they would not have to go down to the plains for anything, and of course, the panchayat would offer all possible help. Everybody clapped when the ribbon was cut. The president entered with his entourage in tow, he peeped in at the door of the house, went around the 'hospital' and asked a few questions before the *vadas* and soft drinks were served to all who came.

The soft drinks were called 'colour' by the village folk, because they were sweet and brightly coloured as opposed to colourless soda. They came in bullet-shaped thick glass bottles; when full, the gas under pressure kept a glass marble compressed against the inside of its narrow mouth. A sharp knock on a wooden plunger with the palm of your hand would pop the marble down into the liquid, which would bubble and froth before tantalising wisps of vapour floated out. Now, the 'colour' was ready to be poured out. The marble was cleverly held back by a wedge at the neck of the bottle, so you had to dip it with the bottle turned the correct way if you did not want the glass ball to fall back and impact at the mouth. Then you would have to use the plunger all over again. Indeed, learning to handle a soda bottle was part of every village boy's growing-up.

The first few weeks dragged by with a handful of patients each day—old people with aches and pains, children with running noses. It was as if the population was gauging his competence with a few simple throws. He spent some of his time making friends and trekking to nearby villages. By the time he brought Malathi up a month later, the daily number had grown to a respectable 20. But all this changed one day about three months into their stay.

Gowri arrived one evening. Boar Hill that towered over the village on the west was already dark against the twilight sky but fingers of sunshine reached out on either side, bathing the surrounding peaks in brilliant light.

She came carried in a litter between four men. As they set her down on the floor, she threw her head from side to side and writhed in pain. Sweat had matted her hair and beaded her forehead; her tired face looked up imploringly as Dr Ravikumar bent down to examine her.

She must have been, at the most, eighteen; obviously in her last trimester of pregnancy. Dr Ravikumar put his stethoscope on her swollen abdomen, moving it around till he heard the foetal heart, faint and distant like the ticking of a watch. The baby was alive and the rate was not too bad. But the rest of it was alarming. The head was still floating. He questioned the mother and another woman, who probably was the self-styled midwife, about the details. She had been in labour since yesterday with no progress; her amniotic fluid had already made its appearance late last night.

The doctor drew himself away with an anxious look on his face.

"She needs an operation; you have to take her down to the plains," he told the parents.

"We don't have anybody, we don't know anybody and we don't have the means," said the distraught mother with folded hands and shaking voice.

The father, a miserably thin man wearing a lungi and banian, proceeded to fall at the doctor's feet. "You do something, master," he cried and as Ravikumar bent down to raise him up, he continued with tears in his eyes, "If you can't do anything, tell us, and we will take her home."

The doctor tried to reason with them for a good 15 minutes but to no avail. Malathi had heard the commotion and was already at the door as her husband came towards her. They both went in and for a time, stood staring at each other.

"They won't take her down and we can't do anything here," said the doctor.

"Can't you try?" said his wife, looking at him hopefully.

The doctor thought for a while and replied, "It's too risky and they might blame us."

"She will die anyway, otherwise. Why don't you call Mr Sundaram Chettiar and bring him into the picture?"

Dr Ravikumar smiled at his wife admiringly as his mind revved and raced to take in all the implications.

"Would you help?" he asked her as he went searching for the stuff they had.

"Sure," she said readily. "Don't forget," she added, "my major was zoology; I have dissected quite a few frogs and rats."

Yes, they could try. He had a few instruments, gloves, suturing needles and catgut. They could tear up a sheet for linen. But how would they sterilise them? An article he had read in a journal, 'Tropical Doctor', some time ago came to mind. They could use the pressure cooker as an autoclave. So that was what they did.

Mr Sundaram Chettiar came readily when sent for and promised to support them in case anything should go wrong. A crude consent form was written, thumb impressions were obtained from Gowri's parents. Gowri's husband, who looked as impoverished as his father-in-law, had by now wandered into the scene. He added his own thumb impression to the rest.

The dining table in the front room would have to stand in for an operating table; the only problem was that the patient's leg and foot would stick out. So a tall stool was roped in from somewhere and it served to hold up the patient's feet. There was just one more thing they would need—a better torch than the small one they had. Night had fallen and even during the day, the room hardly had any light. Mr Chettiar remembered seeing a large and powerful torch in the possession of the manager in one of the estates nearby. The manager used it for hunting and would probably lend it to them, if Mr Chettiar himself went for it. While Mr Chettiar went for the torch, all the other things were gotten ready. Ravikumar was pleased with the torch when it came. *Should get one like this*, he thought, making a mental note.

A good dose of Ketamine, which was a new drug at that time, sent the patient into deep sedation. Ketamine was a safe anaesthetic and the precious little vial was very expensive and now it was half over. Dr Ravikumar thought back on how he had come to have it. The surgeon in Chinalapatti had pressed it into his hands before he left, saying, "At some time, you will find this useful."

The instruments were set out on a small foldable table. The patient had had a shot of penicillin, the only antibiotic available. They were both gowned in full-sleeved shirts and gloved. All was now ready.

The light, held by a stout-hearted neighbour, threw its yellow light on the patient's iodine-wet skin, making it shine. For a moment, Dr Ravikumar looked up at the crude rafters and tiles hardly two feet above his head, and hoped a gecko would not fall into the incision. With that last worrisome thought, he cut down boldly on the woman's abdomen. The blade left a swath of crimson in its wake, warm blood bathed his gloved hands and he entered another world. As he caught the bleeders and searched for the correct planes, he forgot the geckos, he forgot where he was and everything else. In less than ten minutes, he was inside the womb. He wedged his right hand below the baby's head and levered it out through the wound. The shoulders and then the rest of the body followed. He caught the infant by his feet and lifted him high, giving him a smart slap on the back. To his relief, the baby took in his first breath and let out a wholesome cry as though protesting his entry into a cold and cruel world.

Gowri survived the operation and so did her son. She named him Ravikumar after the person who had saved his life, and hers. This watershed event changed everything overnight; Dr Ravikumar's competence was more than accepted by the hill people and patients filled the 'hospital'. It soon became clear that he could not function any more from this thatched shed; he would need more staff and a hospital—and this time, a real one.

Suresh had often wondered how Ravikumar had acquired the present premises and meant to ask him sometime. This thought again crossed his mind now, as he was having his bath. Ravikumar had invited him for dinner and perhaps, this very evening, he would hear that story from the doctor himself.

Suresh finished his bath and got dressed to visit the Ravikumars. He wore the blue shirt, the light blue one, the one he had worn for his graduation. How much things had changed for him from that time. It brought back other happy memories—morning light on mango leaves, the taste of Grandmother's fish and tapioca, an evening walk with Sunithi—there it hit a block! A barb had snagged the train of thoughts and he dragged his mind back to what needed to be done. After dinner, he would take a walk to casualty in case there was somebody there. It would save the ward aide and him an extra trip.

The small torch helped him pick his way through the grass, the wicket gate and onto the road. When he had reached it, he turned right and walked along the driveway that led to Dr Ravikumar's house. The structure had a tin roof, like most of the buildings, and brick wall with no plastering, giving it an earthy elegance. In addition, they said it saved on the plaster and whitewash—things that did not add to the strength of the building. The eaves reached out to shelter the front porch, which was bordered by a simple wooden balustrade but otherwise open on all three sides. Red oxide flooring covered all the rooms and the porch as well, from where a few steps led down to the grass below.

The porch light was on and it threw large patches of light onto the ground outside. Suresh went up to the door and knocked gently. It was soon opened and Malathi ushered him in with a smile; she bade him sit down, saying, "Ravi will be with you soon."

A five-year-old head with ponytails swinging peeped through a doorway and quickly disappeared. That would be Serina, the older one. Puffed up puris and delicious potato mash with plenty of onions made up the main course of the meal. After dinner, Ravikumar and Suresh each carried a cane easy-chair out onto the veranda. They sat down with a hot cup of lime tea in their hands. Just the thing for a cold November night. At three thousand feet above sea level, the evenings could be quite chilly.

They sipped their tea in silence for a time. In the stillness, they heard the sounds of the night—the shrill rhythmic chant of the crickets, the croaking of frogs and the call of an owl.

It was Suresh who spoke first, "What about that X-ray machine, Ravi? It's been lying there for months collecting dust."

"I know," replied Dr Ravikumar, irritation showing on his face. "Those Babus at the electricity board office will not give us permission for the extra load."

"It can be sorted out, can't it?" enquired Suresh.

"Yes, but I don't want to sort it out in the usual devious ways. When the means are wrong, the end can never be right."

"Have you tried?" asked Suresh.

"You bet!" replied Dr Ravikumar with a sneer on his face. "I have gone there at least five times. You haven't been to many government offices, have you?"

"Thankfully not," said Suresh quickly, with a smile on his face.

"Government offices are the unfriendliest places—ever," continued Ravikumar. "There are tables arranged in no particular order, piled up with dusty files, the narrow aisles between them as intimidating as ever. Behind every desk, there is a Babu, each with a mask-like face.

"When you hesitantly enter one of these offices, the masks don't look at you, but you know they have seen you for the expressions change just a tiny bit, enough to let you know that you are as inconsequential as a fly on the wall. If you take another step, the masks become noticeably harsher. 'What are YOU doing here?' they seem to say. 'Get lost! Don't you know that we are busy?'

"I wonder why they are called government servants, they are really the masters. There are about half a dozen of them. There are no signs, no indication as to which desk you should approach.

"The boss sits in a different room at the far end beyond all those desks, as inaccessible as an emperor on holiday. If you do happen to manoeuvre your way through the narrow aisles and then disarm the peon at the door, you get to see him. He listens to you and asks the peon to take you to one of the desks outside, and you are back to square one.

"The Babu this time looks up condescendingly and asks you curtly what you want. He takes a cursory look at your papers and waves you away to another desk across the room. I weave my way to the table I think I have been directed to; it turns out that it's not the one, it's the next one. So I finally arrive at this desk and stand there like a schoolboy until the exalted one deigns to give me his attention. He looks at your consumer bill, and then I think I see the faintest hint of a perverse grin on his face as he pulls out a file and goes through it. After a while, he looks up at you gravely as though you are the relative of a dying patient, and hands you a list of a dozen different documents that I should procure, many of them from equally difficult offices. Crestfallen, I clutch the paper he has given me and walk slowly out of the room. I feel several eyes boring holes through my back, but I dare not look back.

"As I walk away from the office with my eyes on the floor, I am greeted by a cheery voice. I look up into the smiling face of Moorthy the peon. 'You should have come to me first, sir. These are small things, we will be glad to help; of course, there will be a few expenses.' As he sees the hesitation on my face, he adds, 'I don't charge that much, sir, that other peon…he will charge you much more.'

"I realise that he is the pimp for the Babus inside. Seeing no response from me, he walks away with a smug look on his face and disappears into the office."

"If an educated man like me has so many problems," said Dr Ravikumar finally with a sigh, "just imagine the plight of the poor illiterate villager. He stands no chance at all. And then there are agents for all these things. Easiest would be to go through them, they will sort out all the paperwork. You go through a driving school for the road transport department and you go through the auditors for the income tax department. Because I am a professional, I could pay and pass on the expenses to my clients, but to whom will a coolie pass on his burden? It's a vicious whirlpool that breeds inflation and black money—takes us all down."

"It seems very bleak," said Suresh, looking glum.

"We have all got to make a stand, Suresh, do our bit."

"There is another thing I wanted to ask you for a long time," said Suresh purposefully, almost as though he feared the night would go by and he might forget to ask. "I heard that you got this property at a throwaway price?"

"Oh, about Ratanavadivel," replied Ravikumar knowingly. Then he went on to tell Suresh about Ratanavadivel and how he became a changed person.

Chapter 7

Ratanavadivel, The Contractor

Ten years ago, Ratanavadivel was one of the wealthiest men in the area. But he was not born rich. He was the second son of peasants with very meagre means. By the sixth grade, he had had enough of school and quit to help his father with his work and do odd jobs for people. He would sometimes play cricket with his buddies. They had sticks for stumps and a crude bat shaped from the flat part of the large midrib of a palm leaf. But then, this boy was different, he seemed to have his feelers about him and a keen ear to the ground. Between errands, you could see him quickly scan through the newspaper at the tea stall. This boy was inquisitive but not in a nosy sort of way. He would discreetly enquire about people, places and things; a question here, and an answer there, and soon he knew more about the world around him than all his peers.

By the time he was sixteen, his hands had become calloused with working as an assistant to a mason. Before long, he knew not only how to lay on a good brick, but what it would cost to buy one and how much cement it would take to finish a particular job. Along with a few people he met at work, he took on a few minor repair jobs. Soon, he had a band of loyal workmen behind him. Small houses came his way, which he did with not much gain to himself, but it was a fair deal for his clients and his workers. He bought more of his own equipment and hired a shed to store them in. By the time he was thirty, his name had become known and he was getting bigger contracts, often juggling two or three projects at the same time. Then came marriage and a family. His oldest child was Meena, a vivacious little lass who was her father's delight and joy. When Meena was four, her brother was born. So, on the whole, life was good for Ratanavadivel.

By now in his early forties, he was bidding on government tenders and winning quite a few. Small check dams for the public works department, bridges for the highway department. With the government, he learned to adapt to the different tunes that he would have to dance to. He learned how to keep politicians, engineers and clerks happy. He learned who was important and who could be ignored. He also learned that the straight and narrow way would leave him little by way of profits. On the other hand, there was money to be made with a little give and take; a little adjustment here and there.

In time, he became acquainted with a new friend—Greed. He hardly even noticed as it slowly grew on him and its dark roots silently reached the depth of his person. But his workers noticed, and some of the old hands left. But Ratanavadivel didn't care; there were others to be had, to be squeezed. These newer workers were often from other poorer areas, and having no local connections, they worked long, uncomplaining hours.

His newer buildings looked just as good as his older ones; that is, on the outside. But his masons would tell you they were different inside. A case in point was the bridge over the river Neeri. Now, River Neeri was one of the big streams that fed the Parapalar dam. It ran across the main road carrying the traffic from the hills through Pachalur down to Oddanchatram and the plains. Their point of intersection lay about 15 kilometres down from Pachalur. Most of the year, it was only a tiny creek meandering over its sandy bed and flowing through a shallow concrete gutter at the bottom of a large dip in the road. So it was usually no impediment to traffic. But a thundershower could bring out the beast in her.

In a few hours, the rivulet could swell to a raging torrent that could stretch across its full thirty-feet breadth. At those times, the road lay smothered under a brown surging ten-foot torrent of water that nothing could navigate, not even the big trucks. A line of vehicles would pile up for hours on either end of the road. Some of them, especially the smaller vehicles from nearby places, would turn back, most would opt to wait. They would spend the time dozing in their seats or chatting loudly; you could hear the rhythmic thump of music from some trucks. As the rains died down, some would emerge into the open, sit on the grass smoking a beedi or two. The drivers would once in a while take a peek at markings on the steel rod depth gauge set to one side at the deepest point of the dip.

A few years ago, all this changed when the government decided to build a bridge across Neeri at this point. Ratanavadivel got the contract and the bridge was built. It looked like any new bridge with fresh distemper and paint and at the grand opening, the minister had a word of praise for him. It was a few months after Ratanavadivel's 47th birthday and he felt proud of having done something with his life. Yet, the bridge held weakness, the full extent of which could not be easily known. The structural drawings required the central columns to contain a total cross-section of 25 square feet of reinforced concrete. The actual bridge had only 70% of that amount, the rest was a façade built up with bricks and a coat of plastering. The engineers knew this, but by itself, this would have been fine since they traditionally overestimated requirements to meet any eventuality.

But there was another thing that the engineers did not know. Yes, they knew that less cement than required went in the side railings and other non-structural components, and that was one of the places where his profits had gained a lot of weight. But unknown to them, Ratanavadivel and his team had been siphoning off quite a bit of cement. Consequently, even the pillars were not as strong as they should have been. But it would stand for a few decades at least; by the time, all of them would have retired, unless—unless something unusual challenged the structure.

Time passed; Ratanavadivel was almost 51 now. Meena, his daughter—still the special person in his heart—had gotten married more than a year ago. She was now back home for her confinement; the date was almost a month away. She had regularly had her antenatal check-up with a gynaecologist in the plains, who assured them all was well. It was decided that the experienced midwife in Pachalur could follow her up and conduct the delivery. There was nothing to suggest any problem.

As for the bridge, it looked none the worse for use, although the shoulders had broken down in many places. The expansion joints had chipped into a large fissure, which somebody had patched up with tar. At one point, you could see that some vehicle had climbed the sidewalk and rammed the railing; the repair work was shoddy and did little to conceal the damage. Overall, it was well preserved and did its job. But if you had cared to climb down to the water line and remove the moss and reeds that grew around the base of the pillars, you would have seen damage that might have been the cause for some concern.

The plaster was broken and undermined. In many places, the bricks were showing through and some of them were missing. Water was presumably seeping in through these large gaps and it was anyone's guess how the concrete beneath was faring.

It was the rainy season, and one of those beguiling sunny October mornings that gave no hint of the nasty thundershowers that could follow in the later part of the day. Meena woke bright and cheerful. Her mother and the maid waited on her as usual. When breakfast was ready, she carefully waddled her way out of the bedroom. She felt that her protuberant abdomen was hanging down lower this morning and so she cradled it firmly with both her hands as she moved ponderously towards the dining table. She sensed her baby move within her and smiled a little to herself.

After breakfast, her abdomen would not quite settle down; she felt a vague discomfort that did not amount to pain. She did not tell anyone. *Must be that jackfruit I ate yesterday*, she thought to herself and besides, there was another week before the date. By 10 am, mild cyclical pain was upon her and she told her mother about it.

Meanwhile, the midwife had arrived and people were moving about here and there, making preparations. By lunchtime, the midwife said she was definitely in labour and everything was going according to plan.

Outside, the sky was turning darker by steady increments. A strong breeze from the east stirred up the trees, making their limbs shiver and flail about nervously. Heavy sullen clouds moved in above, packing themselves in from one end of the horizon to the other. In a short time, the first ominous peals of thunder rolled across the hills.

But by 7:30 pm, Meena had taken a turn for the worse. An anxious expression had taken over the midwife's face. She soon announced that there was no progress and Meena would have to be shifted down to the plains. Outside, the storm had already started half an hour ago and shown no signs of letting up.

Ratanavadivel soon arranged a jeep and by 8 pm, they started down the ghat road. The wind was coming at them from all directions and the wipers were hard-pressed to keep up with the lashing rain. The headlights could not pick out the road more than five to six metres ahead of them. So they crawled along.

"If it goes on like this, it is going to take us at least three hours," said Siva the driver. "I have not seen a storm like this in years," he added.

Above the squall, they could hear Meena in the backseat as she moaned each time the pains came on her. "Keep going," encouraged Ratanavadivel as he looked at the driver anxiously.

In places, the road was submerged under a flowing mass of water but the jeep could wade through. They saw a few good-sized trees fallen beside the road but fortunately, none of them across their path. They finally came to the bridge across Neeri and they could not believe what they saw.

The Neeri had overflown its banks. The central pillar of the bridge had snapped at its base and leaned over, carrying the bridge down with it. The span had broken in two in the middle, and now lay sloping at a crazy angle. Most of the central part of the carriageway was submerged under a swirling, seething mass of water that flowed over it.

Ratanavadivel got out of the jeep and walked up to the water's edge with the headlights of the jeep fully behind him. His shadow sharpened and fell across the bridge. He stood there, immobile for a few seconds. Then he heard it, what started as a low moan crescendo-ed into a desperate scream that rose above the clatter of the rain. Meena was in severe unremitting pain.

Ratanavadivel did not know what he was doing. He ran to the side of the road, down the embankment and into the surging stream. When the waters reached above his knees, he was swept off his feet. He turned and lunged for the shore, his fingers grasped and held on to some wild shrub and there he was suspended for a few moments, before the driver came to his rescue and hauled him onto the shore. There he knelt with his palms cupped to his face. Then he broke out into great big heaving sobs that swept over him again and again. In time, he regained his equilibrium, got up on his feet and called to Siva, "Shall we take the other road that descends on the east side towards Sempati?"

"That is a very small road, Sar, and there are many streams running across it. Anyway, we have to go back up twenty-five kilometres to reach that road. Why don't we go another twenty and reach the main road to Kodaikanal?"

So they turned the jeep carefully. This was no four-wheel drive and they had a few anxious moments when the rear wheels churned in the mud before they regained enough traction to lift the jeep onto the road. They turned back up the road they had come. Just before they reached the junction, Ratanavadivel said, "Let us try that road to Sempati, Siva; it will gain us an hour."

"Okay, sir," said Siva as he shrugged his shoulders.

They turned left at the junction and took the narrow winding road towards Sempati. They had hardly done ten kilometres when they came up against a line of jeeps and small trucks. Ratanavadivel felt desperation rise inside him as Siva stepped out to enquire what was going on. He came back shortly and announced, "Sir, the road has been washed out and nothing can get across."

"I should have listened to you, Siva," declared Ratanavadivel ruefully.

There was not enough place to safely turn around. So Ratanavadivel walked back, picking out the way with the light of a torch while the jeep followed in reverse gear. They crawled along painfully for another five hundred metres before they found a broad, firm side path that led into an estate. Here, they turned and were soon on their way again.

By the time they reached the main road to Kodaikanal, it was 3 am. There was no sound to be heard from the backseat of the jeep. "Is she alright?" enquired Ratanavadivel.

"She is not bad," replied the midwife and Meena's mother. It was another hour before the jeep turned into the hospital at Batlagundu. As they transferred the patient to the stretcher, Ratanavadivel could see that Meena was far from all right. All the colour seemed to have gone out of her. Her breathing was laboured and drops of sweat stood out on her forehead. She hardly opened her glazed eyes as he held and squeezed her cold hand.

In ten minutes, she was wheeled into the theatre. Ratanavadivel and Siva were frantically searching for blood donors, as Meena's mother waited outside the theatre. It was three hours before a doctor came to tell them the news.

The baby (a boy) was gone. The uterus was so badly torn up and the bleeding so profuse that they could not save it, they had to take it out. After six pints of blood, Meena was barely hanging on to life. Meena survived the ordeal but she would never have a child again.

Ratanavadivel was a broken man. There was an inquiry set up to probe the circumstance behind the broken bridge and in the years that followed, he spent a good part of his fortune fighting the case. His reputation had taken a beating and now he landed only a few contracts. Meena lived a childless woman in her husband's home. The taunts of her in-laws were becoming unbearable and she knew that it would be only a matter of time before they persuaded her husband to marry again. After a year and a half, she returned home to Ratanavadivel's house where she got the comfort that she yearned for.

All the changes that Ratanavadivel underwent were not for the worse. In many ways, he had become a better man and his workers could vouch for this. "Ratanavadivel-Sar is so kind, he has become such a different person," they said.

It was about a year after this time that Dr Ravikumar first came to Pachalur. As his work became known, Ratanavadivel befriended him. One evening, a few months into their friendship, Ratanavadivel told the doctor, "Sir, I have a piece of land that I will give you, for a very small price. Why don't you build a proper hospital on it? A place where children and pregnant women can get good care."

"This is how the property was acquired," said Dr Ravikumar after he had narrated this long story. By now, all the lights in the house, except the one on the porch, had gone off and the house was quiet. To their left, a Rangoon creeper reached up from the ground and wrapped its branches around one of the pillars of the porch, the faint scent of its night flowers wafting in around them. The mosquito coil in the shape of a watch spring had slowly burned itself out, leaving behind concentric rings of ash on the floor beside them.

"You had better get some sleep," said Dr Ravikumar as he got up. They carried the chairs indoors and bade each other goodnight.

As Suresh picked out his way slowly towards the hospital, he thought to himself, *Maybe there are finally no winners in a corrupt society.*

Chapter 8

The Encounter

Tuesday was usually a light day at the hospital. Suresh had finished seeing a few of the patients that had come in that morning. He had done his ward rounds and gone down to the tea shop at the corner where the road to the hospital began. Now he was on his way back, walking slowly, enjoying the feel of the morning breeze. About ten yards ahead of him, a couple with a child was making their way up the road. The man was tall with broad shoulders and the little girl walking beside them must have been about two. Her ponytail danced up and down as she hopped, stepped and jumped along to keep up with the adults.

Suresh could hear that they were having some sort of heated argument. Suddenly, the man turned and took hold of his partner by the hair. He shook her about like a rag doll. The little one, who had caught hold of her mother's legs, started wailing as she was jerked to and fro in the tussle. The young lady's eyes were wide open in fear and she let out a cry when he slapped her across her ears.

By this time, Suresh had run over to them instinctively. He reached out his hand to restrain the man. The man easily plucked his forearm out of Suresh's grip and his fist smashed into the doctor's face with such force that it sent him sprawling to the ground.

Suresh remembered the shock of the blow and nothing more. When he woke up, there was strong light shining down on him, the whole of his head ached. But his lips hurt the most. Somebody, probably Dr Ravikumar, was looking over him. The back of his scalp also throbbed with pain. As he stirred and moved around, they gave him another dose of analgesics and he drifted back to sleep.

Next time he woke up, he found himself in one of the private rooms. He touched his lips, he felt the stitches. His head still ached, but much less. The evening sun slanted in through the window, posting a large patch of light on the wall, within which the shadows of leaves did a lazy jig.

Soon, a nurse came, helped him sit up. He had a little tea from the flask and a sandwich, both of which Malathi, Dr Ravikumar's wife, had left on the table. When the nurse was gone, he searched behind his head and found a large bump the size of a big lemon. He stood to his feet gingerly and moved to the toilet. *No major problems*, he told himself.

Later that evening, Dr Ravikumar came along, pulled up a chair and sat down. They smiled at each other; the senior doctor squeezed his shoulder and chuckled. "That was quite an adventure you had, Suresh. I thought we might have to take you down, but you woke up. Still ideally, I would say you need a CT. Would you like to go to Madurai to get one?"

"No way!" Suresh mumbled through swollen lips. "I will be alright. Who was that lady?"

"That was Usha, one of our staff."

"Yes," replied Suresh. "I thought I had seen her somewhere."

"The guy was her husband, a policeman. He carried you on his shoulder a little way up the road before others brought the stretcher. We did not hear the whole story until much later; by that time, the offender had left the campus with his wife and child."

After some silence, Dr Ravikumar asked, "Should we lodge a complaint?"

"No," replied Suresh, "I don't think anything will come of it, and besides, I am not hurt badly or anything."

"Anyway, you saved that girl a thorough thrashing."

"Did you wear goggles and take the necessary precautions when you sutured me?" asked Dr Suresh after a while. "And I hope the blood-contaminated stuff was properly dealt with."

"Don't worry; everything has been taken care of," Dr Ravikumar reassured him.

In time, Suresh asked how the outpatient clinic was faring and then about a patient.

"You get some rest," said Dr Ravikumar, getting up. "I will send you your dinner."

After dinner, he lay down in the darkness and thought about his life; he thought about his mother and remembered the first time he had told her about his changed status. How it would never be the same for him. About a few days before this, she had heard that Sunithi's father had gone and taken her home. She had not thought much about this. Then she heard that she was not coming back and the engagement had been annulled.

All this had upset his mother, but she had not asked for the reasons, knowing that in telling, he may have to go over pain again. After all, he seemed alright and there would be other girls. But when he told her about what had happened to him, she did not understand at first. Throughout the next twenty-four hours, she asked him many questions. Suresh knew she was constantly thinking about it, searching for ways to somehow find that it was not as bad as it looked. Finally, she was silent. It was as though all these props and hopes had one by one been taken from her, and her spirit lay lifeless within her.

The next day, Suresh saw her many times as he passed a window or a door, sitting in the shadows and weeping silently. If he entered, she would get up abruptly and leave the room without looking at him; as she passed by, he saw the stricken face and the two wet lines coursing down on either side of her face. At other times, she beckoned to him, grabbed his hands, cupped it to her lips and sobbed inconsolably until the backs of his hands were drenched with her tears. He had gone back to his work and study after about a week, but whenever he rang her, he could sense the sadness in her voice.

He would not tell his parents about the encounter he had had today. It would only upset them and besides, what good would it do? His lips hurt a little, but soon the analgesic and sedative that Dr Ravikumar had prescribed went to work and he drifted off to sleep. Later in the night, his mind woke within him and he dreamt that he was running on a railway platform only to find his train well on its way out of the station. With a sinking heart, he watched the large yellow X on the rear end of the last compartment pass by quickly and recede into the distance.

Suresh slept through past the dawn and woke up to the glare of a morning sun already well upon its way. A breakfast of toast and omelette was waiting for him on the table. He sat on the edge of the bed for a while before he walked to the bathroom. He stooped a little and looked into the mirror over the sink. His upper lip was swollen quite a bit and the skin had turned red and shiny, it was almost purple around where the stitches held the wound together. He decided he could not go to the hospital looking like this. What would his patients say? Moreover, the back of his head was still quite sore. He gingerly felt the bump and noted that although it was tender to touch, it had not grown any further.

After a few days' rest, his mirror told him that he was looking well enough to return to the hospital. None of the staff asked him anything, which did not surprise him because he knew that all of them would probably have heard of the matter. His patients were waiting for him and there were more of them than usual because he had been on leave. A few of the more curious among them had questions, which Suresh brushed aside with a summary statement about a 'small accident'.

It was the third day after his return. Suresh examined a patient and was now bent over a prescription. He noticed a figure in white slip in and stand beside the patient. *Probably a staff nurse from the ward wanting some clarification*, he thought, as he finished writing. He looked up and there she stood nervously, and for comfort, her hands clung to each other tightly. For a second or two, he had no clue as to who she was, but then it all came back. The dark and flawless skin. The magical symmetry of that face with high cheekbones and pinched nose. The long eyelashes that now flitted up and down.

"Doctor," she stuttered, "Doctor, I am sorry about what happened. Thank you for helping me." By this time, her lips were trembling and her eyelids fluttered in an effort to hold back the tears. She turned and hurried out of the room before he had a chance to say anything. Indeed, even if he had the chance, he would have had nothing to say.

The weeks rolled into months. Once in a while, Usha would pass him in the corridor or they would meet in the wards. The initial shy smile had evolved into one that conveyed a tinge of affection and he always reciprocated with a polite one of his own. On many a morning, his mirror showed him the faint scar on his lip and he would remember how it came to be there. The rainy season had come and gone, bestowing new life all around. The hills were clothed with a rich blanket of green and if you cared to go closer, you would notice the wildflowers, and if you held one in your hand, you would see that each one was a masterpiece.

Chapter 9

The Tyranny of the Law

It was a Thursday morning and patients were few. Suresh's face brightened as the nurse called out for the next patient—Babu.

Babu came into the room with a swing in his gait and a smile on his face so different from the first time Suresh had seen him. Suresh marvelled at the resilience of youth that had allowed the lad to bounce back so readily.

As he sat down, Suresh clapped him on his back and asked, "How are you, Babu?"

"All right," he replied, returning the doctor's smile. Behind him, the boy's father stood with stooped shoulders; his face still wore some of the pain that they were going through.

Suresh had first seen Babu one night about two weeks ago. The teenager had been brought with severe pain in his right ear and loss of hearing on that side. On examination, the ear was red and bruised in places, but there was more to it than that. The boy's face was drained of colour and he was trembling with fear. "Bring me the otoscope," Suresh told the nurse on duty.

Babu winced as the doctor gently held his ear with one hand and introduced the scope into the ear canal with the other. He could see the eardrum now. Its usual delicate pearly white appearance was gone. The membrane was dull, red and inflamed, a 'C' shaped tear ran through its centre. Suresh could well imagine the force of the blow that would have caused such havoc.

Suresh immediately put the boy to bed, ordered an IV antibiotic and a powerful painkiller. Then he turned his attention to the paperwork. He could not get a word out of the boy. His father was standing penitently in a corner, watching with folded hands. Suresh beckoned him to join him at the consultation table.

"What happened? Did you hit him?" asked the doctor.

"I am his father," said the man.

"I know; did you hit him?" persisted the doctor.

"No," replied the man who, by then, was trembling ever so lightly.

"Then who did? And I don't want any falling down story. The truth: understand?"

Then the man began to narrate a piteous story, reaching to wipe away his tears from time to time.

Babu and his father lived in a tiny village in the midst of the Palani hill reserve forests. The jungle surrounded them, except for a wide swathe of land that belonged to the villagers and few others who lived most of their time in the plains. The dirt road that served this hamlet ran through this strip of land before making a large circle that brought it round to the main road. The few buses that came their way stopped on this road and the villagers had to walk the rest of the way. The village was less than half a kilometre from the main road, as the crow flies, but if we were to take the dirt road, we would have to walk a little more than 2 kilometres.

Herein lay the difficulty, that led father and son into a trap that would change their lives. They were not alone in what they did. Many of the villagers took the same shortcut.

It was a small overgrown path that was barely visible in places. It cut across the forest straight from the nearest point on the main road to the edge of their hamlet.

On that fateful day, father and son had gone down to the Oddanchatram market and bought themselves a new spade, machete and an assorted bag of household goods. They got down on the main road and took the shortcut up through the woods. On the path, they found many dry broken branches that they innocently gathered. They were almost three-fourth of the way to the village when down the path came three forest guards with a ranger coming up behind them.

Babu and his father froze as the men came up to them. The bundle of sticks fell from their hands. The guards surrounded them, their eyes boring into them menacingly.

"Illegal logging!" said one of them who had a thick moustache that spread out like a sickle on either side of his face. "And trespassing on forest land," he added, grinning at his friends. "He has even got the machete in his hands. Come along with us now and no tricks." They went up the path with two guards behind them and one in front. The ranger had already gone ahead of them and was waiting for them in his jeep.

The guards brought their captives up to the jeep and ordered them the climb in. Babu's father dropped the bags he was carrying and fell at their feet, only to be kicked in the side of his chest by one of the guards. Babu came to his father's rescue, falling down to his knees and spreading out his hand protectively over the older man who was now clutching his side and grimacing with pain.

In the next instance, Babu was hauled up by his arm and he found himself looking in the livid face of the guard with the large moustache. Babu could not recall much beyond that because the man had hit him across his ear with such force that he momentarily lost consciousness. When he came to, he found himself lying on the floor of the jeep as it bumped along to the range station. His father, who was squatting nearby, had the boy's head cradled in his hands. He looked to the side and saw just inches from his face the boots of the guard closest to them. Babu felt so terrified that he found it hard to breathe. Thus, they bumped along to the range station many miles away.

Here, they were thrown into an enclosure about 6 feet by 6 feet in size. It had tin sheets for walls and a small window high up with bamboo cross bars. There they stayed till all the paperwork was getting ready. At a rough desk, they were asked their names and address, made to sign (and thumbprint for the older man) on dotted lines, and then back they went to their cell. Evening came, and if you had the chance to look in on them, you would have seen father and son clutched in each other's arms, weeping silently. And where their mingled tears fell, little clods formed in the mud.

Meanwhile, their family had heard of what had happened to them. They had run to the panchayat chief in Pachalur. He accompanied a group of relatives to the range office. After some parleying and exchange of small money, the ranger allowed them to go but they would not withdraw the FIR (First Information Report).

As the man came to the end of the story, he was clutching his side in pain. Suresh took him to one of the treatment rooms and had a look at his chest wall. There was a nasty bruise where the boot had made its impression. Even pressure at a distance along the rib brought pain in that region. Suresh auscultated and heard the faint crackle of a broken rib but the breathing sounds were good, indicating that the lung underneath was intact. *All he will need is some strapping for a week or two*, thought Suresh, as he straightened and proceeded to do just that for him. He prescribed some analgesics for him before he returned to the boy's side. Babu's pain was better and some colour had come back to his face.

"He will have to stay here for the night. Tomorrow, I will see him and decide if he can be sent home. He will need antibiotics for ten days and he should be careful not to let dust or water get into his ear for at least six weeks," said the doctor to the attendee who waited on the patient.

This was two weeks ago. Now here were the two of them again. The boy in good spirits. Suresh did an otoscopy on him again and saw with satisfaction that the drum was healing well and the tear was beginning to close from its ends.

"You have to be careful for another three weeks," he told them. "Why are you looking so worried?" he asked the father.

"It's about the FIR, doctor, they have booked a case against us. I went there so many times to beg them to withdraw it. But they say it has already gone into the files and nothing can be done. I tried to meet the panchayat members, but none of them will help.

"Just two days ago, Babu and I were going for work, and along the road came a big lorry with wood. It was going down to the plains. Babu asked me, 'Appa, what about all that wood? We gathered just an armful and look at what they did to us.'

"'What to do, Son?' I told him. 'That lorry belongs to Shanmugam, a big landlord from a village 10 kilometres away. His men provide every provision for the ranger's family, in addition to handsome gifts. What have we to offer?'"

"Doctor," he continued mournfully, "I also heard that people like us are implicated in small cases so that they can make up the numbers to meet their target. They have to have booked a certain number of cases to satisfy their superiors. That is the system. I don't know what to do, Doctor, we don't have money for a lawyer. It will probably be prison for me, or at best, a fine whose interest I will be paying for the rest of my life. I am finding it difficult to sleep, Doctor. Please can you give me something, just for a few days?"

Suresh wrote out a prescription for them and soon they were gone; but not from his mind, where they lingered for many days. As he trudged home that afternoon, he thought about them, about the system and especially about the target. *How can you fix a target for crime?* he reasoned with himself. *I wish it were not there. True, the big fish get away, which they did anyway. At least the innocent poor won't have to be sacrificed to meet the target.* If he had the power to do away with it, he would have done it that instant.

As he neared the house, Suresh took out the inland letter he had received in the mail that morning. He knew it was from his mom, the small neat handwriting with a lot of standalone letters was so unmistakable, and he had seen it from the time he could remember. He tore it open and smiled as he read. She wanted him to come home. Well, this was nothing new. But Suresh realised it was almost six months since he had been to see her. *He would go next week,* he decided.

That evening, he went down to the phone booth and called his friend in Oddanchatram for a bus ticket to Cochin for

Thursday. Then he phoned his mom and told her; as expected, she was ecstatic.

Chapter 10

A Tale of Two Buses: The Journey Home

Thursday afternoon saw Suresh walking down to the Pachalur village with a backpack on his shoulder. The late afternoon wore a lazy look. The leaves were limp, the air hazy, even a bumble bee that came by seemed lethargic in its flight. The tired sun was waning behind the tops of the tall casuarinas rising on the slopes to the right. Even nature seemed to advocate the idea of the proverbial siesta.

Earlier that day, he had helped the others finish the morning's outpatients and the weekend would usually be light. There were only four buses out of Pachalur, and one was scheduled for 4 pm. This was the one he was planning to catch. It was not an easy task to get sitting space on one of these trips. It called for a good amount of planning and some luck. This service started at K.C.Patti a few kilometres further up into the hills. By the time it reached Pachalur, it would be more than half full.

He reviewed his options as he neared the clearing in front of the temple, which also stood in for the local bus stand. What he saw did not give him much cheer. There were enough people there to fill two buses. *Some would have come to say goodbye and maybe some others were just hanging around,* thought Suresh hopefully. Whichever way it was, the situation called for some scheming.

He could see a few young fellows standing some distance along the road, in the direction from where the bus would come. Clearly, their strategy was to get on the bus while it was still moving. Suresh was not game for this, especially with the rather large pack on his back. There were a few who had crossed the road, and now stood across from where the bus would stop. Suresh had some idea of what their plan was and he decided it would probably be his best bet. So he ambled across to join them.

There was a stirring in the crowd, as the rumble of the bus was heard in the distance. All attention was turned towards the south, from where the bus would turn into the village. Finally, it came into view. While it was still a distance away, the young men started running beside the moving vehicle. The leader of the pack made a lunge for the doorway, his hands found and gripped the rails and his feet found the first step. The others followed close behind him. The old crate was quite a sight. Its dilapidated frame carried a face that bore two square headlights, dull with age. Its radiator grill had vertical lines and the beat-up bumper seemed to curve downwards at the edges. Both the chrome and green paint were worn and chipped all around. It reminded Suresh of a strong, sad, stoic, old man.

Suresh had no time to further dwell on the character of the beast as he ran up to the nearest window. He reached up with the *Reader's Digest* in his hand and begged the young man with a beard sitting by the window, "Sir, please could you put this book by the empty seat next to yours?"

"Okay," said the man as he took the book. That done, he rushed to join the crowd that clogged the doorway. He was carried along as the throng slowly squeezed and shoved its way into the bus.

He had his luggage held aloft over his head as he finally made it up the steps and squeezed his way to the seat that he had booked. The *Reader's Digest* was still on it and the young man in the next seat smiled up at him as he sat down. But the people standing in the aisle next to him scowled down at him resentfully, as though he had cut in on a queue of some kind. But Suresh felt he had only done what he had seen other people do; at the same time, he thought he was lucky that one of them had not brushed the book aside and claimed the seat, for he had seen heated disputes break out over just such a situation.

"You people at the front move forwards, there is room enough to lie down there!"

The irritated voice of the conductor quipped from the back. *Lie down indeed!* thought Suresh. There was hardly room enough for a fly in here. Finally, the driver lugged his vehicle into gear and the engine groaned as it struggled to pull away from the curb. If you had seen it from behind, you would have wondered how it could move at all. There was a jumbled mass of legs and hands hanging out of the doorway; so much so that the vehicle was leaning pathetically towards one side. In addition, there were people on the roof and ladder rungs that climbed up to it. You could see the bus as you might see a hive through a mass of bees.

Suresh shoved his luggage between his legs and under the seat and settled in. A variety of scents assailed his nostrils; among them, he could make out the smell of sweat and cow dung. But soon, these were displaced by the fresh mountain air that rushed in through the windows as the bus picked up speed. In less than 10 minutes, its murmurs and creaks grew noticeably louder, as it took the first of fourteen hairpin bends that would take them down to the plains.

This first leg of the road was steep and soon, his ears popped as the air grew thicker. Then the road ran flat, as it meandered around the shores of the Parapalar Lake. As usual, he was taken in by the beauty of the water and the hills that made up the scene. Little did he realise that so many of his happy memories would one day be linked to this body of water.

As they neared the town, passengers kept climbing on at every stop. Just when Suresh thought that it wouldn't hold one person more, somehow two more would squeeze in. The old behemoth groaned under the weight. Finally, it reached the Chatram bus stand and disgorged its hoard. You could hear its tired muscles creaking and sighing in relief, as people spilled out.

Suresh had a long wait ahead of him, which he spent with some other travellers in a thatched shed outside the travel agent's office. It was 9 pm by the time the coach pulled in. When Suresh saw it, he could not help comparing it to that other vehicle that had brought him down from Pachalur. This luxury transport was a far cry from its poor old country cousin that faithfully plied the hills. It was long, sleek and lily-white in colour, with more than its share of chrome and glass. On the side was painted in bold stylish dark blue font: *Andean Condor*. That was its name and come to think of it, it did look like it could take to the sky at a moment's notice.

Suresh climbed in and found his place. The seats were comfortable and could be tilted back, which suited Suresh who was longing to sleep, tired as he was. However, the onboard TV that was playing a Tamil movie kept him awake. He had no wish to see all the violence and gore, but it pervaded his senses even with earplugs and blinds for his eyes. Thankfully, in another 45 minutes, the film ran to its end. The screen phased out, so did the annoying noise and he fell asleep.

While he slept, the bus steadily bore him westwards across the vast dry plains of interior Tamil Nadu, through a gap in the mountains and into Kerala with its hilly terrain clothed in green. Had not man domesticated the land, it would have remained a dense rainforest to this day. When he awoke, the bus had stopped and the conductor was shouting out, "Anybody for Angamaly? Anybody for Angamaly?"

The few who were to get off were already well on their way down the aisle; no one else stirred, even though the din had awakened everybody. Angamaly was a town about 50 kilometres from his destination—Cochin. Cochin was also the last stop for the bus. Suresh knew that he had another hour's journey left to him. The engines throbbed as the bus started to move again. It lurched and heaved itself over the kerb and on to the highway. Suresh watched the neon and fluorescent lights whizz by, and then darkness as they crossed a river. On the other side were more lights.

It is so different from Tamil Nadu, he thought, *where on a night like this, there would be miles and miles of dark uninhabited stretches between the brightly lit towns*. Here, semi-urban areas coalesced together to make the difference between town and country more difficult to discern. He must have slept again, for when he woke the bus had turned into MG road. It screeched to a halt a few minutes later. "Last stop, last stop," yelled the conductor.

Suresh got his stuff together and climbed down out of the bus. It was still dark outside. A few autorickshaws were waiting for the slew of buses that came into this stop from distant cities; their weary passengers waiting to get to their destinations.

Suresh took one of these, after settling at a reasonable rate. Suresh had discovered that to get into these contraptions without settling the price was asking for an argument at the end of the ride. Few passengers won such a dispute and it left you with a bad feeling.

The three-wheeler puttered its way, twisting artfully through by-lanes and narrow alleys, like a busy black and yellow bug endowed with wheels. Soon, he was on Sudershan Street—his parents' home. Hardly had he stepped onto the road outside the gate when he heard a stirring from within. Papu, his old dog, had somehow sensed his presence. The creature yelped and then whimpered, rattling the door of his cage.

How had this animal found he was there? Was it the smell or his voice? He would never know. Suresh put his hand through the bars and let loose the latch from the inside. The gate creaked on it hinges as it opened to him. He went straight to the door of Papu's enclosure. He saw that the dog was beside himself with joy, jumping up and down in a frenzy. No sooner had Suresh slid the bolt back, when the big canine bounded out and put both his paws on his abdomen and nuzzled into his chest. Suresh rubbed him behind his ears and the animal whined with approval. Then he heard the front door being opened from within and he knew that behind that door stood another one that loved him. Loved him the way only a mother can.

Suresh walked up to the front steps, with Papu trailing behind him, wagging not just his tail, but his whole rear end. There his mother stood, squinting against the bright sun. Papu stopped at the top step, for he knew he was not allowed in. Suresh stepped in, closed the door behind him and stood looking down at his mom. Aleykutty was a plump matronly lady, almost fifty years old, with light skin the colour of dried grass. Her long black hair parted in the middle and came down over her ears, framing a round, pleasant face with a stubby nose. Her dark eyes sparkled and now brimmed with tears, as she hugged her younger son around the waist.

"How long you have been," she said, while her body shook with sobs. "I remember how proud I was when you became a medical student. But now, how I wish you had never gone to medical college."

Suresh held her gently with both arms and patted her back reassuringly. "Don't cry, Amma, it's only been six months," he said. "And I am quite well now; and you will always have Chetan, Ammama and little Neetha Kuttan."

Chetan was the endearing term used for his elder brother and Ammama for his sister-in-law. Neetha Kuttan was his adorable little niece. They lived in Bangalore where his brother was with a software firm.

In time, the weeping subsided and she released him. "Sit down," she said. "I will get your breakfast."

Suresh deposited his backpack under the dining table and followed her into the kitchen. He stood at the door, leaning against its sides, and stared after his mother as she went about her business.

"It's something you like," she said as she oiled the deep concave skillet. She put some batter in its hollow and placed it over the blue flame of the gas stove. In a few moments, she again caught hold of the frying pan by its handles, took it off the fire and deftly rocked it slowly through a circle. The batter climbed up the sides of the vessel all around, leaving a thick centre and a thin, crisp rim all around.

"Ah! Winged appam," Suresh exclaimed.

"And chicken curry," she added.

"What a treat," he proclaimed, with a smile of anticipation spreading across his face. "I will go up and leave my stuff and have a quick bath, Amma," said Suresh.

After his bath, he changed into a lungi and T-shirt. He came down and sat at the table, where his mother sat waiting for him.

"This is lovely," said Suresh as he dug into his breakfast. There was a knock on the door.

"That must be your father, coming back after his walk," Aleykutty said as she went to open the door. Suresh turned to the door as his father strode in.

"Did you have a good journey?" he asked, clapping him over both his shoulders from the back. He went around and sat at his usual place at the head of the table. He leaned forwards, put his elbows on the table, cradled his chin on his palms and proceeded to quietly survey his son as he ate his meal.

Mathachen was of average build. His hair, which was combed back, revealed symmetrical balding at the temples. It was mostly ash-coloured, with streaks of black. His bronzed skin, thin lips, bushy eyebrows and penetrating dark brown eyes gave him a rather stern appearance, which beguiled a rather friendly disposition. Although he shared his mother's complexion, on the whole, Suresh was more like his father.

"So how are the tribals getting along? And how is Dr Ravikumar?" he asked after a while.

After the good food, they talked together for a long time before his father advised him to get some sleep. "You can never get good rest on that bus," he added.

Suresh climbed up the steps to his room, pushed open the door and it was as though thirteen years had fallen away all of a sudden. On the wall to his left was the painting he had done when he was thirteen. It was a silhouette, which showed a maiden with long hair, leaning out over a castle balcony and reaching towards her beau who held out a perfect rose. His bed was in the same place, and so was his cupboard, which held knick-knacks from his childhood. Among these were his stamp collection, an old and now rusting Meccano set and his favourite 'Inderjal' comics.

As he rummaged through the lot, one other object caught his attention. He picked it up in his hands and turned it around. It had belonged to his grandfather who had died eight years ago. As the old Swiss pocket watch lay in his palm, it carried him back almost twenty years, to his grandfather's home in Kottara. The watch was bulky by present-day standards. Although it did not work anymore, the shining stainless steel had lost none of its glitter; you had to flick open the front cover to see the dial with its Roman numerals. It had a winding knob at the top, surrounded by a ring with which it could be attached to your belt rings.

Suresh lay down to nap, but sleep would not come as vivid memories assailed him from every side. The oldest of them concerned their biannual trips from Cochin, where they lived, to Kottara, their ancestral home. These trips were something he had looked forward to as a child. There was much packing and he had his own little airbag. A beat-up old ambassador taxi took them to the train station. As the train rumbled onto the platform and stopped, there was much jostling to find place in their third-class compartment with hard wooden benches. Those metre-gauge trains had only an aisle on one side, and therefore, fewer window seats—and a window seat was Suresh's yearning.

By the time the train chugged out of the station, Suresh would usually have wheedled his way onto some seat with a view, failing which, he stood in the aisle with his face pressed against the bars of the window. There he remained, his eyes flitting back and forth as he watched the world go by.

Everything held a fascination for him. They passed a patch of wild bluebells that grew out of the dirt. Wide-open rice fields stretched into the distance, where they met a grove of coconut palms. The scent of ripening paddy wafted up to him as the lime-green stalks rippled in the breeze. The journey went on. A buffalo was sunning himself in a mud pond, with an egret perched on his spine, busily picking off the nits. He spied a cream-coloured foreign car among those that waited at a crossing. A stretch of garbage made its presence felt by the stink.

On the farther side, he saw a few urchins outside a row of shacks. They jumped up and down, gleefully waving their hands. Suresh waved back with equal enthusiasm. When the tracks took a turn, especially towards his side, he saw the whole string of coaches speeding around the bend, with the locomotive steaming away in front. They went over a river and abruptly, the clattering of the wheels turned into a deep rumble, as the girders of the bridge reverberated under them. So the morning passed. Every once in a while, a speck of coal flew into his eyes, making him smart, tear and rub his eyes till they were red. Hours passed before his mother could coax him from this position for a bite of something. By the end of the journey, his sleeves and collars were sparsely coated with coal dust, but he didn't mind one bit.

They pulled into the large Quilon junction where they were to get off. Getting their things together, they climbed down wearily onto the platform. Did I say wearily; yes, most of them, but not Suresh. He bounded down and seemed to have enough energy for another trip.

As soon as the luggage was gathered together and accounted for, Suresh began badgering his father. "Can we go see the engine?" he begged again and again, tugging at Mathachen's shirt sleeves.

"OK, OK," he said finally, giving in to his son's demands. Entrusting the baggage to his mother, they walked towards the front end of the train.

As they drew close, the sound of hissing steam became louder and the little boy's excitement rose with it. Now they were standing only a few metres from the completely black, towering beast.

The fireman opened the hatch to the firebox. Standing on his toes, Suresh could see the white and orange flames dancing within. He watched in wide-eyed wonder as the fireman dug into the coal bin with his spade, swivelled around and spooned a shovelful into the inferno. They moved back a feet or two, in awe of the heat that came to them in quivering waves. After feeding it a few more times, the fireman closed the firebox. The engine driver leaned out, looked this way and that before he pulled on a lever, sending a piercing whistle into the air. The boy looked towards the source of the sound and saw a thin powerful jet of white steam escaping from the top of the boilers. It hit the insides of an inverted tumbler, setting the air howling around it. It looked like steam did everything around here.

Standing in front of it, the boy wondered if this gigantic mass of steel would ever move, but the whistle meant the train was soon to depart; it also seemed to indicate the start of a wrestling match between steel and steam. The heavy inertia of metal on one side, the energy of steam on the other. The monster appeared to swell a little as steam seeped out of its many pores. The hissing grew louder, as the pressure of superheated steam built up along the pipes and rushed into the cylinder. The beast seemed to snort, as huge puffs of black smoke shot out from its chimney.

Through the cloud of steam swirling around it, they saw the gleaming piston rod move forwards ever so slowly, pushing the giant wheels through a tiny angle. Suddenly, for a moment, the friction on the glistening tracks gave way and the wheels spun freely, struggling to get a grip before traction was restored again. The hulk inched forwards. With each gust of smoke and steam, the wheels rolled faster and the locomotive pulled away, hauling behind it, its twelve carriages. Suresh had counted them, so he knew. Steam had won the day, and as it often was, energy was much the master.

Chapter 11

Reminiscences

As Suresh lay on his old bed, memories fast-forwarded themselves within his mind. Twelve years later, he was out of school and going to college. He had done well in the national medical entrance exam and was allotted a place at Sevur Medical College in the neighbouring state of Tamil Nadu. His father had accompanied him on that first journey to that faraway place. They had boarded the train at the same station in Cochin. Things had changed though. His fascination with locomotives had long since passed away, and with it, those old steam engines of his childhood. Their place had now been taken by the sleek smartly attired diesel-electrics. With a polite tweet on their horns, they would slip out of a station with hardly a whimper; a loud hum was all you might hear. You could not even see their wheels under the chassis. These did not excite him as those old iron horses had. They were too sedate and refined; much like today's soldiers with their dainty guns as against the raw strength of the gladiators of times past.

It had taken Suresh less than five minutes to daydream his way across his childhood and now he was reliving his time in college. He was going away from home for the first time. The rest of that trip, after they left Cochin, somehow held a special place in his memory. Sevur was almost five hundred kilometres away, all the way across the peninsula, on the east coast.

They travelled through the night and across the Palghat gap. By the time the first light of day tinged the eastern sky, they were well onto the reddish-brown plains of Tamil Nadu. The sun rose higher and seemed to gain strength by the minute. Well before noon, its oppression began to be felt inside their compartment. The draught blowing in through the windows was like the warm blast from a furnace.

Hoping to escape its clutches, Suresh spread a wet towel on the top berth and climbed up onto it. He lay there and found it was not much different. It was like being in an oven. He wet his face and shirt, which made him feel a little better. He reached up to touch the tin sheet that made up the inner layer of the roof. It was as hot as freshly baked bread. When he was on the floor, he had felt the two small fans on the ceiling blow hot air down on them and now he knew where it came from. He could only imagine what it would be like to touch the outer steel roof.

Suresh temporarily resigned himself to his oppressive surroundings and poured more water onto the towel. He lay on his back, then on his tummy, then on his sides in an effort to cool each side in turn. He was always on the lookout for slack in the speed of the train for this might indicate an approaching station and the one resource that seemed all important-water. Water was vital on a journey like this; it was their only weapon against the onslaught of a remorseless sun.

After what seemed like a lifetime, Suresh detected a slowing down and then some extra clatter along with the wheels. "Are we nearing a station?" he shouted down to his father.

"Looks like," returned Mathachen, who was sitting with one foot up on his berth, looking out with weary eyes. "I can see some sidings appearing," he added, looking up at his son.

Suresh bounded down from his bunk, grabbed his water-can and made for the door. He could still remember that water-can. Made of aluminium alloy and shaped like an oversized Eau de Cologne bottle, it had a large screw-on metal cap and a tight-fitting jacket made of thick flannel. The jacket served as insulation and when wet, it kept the water cool.

He was not the only one in search of water; there was a crowd at the door, each with his water-can. As soon as the train came to a halt, they rushed out and headed for the nearest water source. By the time Suresh reached the large washbowl, there were already people set around it on all sides. Like the spokes of a wheel, each had his arm stretched out towards the central faucet. The first one had the mouth of his bottle fitted over the nozzle of the tap and water was gurgling into his bottle at a good rate. The tap was one of those robust conical contraptions that needed to be held up to allow the precious fluid to run. If you let it go, it would jam down by default to stop the flow.

Suresh joined the jostling crowd and finally got his turn at the water. No sooner had he got back to his seat, the air horns of the engine sounded and the compartment started moving. *Just in time*, thought Suresh; he had never liked the idea of being left behind on some unknown station with only the clothes on his back and, of course, his prize water bottle.

The day waned and with it the temperature. They were nearing the metropolis of Madras (as it used to be called back then). As twilight came, they saw the green fields being replaced by a smattering of houses; soon, there was no green left. The buildings grew steadily taller and the man-made jungle of steel and concrete closed in around them. They soon passed the gigantic twin towers of the Basin bridge thermal power station, which in the days to come, Suresh would recognise as the one landmark that would tell him that the final stop was only a few minutes away.

At about five to seven in the evening, the train slowed and crept into that vast cavern—Madras Central station.

They joined the line of passengers in the aisle, with their airbags slung over their shoulders and their hands clutching suitcases. Soon, they were on the platform and walking towards the exit when a stout elderly gentleman waved out to Mathachen; as they came closer, the older man had Mathachen in a bear hug.

That must be Uncle Thambi, thought Suresh who had never seen him before. Uncle Thambi was Mathachen's maternal uncle. Mathachen had told his son that Uncle Thambi was a bachelor, and now nearing seventy, he would in all probability stay that way. Dark in complexion, short of stature and built like a bulldog, his balding head held on to a sparse lot of hair around the periphery that fell over his ears and collar. He wore a faded brown jacket, which was a complete mismatch with his dark indigo trousers. With all this, and a round jolly face, Suresh could not help thinking there was something a little comical about him.

"How was the journey?" he asked; his hoarse, high-pitched voice momentarily rising above the noise of the crowd that poured past them. "And this must be Suresh," he added, turning to him and giving him a firm handshake. "Congratulations on becoming a medical student," he said, adjusting his thick 'soda bottle' glasses as though to appraise him a little better.

They followed Uncle into the main hall of the terminus. Suresh looked around him in wonder. Looking nearly as big as a football stadium, he had not seen anything quite like it. His eyes ran up the huge steel columns that reached high above and then gracefully branched away on all sides like a palm. These curving girders met their counterparts and supported a multi-arched partially transparent roof that let in the subdued light of the sun. Its exterior was equally impressive. The brick red facade was topped with a lily-white roof and a tall central clock tower reaching a height of 130 feet. This gothic structure built by the British almost a century ago had become an icon for the city.

They soon found themselves out on the busy street. "It is quite nearby," said Uncle Thambi. "We could have walked it if it hadn't been for the luggage," he added as he hailed down a cab. Within minutes, they were at Uncle Thambi's place. He occupied the first floor of a rather run-down old building, with mildewed tiles and stained, faded whitewash that may have really been 'white' once upon a time.

They climbed up a narrow, creaky, wooden stairway, whose steps were rough and worn down in the centre. It was a modest place—one large hall with a bedroom leading off at one end and the kitchen at the other. The wooden floorboards were chapped with age and the joints between them were plainly seen, although much of it was covered with an odd assortment of threadbare carpets.

"Let's get some dinner," said Uncle Thambi as he moved to the window and bellowed out to someone on the street below, "Muniyandi!" And then, "MUNIYANDI!" much more loudly this time.

"Yes, Sar?" came Muniyandi's voice from a distance.

"I want three chicken biryanis, and make them special."

"Why don't you freshen up?" he told his guests, showing them to the bedroom. First Mathachen and then Suresh had a bath, and were back in the hall when Muniyandi came up with the food. Uncle Thambi took the packet from him and shoved a note into his pocket. "Keep the change," he said as Muniyandi smiled with gratitude, turned on his heels and disappeared.

He brought the parcels to the table, emptied the contents into a large tray. He went to the kitchen and brought out three plastic plates, which he set before them. He ladled huge amounts of the biryani onto their plates, so much so that they had to hold out their hands over their plates to make him stop. "Eat well," he advised as he stood beside them, "it's the best biryani in Madras."

"Please sit, Uncle," exclaimed Mathachen, "we will serve ourselves. After all, we are not guests."

As they ate, Suresh looked around at the mess the house was in. Uncle Thambi's effusive hospitality lay in stark contrast to his utter lack of housekeeping skills. There were books, clothes, luggage and files untidily scattered about the place, with furniture of various shapes and sizes interspaced between them. It was clear that a lady had never been within the four walls of this abode.

"It's not much," interjected Uncle Thambi as he saw Suresh looking around him. "But I have had the rent frozen for more than a decade, that's why I am staying put. And it's so nicely located."

"Why should I move anyway?" he added after a little thought. "I am comfortable here and work is nearby."

Suresh had gathered that Uncle Thambi did some petty business to keep the stove burning, but as to what exactly it was, he would never know.

Dinner was over. Mathachen and Suresh helped with the dishes. Uncle Thambi talked and reminisced about old times. It was almost 11 pm when Uncle's voice rose a pitch as he looked towards Suresh and said: "You better get some sleep," indicating the one bedroom he had vacated for them. "You will have to get up at least at five to catch the morning train."

Chapter 12

College (Sevur)

Suresh slept well that night. He woke up with snatches of a dream lingering in his mind and then fading away. It had something to do with bounding up a beat-up old wooden staircase. Suddenly, the steps in front of him vanished and he was free-falling into space.

They were at the central station by six o'clock in the morning. The burden of their luggage slowed them down. Uncle Thambi walked confidently in front, swinging his arms widely as though the place belonged to him.

This time, it was a short two-hour journey by the east coast railroad that got them to the town of Marivanam. Then a 20-kilometre taxi ride towards the Bay of Bengal and the little town of Sevur, where Suresh would spend the next eight years of his life. A time that would change him from a boy to a man, acquainted with the toils and trials of life.

The town itself was nothing to write home about. It was naturally divided into four quadrants by two roads. The four-lane highway running south and the other smaller one, almost at right angles to it, going due east towards the sea. Most of the commercial and official buildings were in the north-eastern segment along with a temple and school. Shops and houses lay densest at the central intersection and become sparse towards the periphery. It would have stayed an unknown junction between the two roads had it not been for the huge campus two kilometres away. For this reason, this village had outstripped the others around it and stood tall beside them like a conspicuous tree that, alone among its neighbours, had hit on a water source.

"This is Sevur town," said the driver as the taxi crossed the intersection. "The college is only two kilometres from here, Sar," he added confidently, having ferried any number of newcomers to this destination. "The place is very high tech, Sar," he informed them. "Just like Madras. You can see any number of boys and girls in pairs." At this, Mathachen looked anxiously at his son and smiled a little to himself.

Just after the town, they saw, in the distance, the first of many multi-storied buildings rise above the millet fields on either side of the road. There seemed to be more of them on the right or southern side of the road. Later on, Suresh would find this was true because 75% of the land was on the south side of the campus. The small portion on the north accommodated a playing field, the men's hostel and a few residential blocks.

Most of the students were rich kids with motorbikes and branded clothes, who could easily pay a sizeable donation and the sky-high fees. But there was a percentage given to the government, to be filled on the basis of merit. These had only to pay nominal tuition. Suresh had gotten in through this scheme and so had to pay only about 10% of what the affluent had paid for a management quota seat. The system was not without its benefits. It had a good side to it as well since the government would never have had the capital to put up this huge medical complex, which was helping some poor patients and providing doctors for the masses.

"Is it admissions, Sar?" asked the driver.

"Yes," replied Mathachen.

"Then we will go to the administrative block," asserted the driver. They drove up to the main gate of the south side of the campus, where they were stopped and questioned by the security people. Mathachen quickly fished out the admission order from his briefcase and stuck it out to one of them, who had one look at it before waving them through the gate.

They turned into the parking lot of an impressive three-storey building with a brown marble facade. "Murugan, please wait here," said Mathachen before he strode towards the entrance with Suresh in tow and his precious briefcase clutched tightly in his right hand. Money that it contained was not his prime concern, but Suresh's original certificates.

They entered the foyer and turned right under a sign that said 'Registrar's office'. There was another one written in paper underneath, which said 'Admissions'. The receptionist ushered them to room number six where they met the registrar's secretary. After a perfunctory glance at the papers, she gave them a broad smile. "Congratulations," she said as she stretched out a thin hand to Suresh. "Take these there, and they will tell you what to do," she added, pointing them to a side room.

There they sat opposite a senior clerk who took in the originals and gave them a receipt for the same. Numerous forms were signed by father and son in all the right places. "Here is your challan," he said, giving them a coupon with a tear-off portion. "This is for your tuition fee that has to be paid in the State Bank on the opposite side of the road. Keep the counterfoil carefully. Here is a letter to the men's hostel warden. Best wishes!" he ended and got up to see them to the door.

The bank was not difficult to find. They paid the fees and the counterfoil went into Mathachen's briefcase. "I will keep it," he told his son, "in case you lose it." With that exchange of money, Suresh's admission was now secure. You could see Mathachen's face lose some of its creases as his tension ebbed away. They walked out of the bank building into the bright sunshine outside. Mathachen was all smiles and he had a spring to his gait.

"Let's have a look around the campus," he suggested.

"Sure," said Suresh, shrugging his shoulders. They walked along the road further east and came to the gate of the hospital. It was as elaborate as the one that guarded the college campus. But this one had more traffic plying through it. Haggard patients with their precious files, harassed doctors with their stethoscopes and white coats, autorickshaws, cars, ambulances. The larger entrance was for the vehicles and the smaller gate for pedestrians. The security fellows had things in control.

They watched in amusement as a hapless pedestrian walked through the broadway meant for vehicles. The man had crossed onto the road before the guards realised what had happened. Two of them rushed after the man with whistles blowing. They made the poor fellow retrace his path back through the gate and then he was herded towards the pedestrian path. "Ha! That was good," chuckled Mathachen. "I am sure he wouldn't do it again."

They wandered around the corridors and walkways, looking at the tall multi-storied specialty blocks. The hospital was separated from the college by a high and robust wall with barbed wires running along the top. There was a single gate that allowed people with bona fide IDs to cross between the two parts of the campus. Mathachen hadn't any and Suresh had not gotten his yet. So they had to go back out onto the road again before they went back into the college campus. They walked along the concrete ring road that led them around the campus with its residential bungalows, apartment buildings and even a lovely park, till they were once again back beside the administrative block. Beside it stood an impressive structure with a lawn around. Over the years, Suresh would get to know in bits and pieces the story of the man who had created all that they had seen.

The hundred-acre campus was the brainchild of a former bootlegger who then became a hitman for a prominent minister of state. Thereafter, he had slowly but surely squirmed his way into the mainstream of life as a respectable real estate agent and a political wheeler and dealer. He had amassed great wealth during his career, most of which, as they could see around them, was plowed into this institution. The patriarch had since passed on, and the empire was now run by his sons.

Suresh and his father walked over a narrow path through the lawn and now stood and gazed at the hexagonal marble mausoleum erected in memory of the departed soul. His bust looked down on them in mute benevolence. The shining brass plaques below spoke volumes about his great foresight, lofty principles, patriotism and great generosity.

By the time they finished a tour of the campus, the noonday sun was blazing down on them. They found Murugan, the taxi driver, faithfully waiting for them with their luggage safe in the boot.

"Shall I leave you in the hostel and carry on, Son?" asked Mathachen. "Only then can I catch my train back."

"Fine," said Suresh nonchalantly.

They drove through the main gate, past the security folk, across the main road onto another avenue that served the smaller northern part of the campus. There were a few houses on each side and then they encountered this brazen signpost on the right side of the road. It said in large bold letters"

THE MANSIONS OF THE GODS

Enter herein at your own risk.

Mathachen saw what was written and thought to himself, *They are still medical students and already, they think they are Gods. I wonder what will happen when they become doctors!*

Beyond this was the hostel office with a small parking lot into which Murugan drove his taxi. There were a few other vehicles that had brought freshmen and their guardians.

They walked into the building and looked around. On the wall was a large wooden board with the names of previous general secretaries of the 'Men's Hostel Union'. 1967 was Ravishankar. 1968 was Vishwanathan, 1969 was Pramod Gupta and so on. The clerk handed them still more forms to be filled in and signed. They joined the other newcomers who were scattered around the small room filling up the forms. Some occupied the few chairs that were there, some stood and some even went back and used the bonnet of their cars as a table.

Again, there was the challan to be paid at the bank. Even though it was only walking distance, they decided to take a ride for lack of time. So Murugan quickly drove them back down the road to the bank. Suresh's bags were unloaded and then, just seemingly out of nowhere came one of the hostel sweepers, grinning broadly as he commandeered the luggage. "Which room?" he asked as he slung one over his shoulders and gripped the others in both hands.

"125," replied Suresh. They followed him into one of the corridors. They were only a little distance from the office when

Mathachen had a quick look at his watch and tapped the man on his broad shoulders. The man turned around.

Seeing the father's face, he said reassuringly, "I will take him, Sar, don't worry; we will look after him." Mathachen smiled gratefully at him and pressed a ten-rupee note into his pocket. "Thank you, Sar," said the man and resumed his march forwards.

Mathachen stood still and looked at his son silently before they hugged each other. Suresh's face was rather expressionless, while his father's had a tear that brimmed over his eyelids and dropped onto his cheeks. "Bye, and write often," said the father.

"OK, Appa," said Suresh with a confident smile on his face. Then he turned and quickly hurried after his luggage, which was some distance off by then. Pride and sadness churned inside him as Mathachen watched his son for a few moments, watched him walk out of his own immediate circle of life and care.

The taxi sped along, carrying Mathachen back to the station. Melancholy was the better part of his feeling. It was then that he recalled a story that his own father had told him. 'Love, like water, naturally flows downwards from the parent to the child,' his father had said. Then the old man (bless his memory) had proceeded to narrate this parable.

A man's house was being remodelled. He stood, perspiring, bare-headed and anxious in the hot sun and watched his middle-aged son on the roof, helping the workers lay the tiles. "Be careful!" he said to his son once in a while. "Watch where you put your legs." Then, after a while, "Do you want us to get you some water?"

The son had little to say; he hardly heard his father because he was looking down fretfully at his own little boy playing in the sand. "Papa," he finally shouted at the old man, "why don't you ask Ashok (the little boy) to go play inside; he has just recovered from a fever and look at him playing in the sun."

The grandfather became upset and shouted up to the little boy's father on the roof, "What about me? I also had that fever and I am also standing in the sun, but you are not bothered about me. You are only concerned about Ashok."

"That is the way it is," replied the man on the roof. "Love, like water, naturally flows downwards. One day, that little fellow I care about—your grandson—will care more about his own children than he will care about me."

The old man was right, thought Mathachen. *They leave our circle to make ones of their own; that is the way it is*. While such and other thoughts circled through his mind, the taxi reached the station. Murugan kindly held out the door for him. He must have seen the look on Mathachen's face for he said cheerfully, "Don't be troubled, Sar. He will be alright. I have brought many boys to college; they all grow up to be bright young men."

"Thank you, Murugan," said Mathachen. "Give me your address and a telephone number where I can reach you, just in case I have to contact you." And so they parted: strangers only a few hours ago, but now friends.

Meanwhile, Suresh had long since reached his room. The sweeper had put his things down and beckoned him outside. "Those are the bogs," he pointed out. "That is the dining hall. If you need anything, I or one of my other colleagues who look after the place will help you." Indeed, Suresh could see it was well looked after, he was impressed.

It was three stories high, pentagonal in shape, and made out of solid granite like few of the older buildings on the campus. Built at a time when people knew how to work with that stuff, long before steel and concrete took over. The structure had an opening where the road ran in and forked to form a loop that hugged the building all around its inside. Interspaced evenly in the space enclosed by the road stood five huge trees, one against each block of the pentagon. Its top branches towered above the highest floor for a good twenty feet or so. Suresh had never seen trees quite the same before; they said it had been brought from Australia. The centre of the space had a large circular pond with a pathway all around it. Radiating out from this path were six others that cut the lush lawns in-between them into sections like a pie chart.

After settling into his room, Suresh locked it and sauntered confidently onto the driveway and towards the mess. Halfway there, he heard a faint scraping sound that drew his gaze upwards. Just in time to see a yellow bucket disappear back over the third-floor balcony. But not soon enough to avoid its contents that now drenched a good part of him. He looked up defiantly, but there was nobody to be seen where the water had come from. Instead, peals of raucous laughter rose above him from all around. He found quite a few of the inmates staring down at him.

"Hey pisser, what are you looking up for?" said one of them who had a burly voice and a handlebar moustache. "I see that you have wet your pants. Put your head down and go back to your room in the slums." That was what they called the section that housed the freshers. "Come to the room above the mess at 6 o'clock, and don't get out of there before that."

Suresh slinked back to his room, changed into one of his older set of clothes and arranged his belongings mechanically.

He was glad that his father had not stayed to witness this scene. When he had done all that he thought was necessary, he sat pensively on his bed awaiting his fate. He knew what was coming. They had different names for it—ragging, initiation or whatever. A knock shook him from his reverie. He found he had a roommate whose father had accompanied him there. He was a tall, lean, timid-looking fellow from Bangalore. His face reminded him of a mouse on a starvation diet. But he was a nice guy and once they got to know each other, they became thick friends. Ajit Shah was his name. Years later, he was one of the first to be let in on the secret when the crisis hit Suresh.

The college offices closed at five and by half-past, most of the newcomers were installed in their rooms. At six o'clock, they heard a bell. It seemed they were supposed to go to the common room above the mess, and so they went. Seats were arranged in a tight circle for all sixty of them in the centre of the large hall and all around them stood their seniors. Some of them in the older classes looked really fearsome with stern faces, beards and bulging muscles. A tall hulk of a fellow stood up to address them.

"You guys think you are great, huh?" He smirked, looked at them with disdain and went on, "Here, you are dirt, you are spirochetes—germs that need cleansing, a little baptism of sorts. So the next three days, you will do what you are told. Each of you will have a fag master from the final year and he will be your Lord and Master. Implicit obedience is the rule. Any disobedience or breach of code of conduct written on this wall will be met with punishment that will not be easily forgotten." So saying, he pointed to a cardboard notice hanging on the wall and began reading:

"When you meet any senior in the next three days, you will come to attention and salute him, saying, 'I a first-year pisser, salute you, sir, my Lord.' You will move from this posture only when the senior has passed by.

"Every morning at six o'clock, there will be PT, which all will attend.

"You will fulfil all your fag master's requests.

And so on and so forth went the rules.

The next three days were difficult, to say the least.

Some of them had one leg of their trousers cut off, others had one half of their moustache shaved away. Others were made to kneel in homage and recite vulgar poems. At the end of the three days came the grand finale. Gathered together in front of the mess, the weary ragtag bunch heard the field marshal announce over a loudspeaker. Incidentally, this megaphone was in use all the days of their ordeal. Bawling out at them to come for a forced march at three in the morning, another talent contest or yet another session of PT.

Now, for one last time, it spoke, "How many of you guys don't know how to swim?" About half the hands went up. "Anyway, I hope you don't drown. The pond that you see in the centre is seven feet and four inches deep. There have been accidents in the past. I am sure most of you will make it. There is an ambulance waiting, in case, you know…"

Suresh turned like the rest of them to follow the pointing finger and sure enough, there was a fair-sized ambulance on the driveway.

The sun was almost setting when they were blindfolded and lined up, one behind the other, to face the pond. Over the course of the preceding days, when they were doing silly errands for their seniors and generally being paraded around the hostel, their fag masters made sure they saw the depth gauge displayed prominently against the side of the pond. The water was just above the seven-foot mark and through the greenish murky waters, they could see marking going down into the depths. Suresh knew how to swim, so he was not excessively worried but some of those who did not were far from comfortable. He heard one desperate fellow shouting in a hoarse voice, "I don't know swimming, sir! Please, sir. I don't know swimming, sir!"

One by one, they were yanked off the ground by their hands and feet, swung to and fro amidst a chorus of loud voices that roared, "One. Two! Three!"

Into the pond they went. Each body was released up into the air and fell into the water with a mighty splash. To add to their fright, there were urgent appeals over the loudspeaker. "He can't swim, somebody help him! That fellow has stopped breathing, rush him to the hospital."

Suresh felt himself flying through the air and then a cold splash. As he hit the water, he instinctively went into a semi curl with legs partly down to meet the floor. Suresh was expecting to go down deep, so when less than a second later, his feet struck the bottom, he was jarred by the suddenness of it and stood gingerly to his feet in water that just about reached his waist. He waded to the edge and strong hands hauled him over the edge. No matter he was wet to his bones, but there were hugs all around. Fearsome smirks were replaced by open smiles and vigorous handshakes. They had half an hour to change and come for a grand dinner, where they sat side by side with their fag masters and others.

The general secretary stood to address them. "It's all over, fellows. Congratulations and welcome to the Men's Hostel brotherhood, and the Mansions of the Gods." They all raised their glasses of soft drinks above their heads and the room was taken over by rounds of applause. And what became of the commander? You could hardly have recognised him. Gone was the baton in his hand, the military fatigues and even the megaphone. In their place, he sported a benign grin as he sat quietly at one of the tables.

Classes were supposed to have started the day before, but their teachers knew the 'freshers' would not show up, nor would most of their seniors. So they graciously looked the other way and condoned the absence. But from eight o'clock the next morning, there would be no excuses. They had had their fun and now it would be back to the books. And what books they were—fatter tomes Suresh had never set his eyes on. Why, it would develop your upper limbs just to carry around *Gray's Anatomy* for a few days. Then there were introductory lectures, labs, etc. But what Suresh could remember most clearly was the dissection hall.

The first day that Suresh entered the large hall, a pungent, almost overpowering odour hit him in the face, making his eyes smart. It was the smell of formalin. A smell that would become as familiar to him as the smell of sambhar and chutney. Out of a class of a little more than a hundred, only half of them were here; the other batch was in the biochemistry lab. They sat down on benches with long stainless steel tables in front of them.

The professor of anatomy, an elderly spinster, stood to address them, a small microphone clipped to her white coat lapels. Soon, her sonorous voice came booming over the PA system.

"This is a sacred place," she said gravely. "Here, the dead teach the living. Each of the bodies you dissect was once a living, moving, vibrant, thinking human being like us. The fact that their earthly remains are now available to us is because of the largeness of their heart, or the unfortunate circumstances that befell them. Each body and limb should be treated with the utmost respect.

"Each of you will be assigned tablemates, and there will be eight to a table sharing one cadaver. Four of you will work on one limb. The head and neck will be common for the eight of you. There will be a weekly test and these marks will count towards the final assessment."

While this lecture was going, Suresh saw the lab assistants dip into large rectangle tanks, each at least six feet in length. They used large L-shaped instruments to dig deep into the receptacle and, between three of them, they slowly lifted up something. It was difficult to believe that it was a whole human body that emerged from the murky formaldehyde (formalin) solution it was immersed in. It was as stiff as a wooden board; more like tree trunks than like the remains of human beings. The chemicals had dehydrated it; turning it into the likeness of a dark shrivelled fossil—its face set in death: gaunt and hideous.

In the subsequent months, Suresh enjoyed his work with the cadaver they were allotted. Some of the others did not like dissection as much as he did. He, being surgically inclined, liked to cut into the skin and tease it off the underlying fascia. He had to be careful not to buttonhole it. But his skill was up to it. The incision ran vertically right through the centre of the leg and the skin was reflected off latterly in two halves. The calf muscles had to be then delineated, taking care to preserve the nerves and vessel in their relative positions. A mistake here would not mean much, but in real life, a slip of the scalpel would mean the loss of life or limb. At the end of each session, the muscles would be covered with a thin layer of coir fibre dipped in formalin. The skin would be replaced over the whole, providing protection for the underlying structures, much like its function in the living man. A large plastic sheet was draped over the whole table and everything on it, until the next session. Each of them was given a box of bones to take to their room, which included a skull as well. In this study of osteology, they had to learn the names of each major crease and tubercle. The entire set would have to be returned at the end of the third semester.

Anatomy was the study of structure. In the physiology classes, on the other hand, they learned the function. They learned how the skin was actually the biggest organ in the body, serving to regulate its internal milieu, at the same time sending vital information to the brain via the sense of touch. Nevertheless, Suresh liked the structure and form over function. He found biochemistry particularly boring.

The first year was a busy time full of welcome parties and academics and before he knew it, the university exams were on him. The 2nd year, which actually started with the fourth semester, was a breeze, leaving him time to do a few other things, for he was a kind of an all-rounder. He dabbled in a little bit of music, a little bit of sports. He had a good number of friends: but there was one, who in time became more than a friend, Sunithi.

She was not on his dissection table. In fact, she was right across on the other side of the hall. But Suresh could not help stealing a glance at her once in a while. And when he did, everything around seemed blurred and out of focus in contrast. *My! She is cute*, thought Suresh, but then left it there. In truth, most would have thought her not beautiful but almost pretty, comfortably pretty.

She had the colour of ripe yellow mangoes with a certain transparency, almost like marble, shining dark eyes, a round face and a flat, unobtrusive nose. She was not very tall and had a few extra kilos about her. She wore her straight shoulder-length hair loose and as she turned from side to side, it whirled around her neck like the long pleated skirt of a flamenco dancer. A chubby jovial doll—that was what she looked like. *A happy-go-lucky type*, thought Suresh, but again, he thought no more about it.

It was not until they were into their fourth year when Suresh first made friends with her. They found themselves seated beside each other on a bus trip to a village community health programme. They got talking a little and then lingered for a few minutes, even after the bus had dropped them off in front of the library. Thereafter, at least once in a week, Sunithi would notice Suresh looking right at her in a funny sort of way, with something more than just an innocent smile.

By the end of that academic year, Suresh was well and truly smitten. And he somehow knew that she knew. Maybe it was the not-so-random acts of kindness he dropped around her or the body language or something else less tangible. It came to a point when he just had to know what she thought of it. So he got up the courage and asked another lady classmate to ask Sunithi for a date. Thilaga was a good friend and his dissection partner; besides, she was Sunitha's roommate. Thilaga was a bit surprised when he asked her, "Why don't you ask Sunithi to meet me at the sunken garden at about 6 pm tomorrow?"

"Don't raise your hopes too high," she replied in her usual motherly fashion. "I will ask her." And so she did. Suresh waited impatiently for the next day. Thilaga had a faint smile on her face when he walked up to her. "She said she will be there," she announced. "I think it will be alright," she added reassuringly.

"Thanks a lot, Thilaga," said Suresh gratefully.

Now he had all day till 6 pm and time seemed to crawl along. While the lecturers were droning on, he found his mind wandering away to the sunken garden. Would she really come or would she send word at the last minute, declining?

The sunken garden lay between the library block and the women's hostel, the size of an ice hockey rink. It sank in tiers towards the centre, where there was a pond. Each tier had exotic palms, creepers and flowers of every hue. It gave you the feeling of being in a huge green nest. The body of water in the middle had a broad pathway around it with a few stone benches. This was where Suresh was sitting at 5:45 in the evening, nervously awaiting what he at that time thought would be the most pivotal point of his life.

A little after six, he saw her glide down the steps towards him wearing a grey sari with little red butterflies on it. He was not one to notice things like this, but this sari he would always remember. Suresh rose to meet her. And they sat on one of the warm granite seats. "It seems you wanted to meet me," she opened with a playful expression on her face.

"Yes," Suresh said with trepidation.

"So, what is it about?"

"Just thought we could get to know each other a little bit more," returned Suresh.

"A person like you would be nice to know," she replied and this time, she had an unambiguous joyous smile on her face. The ice was broken. They talked for a long time that day.

She was an NRI candidate. Her father, Mohan, worked as an engineer in the Middle East and her mother was a nurse. In their final year, the relationship bloomed with long walks in the evenings. There were others like them, and so the internal phones in the hostels were always in demand.

What Suresh remembered most was their evenings on the beach. They had to go through a fishing village and out onto the shore. Many a day, they sat on the sand with their backs to the setting sun, watching its thrilling display of colour—a fitting finale to the day.

Chapter 13

The Making of a Surgeon

The final year was soon over and then the examinations. They were in different batches and so had varying subjects on each day. They met every evening to exchange news. The medicine clinical exams were over for her batch when she came to the same spot that had become their rendezvous point since that first time. The sunken gardens were as beautiful as ever, but this time, her eyes were bloodshot and her face puffy. She began crying as she collapsed onto the granite seat beside him.

"What happened?" he asked gently, wrapping his arms about her shoulders.

"It was awful," she said. "He just finished me off. I got the diagnosis wrong for the long case. The right one was not even on my list of differentials. The short cases were not any better; I got some important findings wrong. There is no way I will pass."

"Don't worry," he said reassuringly. "You never know until the results are announced."

"The skilled assistants have told people," she continued between sniffles and through her handkerchief, "that only half the batch has passed."

"It will all be alright," Suresh said, trying to comfort her.

"It's easy for you to say, you are a clever open candidate," she shot back. Suresh remained silent, knowing the mood she was in.

"Looks like we won't be starting internship together," she said after a while.

"How will that make a difference to us?" he said emphatically. She only looked up at him and smiled faintly.

The next day, they heard all about it. It was a massacre alright. The external examiner, a senior man, was particularly mean and seemed to have needed only the slightest reason to flunk a candidate. The internal was a young fellow who really could not stand up to him.

She got over her disappointment in time. She left to be with her parents in Dubai for some time. Meanwhile, Suresh started his internship.

In spite of hearing some nasty tales from his seniors, he was ill-prepared for the change when it came. From the bliss of his years as a student, to the grind of being at the bottom of a long chain of command, was a sea change. It was like being thrown from the comfort of a warm bed into icy waters. Over a matter of days, his life had changed beyond recognition.

Surgery was his first posting. Now they were on grand rounds that happened twice a week. The entourage was on their way to A-ward where the male surgical patients where admitted. The chief, Dr Madavan, was up front, flanked by his assistant on his right and his chief resident on his left. A few junior consultants and the other residents made up the middle. Bringing up the rear was Suresh with his fellow interns. As the company turned into the foyer of the ward, the chief stopped and by the time he turned around, the stragglers had caught up to the group.

Dr Madavan in his mid-fifties, a dark-skinned massively built man, well more than the average height. His razor-sharp eyes peered at you through a thick pair of wire-rimmed spectacles held up by a broad-based stubby nose. His puffy eyelids and sagging cheeks were a testimony to his camaraderie with alcohol and tobacco. If you were to meet him in his office or the theatre lounge, he would in all probability have a cigarette dangling from the corner of his lips. But in all truth, it must be told that he was never once found to be even remotely smelling of alcohol when he was in the hospital.

His temper was proverbial. He could be violent and vitriolic at times, but at certain other times, he could be tenderly kind and generous. He ran a bachelor's home to which the whole department would be invited at least once a month for a lavish party.

The man surveyed his lot and began to speak, "There is a food chain here, and I am right at the top. You are here to work and perhaps to be trained, if that is possible and you have got it in you. You are my pack mules and you will do what you are told. Mistakes maybe condoned, but laziness and wilful disobedience will be dealt with a strong hand. You can meet me with your concerns at any time of the day or night. But don't come to me saying you have had only five hours of sleep. Count yourself fortunate if you have had four."

After a few more words, he wheeled around and continued his tour. This was the twice-weekly grand rounds and each case was discussed threadbare. They had passed the first two beds without major incident. But the third one was different. This was a patient who had had an intestinal perforation. This was his third day after surgery.

"Has he passed wind?" asked the big man.

"No," came the reply.

"And why not?" asked the chief as he bent down to look at the plastic drainage bag hanging by the patient's side. "How much was the drainage last evening?"

"Ten ml, Sir," said the junior resident in charge of the patient.

"And why, for heaven's sake, is that drain still there? It should have been removed last evening."

"I told the intern to do it, Sir," said the junior resident, looking daggers at Suresh. "I will do it after the rounds, Sir," he added meekly. The Lion was roused.

"Do it after rounds!" roared the man. "Then why the hell do we have rounds in the first place? You had the whole night, you stupid fellows." By this time, the decibel levels had increased to the extent that he could be heard on the other side of the ward. "How many times have I told you, idiots, that a drain should not be kept one minute more than is necessary?"

"Shankar," he said, motioning to his assistant, "see to it."

"What are grand rounds coming to?" he muttered as the whole team moved to the next bed. Meanwhile, the resident had drawn up to Suresh and cursed him under his breath.

"Sorry, man," mumbled Suresh as he ran towards the nursing station to get a suture removal pack. As he mechanically went about removing the drain, he pondered the fact that a second instalment of the bawling out would be coming his way later that day. And he mentally braced himself for it. Suresh was interested in a surgical career and was determined to give a good account of himself here. This would stand him a better chance if he were to apply for a resident's post in this hospital.

Sunithi wrote him long letters, but his replies were always short and to the point. For that was all he could afford. He hoped she would understand; at least she would when she got into internship. Sunithi came back to the hostel a month before her examinations, at which time Suresh was into his public health posting. He saw her more often but not for long—their days on the beach were behind them, at least for now.

It was soon time to apply for his post-graduate entrance exam. General Surgery was a sought-after specialty, but with his grades, Suresh made it in his first attempt. This was how Suresh again found himself in Professor Madavan's unit.

It was a Thursday and they were in the theatre. The large multifocal dome light was shining down into the open abdomen. The intestines hung out to one side, revealing a large cyst arising from the head of the pancreas. They were one hour into the operation and Chief had just dissected off the lower surface of the tumour. Suddenly, the intern to his right, who was retracting the liver, disappeared from sight. They heard a dull thud and then a loud clang, as the large retractor fell to the floor and slid to a corner. Dr Madavan looked down to find his intern sprawled on the floor at his feet. "Remove him," he commanded in a loud impassive tone before he turned his attention back to the tumour at hand.

He had carefully dissected to some extent all around. He gently turned the mass down to get at the central bit of tissue that was holding it down. The next nip of his scissors saw a spurt of blood that hit the assistant's face before Chief put a mop on it and then one more.

"Arrange for blood," he said gravely to his senior resident standing on the floor. He turned on the intern standing around and then sent him packing. "Go out and get some donors," he yelled.

The anaesthetist was in a flurry and sent her technician hurrying to the theatre blood storage unit. "Get some good suction ready," he told his team as he gently peeled away the mops. No sooner had the last one been removed, the blood gushed out and began to rapidly fill up the abdomen. This time, he blindly reached into the red pool and with his thumb and finger, he clamped down on the site he thought was the cause of the problem. His left hand stayed there, while he looked blankly at the wall. The blood that was up to his wrist had receded with the powerful suction on the job. Meanwhile, the anaesthetist was rapidly losing her cool.

"Do something, Sir," she told the surgeon anxiously. "He is dropping his blood pressure."

He glared at her over his spectacles, but said nothing.

The field had become reasonably clear; whatever was bleeding was under Chief's thumb. "Get me an artery," he said as he stretched out his right palm to the scrub nurse. She handed him the usual medium artery forceps. He took one look at it before flinging it across the room to its furthest corner. "Where is Manjula?" he bellowed. "Why can't they post her with me, at least on the majors?"

Manjula was an older hand who had spent years assisting him. All this time, his left hand was firmly in control in the depth of the abdomen. He reached out once more and this time, he was given an instrument long enough to reach to the bottom of the abdomen. He rested a moment and then made sure the retractors and the suction were in their place but yet out of his way. While his left thumb and index finger gradually relaxed their hold, the slightly opened jaws of the forceps darted downwards to take their place, biting down on the tissue that held the bleeder. He made sure that the instrument was ratcheted safely up to the third notch before gingerly relaxing his hold on it.

He gave a big sigh and looked up to smile at Shankar. "Now for some thick atraumatic silk on a round body," he asked. "No hurry," he added, knowing that the emergency was over. Having got what he asked for, he checked its tensile strength by stretching the ligature with both hands and giving it a good tug. Satisfied, he put the needle back onto its holder and reached into the wound; he deftly directed the round body needle into the pancreatic tissue, making sure to encircle the area around the tip of the precious forceps that was holding things together. He took the ends of the suture in his finger and he directed the vector of the tension with an outstretched index finger.

"Ready now?" he asked Shanker, who was holding the artery clamp. "When I tell you, release the clamp and get it out of the way." After a few deep breaths, they were ready to go. "Yeh," said his boss and Shanker released and withdrew the forceps in one fluid motion. At the same time, his boss tightened the ligature in a flash, with enough tension to singe down on the tissue but not too much so it cut through. Something that only the sensitive fingers of a surgeon could determine. He threw another knot on the first one to secure it, and then two more for safety.

"Always leave an extra knot just in case your assistant decides to cut it too fine," he commented, looking at Suresh. Then, holding his gloved right hand in front of him, he flexed his fingers and declared, "Shankar, you may be having all those new-fangled scopes and instruments coming. But mark my words. Nothing like these hands."

The patient survived and so did the intern. The tender part of this great surgeon made its appearance after he had scrubbed off and gone to the professor's lounge. Suddenly, he remembered his new intern who had taken a fall. He was soon seen carrying a cup of his own coffee to the junior doctor's lounge and giving it to the poor chap. Tears ran down the young fellow's face as Chief left the room.

Sunithi had meanwhile gotten over the temporary setback and cleared medicine in the next attempt. She had sat and really worked hard for her entrance exams. She made it from being second on the waiting list to getting onto the diploma course in paediatrics. She had always liked children and this was what she wanted to specialise in. She said a diploma would be enough to allow her to practice in most places. Suresh was pleased as long as she was happy.

They got engaged at the beginning of Suresh's final year. It was a small but elegant function, held in one of the finest hotels in Cochin. Sunithi's diploma course being two years, they would pass out at about the same time. The wedding was slated for that time, about a year from this present function. Suresh could just about wrangle a few days for it.

Suresh was lying on his own bed, while all these years tramped through his memory. Then another incident from those residency days came to mind. This time, the patient had not been so lucky.

It happened during his one month posting in thoracic surgery. In that super-specialty unit, he was again at the bottom of the food chain (as Chief would have put it!). There were no interns and so he found himself doing first-call duty once again. And again at the mercy of the nurses who would call him up at any time of night and day—for an IV line gone sour or an order that had to be initialled.

One theatre day, he was the third assistant on a patient in her late teens. She was a cheerful girl, who quickly made friends with her caregivers, including Suresh. From her childhood, she had suffered repeated attacks of dyspnoea and could not run or play as other children did. She was diagnosed to have a PDA (patent ductus arteriosus), a defect that lay between her aorta and pulmonary artery. This conduit was useful inside her mother's womb, but should have closed at birth with the expanding lung. In her case, it had remained open, shunting large quantities of blood through her lungs and putting her cardiopulmonary circulation under stress.

The last time that Suresh saw her alive was during the previous day's night-rounds. "Goodnight, doctor," she had called out to him cheerily, her big circular earrings swinging as she shook her head from side to side. He was the last one to leave the ward among the doctors on duty.

The next day, her chest lay open before them. The heart was pulsating under the pericardium, like some restless beast waiting to be released from its cage. Suresh was standing to one side, retracting on the lung. The surgeon had dissected into the mediastinum from one side. The aorta came into view, throbbing with the pressure that it drew directly from the body's amazing pump. The blood that flowed through the great vessel at this point would have been enough to fill a bucket in a matter of minutes and the pressure enough to drive a fountain a metre and a half into the air. The ductus was dissected out, a loop of thick silk was passed under it and the knot was carefully fashioned. The operator was tightening down on the ligature when it happened.

Suresh would never know exactly what went wrong. Perhaps the silk broke or his hand slipped. He only saw the surgeon's elbow jerk awkwardly for a second. The next moment, the chest was filling up with blood at an alarming rate. Dr Saha frantically tried to stop the flow with his hands, blindly groping under a rising tide of crimson. "Satensky!" he cried out frantically and was immediately handed over the large instrument used to clamp large vessels.

He closed down on something, which must have been the aorta, for the bleeding slowed down a bit but still kept coming. The red deluge filled the chest and spilled over the sides, drenching drapes and gowns on its way to the floor. Suresh found he was standing in a pool of blood with his feet soaked in the stuff. It was all over in about a minute. The monitors had thrown all their alarms and tracings were all flat. The jerk of the knot, for whatever reason, had torn a hole in the aorta, pulmonary artery or maybe both. One of them might have been fatal, but if it were both, it was beyond help. They staunched the bleeding with mounds of mops, called on the pump technicians and put her on the heart-lung machine while her great vessels were repaired.

After this, they shocked the heart back into action and it faithfully but feebly got back to work. The patient was brain-dead by now and on a ventilator. She was transferred to the ICU on a heavy dose of inotropes to keep her BP up. She died the next day, never having gained consciousness.

The only thing worse that Suresh could think of was for her to have become a vegetable, like some patients he had seen. Dead yet alive; alive yet dead to all that mattered. *What was life anyway?* thought Suresh. *Without choice, what was life?* These living dead had no choices, not the smallest, tiniest choice. Unless… Unless the choices were made somewhere deep within them, and this we would never know.

Even while they were working like dogs to save lives, death was always around the corner. Like the young mother in the burns unit, shrieking her way to an untimely delirious death, her bloodstream taken over by bacterial toxins. The most powerful antibiotics did nothing to save her. Then there was that patient with terminal cancer being sent home to die. The man did not know his prognosis, for his relatives had refused to allow them to tell him he had only a few weeks to live. This being the case, he cheerfully bid Suresh goodbye in the usual Tamil greeting—Poyitu Varren. (I will go and come back.)

Looking into his face, Suresh felt a tinge of sadness, for he knew that he would not see that old man again, nor would he ever come back. He also felt a little anger at his relatives. Like it so often happened, the relatives would not want to tell the sufferer the diagnosis of an incurable disease. *I would certainly like to be told if I were the patient*, Suresh remembered thinking during those times. He was thankful that he did not know then, how little it would take to go from being a doctor to being a patient.

The last year of his surgical residency seemed to drag on and on. It was one of those nights again. His unit was on admission duty and when this came on top of a regular operation list, it was enough to exhaust even the toughest of them. And so Suresh found himself at 5 am, groggily entering the theatre yet another time. He had hardly slept over the last twenty-four hours, but he still had a few more hours to go before handing over his pager to the next guy at 7 am.

The patient had come in at 1 am with a duodenal perforation. *This should be an easy one, open and shut*, he thought to himself as he tumbled into his theatre overalls. And so it was, except for a minor incident, which had been totally erased from his memory in a few days' time. The patient was being prepped when he noticed that the patient was inordinately emaciated for a disease of such short duration.

"Are all his other tests normal?" he asked the second call. Having gotten a 'yes' for an answer, he dismissed it from his mind without further thought.

Suresh had finished sewing up the perforation with four bites taken across the small hole, adding a piece of omentum in-between to bolster the repair. He washed out the abdomen and thought he would just put in the drain before scrubbing off. The junior resident could do the rectus and the intern would probably get to do the skin. He had his left hand inside the abdomen, his index finger tenting up the skin at the point where he wanted the tube to exit. The finger was protected by many layers of muscle and fascia. The scalpel that his right hand held was only expected to reach the subcutaneous tissue, the rest of it being achieved by a blunt hemostat.

Whether the blade was unusually sharp or if he was in an inordinate hurry to finish, whichever way it was, the scalpel went right through the skin and several layers of muscle and fascia. Suresh felt a sharp pain as the knife point made contact with the tip of his finger. He yanked out his hand and held up his finger to examine it. The glove had been pierced and a touch of blood was visible beneath the ivory of the latex. He finished pulling the tube through with a curved Koker-clamp before scrubbing off.

"Wash it with water and betadine," advised the worried anaesthetist. It was a small wound, about 5mm in length and less than half that in depth. The bleeding had stopped. Somebody brought him some Band-Aid. He walked out of the theatre, looking forward to a few hours of sleep. He felt comfortable, except for a mild throbbing pain in his finger. It would take about a week to heal. He would have to tell his unit head, and this would mean no operating during this time. He was relieved in one way, as it would mean a few more hours of sleep and a little more time with his books.

All this seemed so far away to Suresh, as he lay there in his own childhood room and on his own childhood bed. His long reverie had made him oblivious to time. He must have slept and dreamt some of it. He did not know. He was awake now. Later on, his mother would tell him that she had come up to call him for lunch, but found him so soundly asleep that she did not have to heart to wake him up.

Dusk was well on its way outside. The brief twilight had stolen its way into the room, lending it a strange brightness. Suresh stared vacantly at the blades of the ceiling fan that cranked its way through circles that never seemed to end, and wondered if his life had not become something like this—going round and round and nowhere in particular, nowhere that meant anything.

Sunithi had gone from his life many years ago. He could not operate with confidence any longer, even though all his faculties were as sharp as ever. He was looking forward to being on his way back to Pachalur on the day after tomorrow. Those quiet hills were his only comfort. There, he was accepted and there, he had a purpose. He loved seeing his parents again, but soon would come prying relatives with veiled questions. His mother would start weeping again. It was much better that he left and saved them some trouble. It was not that he loved them less, but that he felt most at home in the Hill People's Hospital. If indeed home is where the heart is, then Pachalur would soon have more reasons for inviting him to make it his resting place.

Chapter 14

Back to Pachalur

The luxury coach deposited Suresh on the kerb at about ten minutes to five in the morning. Suresh heaved his bag onto his shoulders and trudged towards the bus stand about a furlong away, where he knew he would find a cement bench that could afford him some solace.

He could not remember seeing Oddanchatram so still and silent. Where were the bustling crowds and the churning traffic? Yet there were signs to say that the town was waking up from its night of slumber.

A well-groomed lady was sprinkling water over the earth about her front door, in an effort to keep the dust away and lend it some freshness for the day that would soon begin. A lone chaiwallah had gotten up his shutters and was now firing up his kettle. A beggar, prostrate on the veranda of the bank building, was stirring from his sleep, muttering to himself in the twilight zone between dream and wakefulness. Suresh had just found himself a seat when the mullah's cry from the loudspeakers of the mosque broke and rippled through the quietness of that early hour.

The first trip to Pachalur would be only at 6 am and so Suresh sat and waited on the concrete bench. He found himself nodding off to sleep from time to time. At length, the dim light of dawn, the incessant chatter of the increasing throng of travellers and the loud blare of bus horns goaded him wide awake.

There were few who set out for the hills this early and so getting a seat on the ramshackle bus was not a problem. The old behemoth laboured up the mountainside. The sun's cheery face broke upon them over a small hillock on the eastern horizon. The gentle light fell on Suresh's face and its warmth kindled fresh hope and courage within him.

Suresh fell asleep 10 minutes into the journey up the ghat road. He had fits of lucidity, when his neck would involuntarily snap back erect to prevent him from falling forwards completely and hitting his head on the seat in front. In time, he woke up feeling chilly, because the bus by then had reached almost 3,000 feet in its climb and was now struggling around the 11th hairpin bend. As it swung back into another steep incline, Suresh briefly glimpsed the blue waters of the lake far below them.

He rummaged in his backpack for a shawl that he wrapped around his ears and neck. Soon, the bus had conquered the last switchback turn and ran along the edge of a vast green valley to his left. Ahead, the soaring ridge of the higher ranges of the Palani hills came closer. Suresh could clearly see the pine trees that marked the northern end of the hospital grounds. Indeed, these pine trees could be seen from the plains if one had a pair of binoculars. It wouldn't be more than ten minutes to their destination now.

An open space in the front of the temple was the designated drop-off point. Suresh picked up his luggage and lumbered down the steps. The cool crisp mountain air caressed his face gently. The sun shone down on the brown roofs. On the sidewalk, an old man wrapped in a shawl squatted on the ground, comfortably soaking in the warmth and light, his breath escaping in a faint mist.

It was a good walk to the campus. He reached the edge of the village and onto the rough gravelled road. The hillside to his right was densely wooded. He could see that it had been raining while he was gone. Everything was looking so green and alive. The bare branches had put out tufts of tiny leaves. In carefree expectancy, the thorny branches of the sacred datura had put out its white moonflowers. They looked so much like a company of maidens dressed in white, their hands raised, grateful for the rain, for the sod and for life itself. It made him think.

These wild things responded so readily to nature's touch, no trace of reluctance there. They did not ask for a 'package deal'. They did not ask for a guarantee of three showers of rain during the week. We, humans, want the weeks, or at least the day's plan set out in neat array, before we can be happy. But for these plants, a single shower was enough to make them burst forth with outstretched arms and smiling faces. They switched to 'celebration mood' so willingly. These free growing children of nature had such *hope*, and walking beside them, he suddenly felt ashamed.

Contemplating thus on these matters, Suresh reached the forest guesthouse on his left; it was then that other thoughts came back to him. This was the spot where seven months ago, he had intervened in a quarrel not his own. It was here that the brute had the lady by her hair. As the images crowded in, his fingers instinctively reached for the faint scar on his lips.

In time, he passed the hospital gate where a few patients were standing around. The night-duty nurses came down the steps that led up to the hospital. They greeted each other cordially. He continued along the winding path through the eucalyptus grove and finally reached his house. *I need a hot bath*, he told himself, and he went about getting a pot of water onto the gas stove. The cheese sandwiches his mother had packed for him would do for breakfast. His patients would be waiting for him.

In a few days, he had fallen into the routine of seeing patients and doing some surgery—always very carefully and with double gloves on. December gave way to the middle of February, the month he thought brought the greatest change in the weather. The hot season would soon be upon them. Even now, the sun was setting a little later every week.

One evening in the second week of June, Suresh was walking back up from the village, where he had gone to get some provisions in the grocery store next to the post office. A few days ago, after months of baking heat, a shower had arrived. This marked the beginning of the monsoons in Kerala, on the other side of the mountain ranges to the west. The monsoons in Tamil Nadu would come only in October, and what they were getting now were the leftovers. It was frustrating to watch whole battalions of clouds pass by on their way east, but most of them were already spent. A few would be generous enough to give Pachalur hills a sparse rain or two. Even these were gratefully received, as any little water from the sky was welcome in this parched inland part of the state; it would at least get the temperature down a few notches.

Like everybody else, Suresh loved the rains and deemed it excellent weather whenever it came around. He sometimes reckoned that the old nursery rhyme would have to be turned on its head to make it relevant to folks here:

Sun, Sun, go away, come again another day

The rain is falling, don't you see, so please let it be.

For good earth, for baby and for me.

Suresh liked everything about the rain. He found the first rains particularly fascinating. The dry and weary season seemed to go on and on, and then they came. Suresh listened to its staccato rhythm on the tin roof and thought it the sweetest thing he had ever heard. There was that earthy aroma that rose up from the ground as dry dirt met the first drops of water. Many a time, he wished someone would bottle up this smell for him. Then he could take a whiff of it at any time, close his eyes and imagine it was raining.

A fortnight later, on a Wednesday morning, they were sitting around in the doctors' meeting room when a tall distinguished gentleman stood at the door. Ravikumar's face lit up in happy recognition as he got up from his seat and beckoned for him to come in.

"Please, have a seat, Jagdesh," he said, waving him into a plastic chair next to him. "So how are things in Natham?"

"Not very different, doctor. I came to Chinalapatti and then thought I would come and see you. Things okay here? No more trouble from those people?"

"We are all doing well," said Ravikumar and proceeded to introduce the newcomer to the others in the room. "This is Doctor Suresh."

"Vanakam, doctor," said the tall man, bringing his palms together in greetings. "This is Dr Jhansi," said Dr Ravikumar as he continued around the circle.

"Come, let's go home," said Ravikumar. "Malathi will be happy to meet you." With that, the two men rose to leave.

Later that day, Ravikumar told some of them how he came to be good friends with Inspector Jagdesh.

"It was a difficult time for me," began Dr Ravikumar. "We were just settling into these new buildings. We had a laboratory technician who was a trouble maker of sorts. Finally, after repeated warnings, I had to give him a termination order. But things did not settle down. Apparently, the offender had political links in important places. He belonged to a caste who were a violent lot, and they had a sizable presence in this area. I got some threat letters.

"There was one patient who was also from his community, who developed a reaction after a test dose for penicillin. We saved her, but she had to be in the ward for a couple of days. Far from being grateful for our care, she—no doubt instigated by the lab technician—lodged a complaint saying the doctors had given her the wrong injection. The member of the state assembly also got involved on the opposite side. It was a tense situation. Pachalur came under the jurisdiction of a police station twenty kilometres away. This was when Inspector Jagdesh rang me one day. 'Doctor,' he told me over the phone, 'I know you are doing good work. You see, these fellows have made a criminal complaint against you, in addition to that other one about gross medical negligence. That patient has reported that you tried to assault her. There are about two hundred of them now outside my station; they want me to arrest you immediately. I will delay the arrest. But this is what you do. You leave the place immediately; go down to Dindigul town, contact a good advocate and get yourself anticipatory bail. Tomorrow, when I come to make the arrest, you can hand it over to me. Don't worry, things will settle down.'

"As predicted by Mr Jagdesh, the case was dismissed in a few months, after preliminary inquiry. Because of this incident, we became good friends. He had often shared with me how difficult his job was. The area that his station looked after was quite large and on paper, two inspectors were allotted to it.

However, one of these posts lay vacant for years. So he was forced to be on call around the clock. Emergencies would come in at all times of the night and day. He often knew who the offenders were in a particular situation, but he had to sometimes let them go because of political pressure. Inspector Jagdesh was a good man, and he would not bend beyond a certain point. That is why the threat of transfer hung over him constantly. And so he was transferred out of our area six months after he took charge. They often shunt these honest officers to noncritical arenas like the prisons department or the police training college. That is how it is," finished Dr Ravikumar.

In August, the bed strength of the Hill People's Hospital increased from 12 to 18. This meant they would have to work a little harder. Usha was posted in Casualty, and Suresh would see her once in a while. But late in August, it occurred to Suresh that he had not seen her for more than a week. "What happened to Usha?" he asked Dr Jhansi.

"She is on leave," was her reply.

Then the stories started filtering in. "Didn't you know, doctor, her husband is very ill?" said one. Someone else said he had a motorbike accident; a third person said he was stabbed in a drunken brawl. Whatever it was, the man had been seriously injured. In a few days, he learned that he had died. Dr Ravikumar and a few others got ready to attend the funeral. Suresh was invited to join them, but he declined. During the next week, Suresh often thought of what had happened and wondered at his own feelings about it. There was sadness for Usha and her daughter Jasmine; at the same time, there was a sense of relief that some closure had been achieved on a past episode, and that in some strange way, things had been made right for him.

It was three weeks before Usha came back. In the meantime, Suresh wondered more than once if he would ever see her again. She had become a little thinner and her face bore marks of weariness. As soon as she saw him, the spark came back to her eyes for a fleeting moment. She smiled ever so briefly, it would hardly have been noticed by anyone else. Then she looked away and down.

The next day, they again met when she had to assist him, while he drained an ugly injection abscess on an old man. The poor fellow had gone to a quack in a village nearby, who had injected him with heaven knew what. The fever for which he sought treatment had gotten better, but here he was with this large angry-looking protuberance on his buttocks. Soon, the blade had done its work and yellow pus was pouring out of the wound it had made.

"How are you, Sister Usha?" asked Suresh.

"OK," she said matter-of-factly.

"I am sorry about what happened," he offered sombrely. A stoic silence was all he got and a face that betrayed no feelings.

There was a path that took a shortcut to the hospital from the residential area. It cut across Dr Ravikumar's driveway and then through a little play area with a swing and seesaw. This was where Suresh met her a few weeks later when he walked towards the ward one evening. Usha had her back to the path. She mechanically rocked the swing that Jasmine was sitting on, while her eyes stared blankly into space.

Suresh walked down the path towards the ward. "Sister Usha," he called. She started momentarily, and then quickly turned to face him. This time, her smile unfolded to its full without any impediment. Its strength and beauty seemed to overshadow any weariness that was left.

"How are you getting on?" he asked with a concern that he didn't bother to hide.

"We are getting along," she replied amiably.

"Is there anything you need?" he enquired.

"No," was her quick response.

Suresh bent down and patted Jasmine on the head. "You like this swing?" he enquired. The child looked up at him with a quizzical look on her face and then reached for her mother's sari.

"She likes the park and so we come whenever I can manage it," Usha stated.

"That reminds me of something," Suresh uttered and with that, he retraced his steps back up the path and towards his house. In a few minutes, he was back beside them. He squatted on his heels and held out a big bar of chocolate to Jasmine, who looked up at her mother enquiringly.

"You can take it, Thangam," Usha reassured her daughter. "It's all right; you can take it." At this, the child slid off the swing and stretched out one and then both her little arms to receive what was offered.

"Thank you, Doctor," said Usha, "it was nice of you to take the trouble."

Suresh straightened up and stood before he turned towards the ward. "I go and come," he said in the traditional Tamil way. This meant 'bye' and 'see you later'.

Suresh went down to Oddanchatram about once a month to get what was not available in Pachalur. The next time he made the trip, he bought some cake. He did not want to go to Usha's house, so he waited for an opportunity. He knew mother and daughter would be in the park very often and kept a lookout for them. Walking back from work the next day, he spied them in the park. He quickened his pace to his house and was back in no time. Usha had seen him coming and somehow knew that he was coming for them. She called to Jasmine, who was playing on the grass, and picked her up onto her hips. This time, Jasmine showed no apprehension. She even gave Suresh a faint smile of recognition.

"I went down to Oddanchatram yesterday and I bought some cake for Jasmine." As he offered the packet, the child reached for it with her left hand.

"Not that hand, Thangam," Usha corrected as she took Jasmine's right hand and pushed it forwards. "You never take something from someone with your left hand," she added.

Jasmine's arms were just big enough to go around the carry bag. "You better hold it, Sister," said Suresh, still holding onto the parcel. "It's too big for the child."

"Say thank you, Thangam," Usha said. "Why did you take the trouble?" she asked Suresh.

"No, it's nothing," Suresh replied.

"You said it's for Jasmine," Usha asked with an impish grin on her face. "May I have some of it?"

"You have to ask Jasmine," Suresh shot back with pretended sternness. "She is its owner now."

They both laughed, while Jasmine looked on in amusement.

"How are your parents?" enquired Suresh. "Do they live with your brother?"

"No," replied Usha. "They are quite capable of looking after themselves and would rather have their independence. So they live in the government-allotted house in Virupatchi."

"What about your parents in Kerala?" she asked.

"How do you know?" enquired Suresh, looking surprised.

"Oh, I have been asking around."

"They are doing well."

"Do you write to your mother often?" she asked.

"No," replied Suresh honestly. "She writes two for every one of mine."

After a couple of minutes, Suresh excused himself and went back to his house, while Usha followed him with her eyes until he passed the hedge and wicket gate.

In the weeks that followed, Suresh noticed that Usha had quickly regained her former disposition. If anything, he thought she looked a little more relaxed and carefree compared to the person she was before.

The northeast monsoon came in October. But it was rather weak, with only about three good showers. Rain was so precious that people here kept track of exactly how many good rains they got each season.

Very often, when their paths crossed, Suresh and Usha would tarry to talk. Most times, Suresh was the one to call it off. And for little Jasmine, there were more chocolates, at least one every week. There was not much of a winter in this part of the world, but up in the hills of Pachalur, it could dip down to a nippy 9 degrees in January. One evening, Suresh walked over to the park, for he knew the two he wanted were there. It was almost dark, even though it was only six. Jasmine saw him from a distance, perceived his gait and ran to meet him. He bent down and she was in his arms in no time. He carried her to her mother, tickling her along the way. This time, he had more than chocolates for her. It was a mid-sized doll whose eyes would close when you laid it down.

Usha took one look at it and put her fingers to her mouth. "Oh doctor," she exclaimed, "this is too much."

"No, not for her," replied the doctor, tickling Jasmine till she squealed with joy. "And there is another thing. Why don't we chuck this 'sister' 'doctor' business? At least when we are not in the hospital. Just call me Suresh." By this time, their more than cordial relations had been noted and some of her colleagues were even subtly teasing her about it.

"Sure," said Usha, "it's fine with me."

One evening, Suresh was over at Dr Ravikumar's house chatting over a cup of coffee. "It's been three weeks since the cautery machine has packed up. We have been managing with the old machine."

"That is the problem with being in a remote place," Ravikumar put in. "If it was a city, we would have someone come in on the same day. Our people's paying capacity is poor. On the other hand, the logistics and service we get are also dearer and poorer. We get hit from both sides. The office tells me that they have written to their office in Madurai and even telephoned them."

"Next time, we should go to a better company," said Suresh.

"I don't think that is going to help," replied Ravikumar. "They are all the same, they will promise you the moon till the payment is made. Then we are at their mercy."

"Before I forget," declared Suresh, "there is something I have wanted to ask you, Ravi. Something I wanted to ask you for a long time. How did you decide for service in this out-of-the-way place, instead of going for the big bucks and the comforts of the city? When exactly did this happen?"

Dr Ravikumar was silent for some time before he told Suresh about it.

"It was in my final year, Suresh. We were having the gala banquet in the central garden of the men's hostel. You know what happens every year, don't you? The lights were brilliant, the tables were set out in spotless white on the green lawn. Young men were clad in their best and the ladies who were their guests were decked out in finery. The sumptuous meal of chicken, fried rice, salad, brinjal curry and papad was coming to an end. I got up to wash my hands before the desserts began. Since there was a crowd around the taps for the guests in the central quadrangle, I did not use these but went to the regular bathrooms jutting out from the hostel. As you know, these washbasins overlook the unkempt outer space that few cared about. It was a filthy place littered with junk and garbage. The lazier inmates threw their trash right out of the window.

"In the time I was there, through the cement latticework, I saw something in these foul surroundings that riveted me to the spot for almost half a minute. A miserable thin boy, maybe about six or seven, was scrounging around looking for anything of the slightest value—a plastic bottle, a piece of wire, a cardboard box—all of them would be picked up by tiny hands. He had no shirt on, so I could see his ribs sticking out. The threadbare knickers that covered his nakedness was held around his protuberant abdomen with a piece of string. Even this attire was torn across the back so some of his buttocks stood exposed.

"I went back to my table in a daze. Everything was as gala as before. The music was wafting over the gathering. But I suddenly found I had lost my appetite for the cake and ice cream that was to follow. I excused myself and went back to my room as early as I could.

"That was the day I decided, Suresh. That night I decided I would not spend my life rolling into oblivion on radial tires and mosaic floors."

They talked on about the hospital. Suresh shared some circumstances from his own life. Things that he had not shared with him before.

Suddenly, Dr Ravikumar said, "You know, Suresh, Sister Usha asked me a few days ago why you were not married yet. I did not tell her any specifics but simply stated that you liked to be single."

Suresh understood why she had asked. Bits of his hair was growing grey prematurely, and most everyone knew he was into his early thirties.

In the months that went by, Suresh would often catch Usha looking at him and at other times she would catch him looking at her, and their looks would linger. Suresh admitted to himself that her happy face had barged in on his thoughts more often than was warranted. It was a pleasant feeling; more than this, he did not know what to make of it.

April rolled around and it was Jasmine's birthday. By this time, the tiny tot, who was going to be three, was saying things in full sentences. She had gotten to referring to Suresh as 'Chocolate Uncle'.

As she saw preparations being made for the small party at their cottage, she asked her mother, "Chocolate Uncle coming?"

Usha's brother and family had come up for the occasion, so had her parents. When most of the guests had left, Jasmine could not contain her curiosity any longer and started opening her presents with her mother's help. There was a book, some colour pencils, etc. Soon, she came to Suresh's box on which was written: 'To my dear Jasmine. From Chocolate Uncle.'

They removed the lid and there lay before them the loveliest dress they had set their eyes on. It was made of shiny dark blue satin, with delicate lace around the edges. The sleeves were puffed. The collar had more lace and it had a snowy white sash around the waist. As the child eagerly caressed the dress, Usha looked up and stared at Suresh with an incredulous expression on her face.

Suresh was the last guest to leave.

"Everything was so good, Usha," he said as he bade goodbye.

"Thank you, doc—" She stopped short, seeing the expression on his face and remembering their decision. "Thank you, Suresh," she repeated through moist eyes and for some reason, she clasped his hands for a brief moment before letting go. "Thank you for arranging for the cake, and especially for the dress. Where did you get it, Suresh? It must have been very expensive. She has never had anything like this before."

Suddenly, Jasmine darted out from amidst her toys and came between them. "Don't go, Chocolate Uncle," she whined, with one arm around her mother's knees and the other hand extended to clasp Suresh's trouser legs. Usha's brother, who had seen all this, smiled politely as Suresh shook hands with him before leaving. As far as he could make out, there was no hint of disapproval there.

Chapter 15

Shared Sorrow

The work in the Hill People's Hospital was taken to another level when finally, by sheer persistence, the electricity load for the X-ray machine was sanctioned. Now, at last, they could see a fracture without guessing if there was one. It made a lot of difference for the horde of patients with cough and breathing troubles of various sorts.

Almost a month after Jasmine's party was Ravikumar's daughter's birthday. But Serina was older; she was going to be seven. It fell on a Saturday so they decided to go for a picnic down to the lake. Some of them squeezed into the hospital jeep and the rest piled into the ambulance. They started at about 3 pm, after a busy OPD. It was just the day for a picnic. Bright blue sky, with quite a few clouds for shade. The jeep went ahead; Dr Ravikumar being a fast driver, they soon left the ambulance far behind.

They turned and twisted around the hairpin bends, over the bridge and on to the flat road that ran along the fringes of the lake. They stopped the jeep in a clearing from where Dr Ravikumar knew a path that would take them to the grassy banks of the reservoir. While they unloaded the jeep, the ambulance arrived with the rest.

There were quite a few things to carry. A cardboard box with biscuits and murukku. A plastic wire basket with two large flasks of tea. There were reed mats to sit on. Their group included a few ward helpers, Dr Jhansi, two lab technicians, a junior pharmacist and the accountant with her child. Then there was Ravikumar and his family and about half a dozen nurses. Suresh was glad to note that Usha was there.

The path that Dr Ravikumar had chosen wasn't used frequently. The grass was beginning to grow over its sides. The bramble bushes reached out and blocked their paths, their tiny barbs snagging on their clothing. However, once this rough patch was done, they were into a eucalyptus groove, beyond which lay a carpet of green sloping down to an expanse of shining water. An outcrop of rocks between the patches of grass provided a place for some to sit on.

Once everyone had settled down, they sang a few songs that everyone knew. The next one was Surangani—a Sri Lankan Baila with a snappy tune. As they belted out the rhythm, it did something to Usha. No one noticed that she had stopped singing and a faraway look had come over her. Memories from another world came flooding back to her. Her eyes became teary; soon, she was hastily wiping them with a pink flowery hanky. By the time the song was over, she had regained her composure.

Mrs Ravikumar had been carefully carrying an aluminium box, even though others had offered to take it from her. She now proceeded to open it and carefully take out the birthday cake. She laid it down on a plate and placed it on the flattest rock they could find. She fixed seven candles on it, and the father of the birthday baby lit them up. After they sang 'Happy Birthday' for her, the girl blew on the candles and managed to extinguish four of them. One more blow took care of the rest. Everyone clapped as the child beamed about in delight.

After this, they sat around eating, drinking tea and exchanging anecdotes and funny stories. In time, someone produced a ring through which was threaded a thin nylon rope about five metres long. They stood in a circle holding the rope. One of them, who would be the catcher, had to go outside the circle and face away from them till all was ready. Then he would come in and guess who had the ring that was being passed from hand to hand—of course, without the catcher's knowledge and most often behind his back. If he found the hand with the ring, its owner would now become the catcher, and so it went.

As the evening wore on, they had dispersed in twos and threes. Ravikumar was talking to the pharmacist about some drug problems. Serina, the birthday baby, was playing at the edge of the water; she threw little pebbles into the water, as far as she could get them to go, and squealed as each one landed. Some went for a walk along the shore, others sat in circles talking. One young man had brought his swimming trunks and was now wading into the water. "Do you know how to swim? Do be careful!" Dr Ravikumar shouted anxiously after him.

Suresh sat on a rock, daydreaming. He looked around for Usha and noticed that she was sitting by herself, looking up into the hills, while leaning against the trunk of a eucalyptus tree some distance away. Suresh picked himself up and casually made his way towards her. She saw him coming and straightened up a bit. "May I keep you company?" he asked.

"Sure," came the willing reply.

"Why did you not bring Jasmine?" he enquired.

"My mother had come, so I thought I would come without her for a change."

Neither said anything for a while.

"I think Jasmine needs a father," she suddenly blurted out.

She could see that Suresh was a little taken aback and had a puzzled look on his face. "Would you be her father?" she asked boldly.

"What do you mean?" replied Suresh. "You are doing fine, as far as I can see."

"But still, she needs a father," persisted Usha.

"You want me to adopt her?" Suresh enquired.

"No," came the firm reply.

In the silence that followed, it gradually dawned on him.

"Are you asking me to marry you, Usha?"

She nodded, but said nothing. "I wish I could, Usha," he said haltingly. "But I cannot." Then after a pause. "I should not."

"Why not?" she demanded. "Is it because I am from another class and race? Don't you like me? I thought you did."

"I like you, Usha, but I must not marry you."

"Why not?" she repeated insistently.

"I cannot tell you now, Usha, maybe someday you will know about it."

For the second time that evening, Usha found herself crying.

A cricket chirped in the woods behind them, a koel repeated its soothing call, each time a little louder. In the distance, on the opposite shore, some wild bison had gathered to slake their thirst. They heard cowbells tinkle along the road nearby.

But the silence between them grew into a wide chasm that seemed to take them further apart by the second. Immersed in their thoughts, they forgot the passing of time, until they heard Dr Ravikumar's loud voice booming out to everyone, "It's time, pack up, everyone."

Usha stood up abruptly and walked away in the direction of the rocks towards which the others were converging. She gave not a backward glance and her gait was steady and purposeful. As for Suresh, he sat there for a few more minutes, trying to take in all that had happened.

Chapter 16

Shared Joy

The next few months seemed to drag along. It was a difficult time for both of them. Usha would not give him as much as a glance. If she had to help him with some procedure, she would do so sullenly, making sure she did not turn her face to him. For a while, Suresh did not dare to even try and renew some contact. Then, when he had plucked up the courage, she rebuffed him so rudely that he did not try again. He was sorely missing his time with Jasmine. And unknown to him, the child was missing him too.

"Where did Chocolate Uncle go? Why is he not coming to see me?" These were the questions the little one would ask her mother, who only glared at her in reply. In time, she understood that any mention of Chocolate Uncle had somehow become taboo.

Meanwhile, Chocolate Uncle had decided that, for the child's sake, he would make another attempt to see her. He had her favourite brand ready in his pocket. As he neared the park, Usha saw him from a distance, hastily went after her daughter and swept her up into her arms. Clutching her tightly, she stomped past the doctor and made for her house before he could utter a word. The child began to smile at him, but then she noticed her mother's livid face. She looked back at him;

this time with bewilderment on her face. She did not turn away till they had disappeared behind some trees over the ridge of the hill. In the last few moments, Suresh thought that Jasmine smiled again. He did not know; perhaps it was his imagination.

In the last week of July, Usha noticed a persistent soreness in her mouth. She went to see Dr Ravikumar. "Come in, Usha," said Dr Ravikumar with a welcome smile. Noticing a chart in her hand, he added, "Is the patient a relative, or is it someone sick that I have to look at without delay?"

"No, doctor," said Usha as she let herself down onto the patient's chair. "It's my chart."

"And what is the matter with you?" he asked jovially.

"It's my mouth, doctor; I have this mild irritation in my mouth. It started a few weeks ago. I showed Dr Jhansi who ran some tests and gave me a mouthwash with which I was completely alright for a week or two. Now it's come back again so I thought I would show you."

As he listened, Dr Ravikumar was going through the previous pages in her chart. He saw that Dr Jhansi had made a differential diagnosis of angular stomatitis and oral thrush. *Oral thrush was not common*, he thought, as he examined Usha's mouth with a torch and took a scraping for the lab. He also noticed a diamond-shaped lesion on her tongue. *Median rhomboid glossitis*, he thought to himself.

"Have you had any antibiotics recently?" he asked her.

"Yes," she replied. "I had taken a course of Septran about a month ago for sinusitis."

"This could be the reason," Dr Ravikumar told her reassuringly, as he went back to her chart. He noted with satisfaction that Dr Jhansi had run the usual tests to rule out diabetes, blood disorders and such like. All of them were negative and yet it had recurred. Then a possibility occurred to him that creased his brow ever so slightly. Usha noticed the seriousness on his face.

"Is it anything serious, Doctor?" asked Usha anxiously.

"I don't think so, but I think you should take some vitamins, maybe a longer course of local antifungal mouthwash and maybe some change in diet. However, I will talk to Dr Jhansi; I think you should go and see her again today or tomorrow."

Usha did not have time that day, but she did go on the next. Dr Jhansi saw her at the door and smiled. "Just wait two minutes, Usha, while I finish seeing this patient," said the doctor. When she had finished with her case, Usha went in. "Come, sit," welcomed the doctor, then she turned to the nurse who was assisting her and said, "Sister, please could you wait outside and shut the door after you?"

Once they were alone, the doctor said, "I am sorry, Usha, that the problem is back. Dr Ravikumar and I discussed it, and we feel that we should do one more test. He asked me to counsel you about it. You see, we are hearing about this new disease, HIV, and we are beginning to occasionally see a few patients here."

Usha had heard about the disease recently, but had not bothered to find out more. Indeed, why should she want to know! While she was thinking thus, the doctor asked her, "We were wondering if you would like to be tested for it."

Usha straightened herself and braced her shoulders; a cloud came over her face. "How would I have gotten it, doctor?"

"It is very unlikely that you have it, but it is good to check."

After a few moments, when neither of them spoke, Usha ventured, "Could it be from my deceased husband? But that is so long ago."

"It can come on years after exposure," replied the doctor.

"Oh," said Usha.

After some hesitation, the doctor slowly continued, "I hope you don't mind me asking you if your deceased husband had risky behaviour."

"Yes. I have heard that he used to fool around quite a bit. It is a serious thing, isn't it, doctor?" asked Usha anxiously.

"Yes," the doctor replied gravely. "You know, you need not get tested if you don't want to, but it may be good to know."

"Where is the test done, doctor?" enquired Usha.

"Oh, we have to send the blood to Oddanchatram, the result will take about a week and it will come straight to me, nobody will know."

After a while, Usha said she would think about it. "Okay," said Dr Jhansi. "That is fine, let me know what you decide."

With the second course of antifungal, the problem cleared up completely and did not bother her again. Over the subsequent weeks, she asked around and read what she could. She found out that there was no good treatment and that it was communicable to some extent. She could not get the possibility out of her head, especially when she thought about her daughter. The more she thought, the more convinced she became that, at least for Jasmine's sake, she should get herself tested.

And that was how Usha found herself in Dr Jhansi's consulting room one morning towards the middle of August.

Cognisant of the implications, the doctor took the blood herself, labelled, sealed and packed it with her own hands. And on the next Monday, it was sent off with the rest of the specimens.

It was nine o'clock that same night. Jasmine was almost asleep. She was hearing the story of the hare and the tortoise for the third time now. And for the third time, she was asking, "Why did the hare sleep, Amma?"

"Because he thought more of himself than he ought to have," replied Usha once again.

"Then what happened?" asked Jasmine, goading her mother on. As the story went on, eyelids drooped as they fought somnolence but soon they surrendered to sweet slumber. Usha kept awake a long time.

She wondered, *What if the test came back positive? What would change?* Anyway, she was now living only for her child, for whom it would make little difference. But Jasmine would be too young if anything should happen to her. *How will she manage without me? She would live*, she told herself, *somehow she would live, Jasmine needed her*. She thought about her childhood and Sri Lanka. She thought about Suresh. *Maybe it was just as well that he did not agree to my proposal.*

Her thoughts returned to her daughter. She wondered why this innocent child, for no fault of hers, should become an orphan. Then hope fluttered back to life within her when she remembered her parents and brother who were still pretty healthy. *Should anything happen*, she reasoned, *they will look after her*. This deliberation kept echoing in her mind. *I shall not die but I shall live. I will live for Jasmine's sake.* Cradled thus in the arms of hope, she drifted off to sleep.

The next day, apprehensions about the impending test results intruded her waking hours a few times. But by the third day, the business of everyday living had pushed it from her mind and she forgot all about it. A full ten days went by before she was summoned by Dr Jhansi. On hearing that Dr Jhansi wanted to see her, Usha's mouth became dry, her heartbeat quickened and the short walk to the doctor's room seemed to take a long time, as she forced herself to walk slowly. She took a few deep breaths to steady herself before going in.

There was nobody else in the room. "Close the door behind you, Usha," said the doctor with a smile. When Usha turned, the smile was gone and in its place was a deep concern. "Sit down, Usha," said the physician.

"What is it, doctor?" asked Usha through tremulous parched lips.

"It's positive, Usha," said the doctor as gently as she could.

Usha looked down and remained silent and motionless for what seemed like ages; only her hands moved as they clasped and wrung each other in a desperate search for comfort. A sharp indrawing of breath signalled the start of a series of sobs that appeared to convulse her entire frame. The doctor quickly pulled her chair beside her, put her arms around her and pulled her close. Thus they remained for a long while, and then some more.

"It will be alright, Usha," said Dr Jhansi.

"How much time do I have, doctor?" asked Usha, her tear-stained face looking up.

"We cannot be sure, Usha. It will probably be many, many years before something serious happens, and besides, we are all here for you. Let us go home."

That night, the doctor stayed with her and helped her look after Jasmine. Usha considered a few days leave, but with advice from the doctor, she decided that it would perhaps be better if she threw herself into her work. And so she did. She went from one task to the next with cold deliberation. She tried to hide her sorrow from Jasmine, but on some evenings, the tears would start even when the child was in her arms. At those times, little fingers would reach up to wipe them away and little lips would say, "Don't cry, Amma, Jasma is here." Usha would return the child's poignant smile with one of her own, which she hoped was equally brave and optimistic.

The weeks went by and Usha learned to live with her diagnosis. But around her, things were happening. The wheels of fate turned and clicked, but she knew nothing of these.

Dr Ravikumar invited Suresh home for tea one day. This was not unusual and Suresh did not think much of it.

Over tea, they discussed odds and ends before Dr Ravikumar took on a more serious demeanour and said, "I called you over so that I could be sure we are not overheard. A while ago, you shared with me how it is between Usha and you. Things have changed."

Then he told Suresh about Usha's diagnosis. "Keep it to yourself because apart from Dr Jhansi and me, no one else knows. She needs some comfort now. So I think you should start talking to her again."

"I don't think she will let me do anything of that sort," said Dr Suresh.

"Then I will invite both of you for tea tomorrow. Perhaps it helps to be in a different setting," suggested Dr Ravikumar hopefully.

"I am willing to give it a try, Ravi," said Suresh.

The next morning, true to his word, Dr Ravikumar casually invited Usha to come over for tea. This she accepted gladly. She had been invited before, and was grateful for the comfort and counsel that Malathi had given her at that time.

Dr Ravikumar had wisely asked Suresh to come half an hour later than the time he had told Usha.

Usha came with Jasmine, and soon the child was happily playing with Serina and her little brother. Malathi and Usha sat at the table talking. Meanwhile, Dr Ravikumar had gone out and now stood waiting for Suresh at the beginning of the driveway. When he came, he locked the gate behind him and they walked silently and climbed onto the veranda. The older man waved Suresh to one of two chairs that he had placed there. Then he pulled down the bamboo curtains that bordered it on all three sides, essentially making it a closed space. This being done, Dr Ravikumar went into the dining room with a mischievous grin on his face.

"Excuse me," he told the ladies. "There is someone here who wants to see Usha."

Usha got up and followed him with a questioning face. As she came onto the veranda and saw Suresh, she could not help but show the resentment and scorn she felt. She said nothing, especially because the senior man was there. When Suresh rose and offered her a seat, she took it reluctantly.

By this time, Dr Ravikumar had quietly let himself into the dining room and closed the door. Now, like it or not, they were by themselves.

After a time of silence, Usha asked with blazing eyes, "Is this some kind of plot? If I had known you would be here, I would never have come." Then, after a pause when they could almost hear each other breathing, she continued, "Why did you call to see me after all these months? Did Dr Ravikumar tell you something? If it is to console me, then you had better think again. I don't need your comfort."

Suresh sat there as though he had had a stroke, and then plucked up the strength to speak.

"No, Usha," he said, putting out his hands. She withdrew a little and glared at him. "I wanted to ask you if you would marry me."

"Is this some kind of joke?" she shot back venomously. "I know that you know."

"Listen," he pleaded, "that is why we are here. Usha, will you marry me?"

"Mad fellow! What are you talking about?" she said with a wild look on her face. "I have HIV—"

"And so do I, Usha!" he interjected before she could utter another word.

For long moments she sat there, stunned, as if turned to rock. Then she took his arms and placed it on her knees. She bent down till her face was cradled in his hands. She sobbed till his palms were drenched with her tears. The spasms gradually abated and stopped. As she straightened to look at him, an exultant smile broke out on her tear-stained face.

They talked feverishly that day. One hour was a long time to talk. But it seemed to them like a moment. "How did you get it, Suresh?" enquired Usha.

"I will tell you another time," said Suresh hastily for, by that time, Dr Ravikumar had come into the drawing room with Jasmine in tow, asking them if they were through.

Chapter 17

Weathering a Stigma

Over the next few days, starting with their long chat in Dr Ravikumar's house, Suresh told Usha all about his life with the dreaded disease.

Six months before the end of my surgical training, I had an accidental wound with a scalpel while I was operating. I didn't think much of it, but six weeks from that time, I developed what I thought was a viral fever with some rash. I did not think much of that either. It was only another six weeks later that all my life stood on collapsed beneath me. One of the patients in our unit needed blood before surgery and try as hard as I might, I could not get a donor. So I decided to donate a pint myself; something I had done before on numerous occasions.

In the blood bank, I lay down and the process was soon over. After consuming the customary pastry and orange juice they gave all who made a contribution, I rushed off to the ward to prepare for rounds. The next day, the unit chief called me into his room and said that the medical superintendent would like to meet me in his office. Professor Madavan had a serious look on his face and I felt a sudden heaviness in my tummy. I knew I had not done anything drastically wrong, I had followed all the protocols and filled all the correct forms, so what kind of problem could this be? I quickly made my way to the superintendent's office.

I entered and there was Prof Prakash sitting behind his huge desk. Beside him was the head of the Department of Clinical Pathology, a kind lady in her fifties. "Please sit down," they both said almost simultaneously, showing me to a chair. After a bit of silence, the lady opened gravely.

"Suresh, you donated blood yesterday, didn't you?"

"Yes, I did," I confessed.

"Well, we had to throw that bottle away."

"Oh!" I said in surprise.

"We are now testing for a new retrovirus—HIV—you know about it. Your sample was positive for the antibodies."

I just stared at them, and to me their faces became indistinct. I don't know how long I remained like this but it was Professor Prakash's voice that I heard next. "Suresh," he said in the kindest voice. "We still don't know many things about this disease, and you know there is no proper treatment as of today, but intense research is going on and they may soon come up with something. So don't worry. I have told your chief to let you take some leave."

My ears heard the words, but my mind was elsewhere. It raced all over the place. I thought of my parents, then about Sunithi. Again, Dr Prakash's voice broke the silence, "Is there anything else you would like to ask us?"

"No," I mumbled.

"Do you want us to get you something to drink, a little tea perhaps?"

"No, sir," I replied, giving my voice a little volume to hide the despair growing within me.

After a while, they got up. So I was forced to follow suit. Professor Prakash said as I left, "Please let us know if there is anything we can do for you. Your chief will be expecting you back in his office."

I hardly remember the walk down the corridor and up the stairs to the surgery office. I knocked at Professor Madavan's door. "Come in," said his booming voice. "Sit down, sit down," he said as he urged me into a chair. "They told you, didn't they?"

"Yes, sir."

Then the big man came around his table and held me by his shoulders.

"I am so sorry, Suresh," he said solemnly after some time and then returned to his side of the table. "You see, we have not yet started testing for this virus on pre-ops as a routine. We did not know the patient had this infection."

"It's alright, sir," I lied valiantly. "I understand."

"Take a week off, or maybe even two. Don't bother about the duty roster, I will rearrange it. You have to tell your parents. Don't let it upset you too much; I hear they are making progress on research in this field."

"Thank you, sir," I said firmly as I got up to go. I did not want to prolong what was becoming for both of us a difficult exchange.

"If there is anything at all any of us can do, please call," he said as he saw me to the door. *"Here is my residence phone number,"* he added, depositing a piece of paper in my shirt pocket. *"Any time of night or day, you are welcome."*

Again, I hardly remember the walk back to my room. Once I had shut the door behind me, I collapsed onto the bed and then the emotions broke through. I cried till my lachrymal glands had nothing more to offer. I didn't have lunch that day nor dinner. Went for a walk in the evening. Night had fallen before I went down to the pay phone across from the hospital. I gingerly rang my parents' number. It was a trunk call and so I had to wait a bit. Finally, my mother's familiar voice answered. "Ena mone?" she asked.

"Amma, is Appa there?"

"He just lay down a few minutes ago. I don't think he is asleep yet. I will call him." Then he could hear her calling her husband.

"Appa," I started when he had come on the line, "I donated blood a few days ago."

"Ah, what about that?"

"They found a virus in it. It's called HIV. That is what causes AIDS."

"AIDS!" he remarked, now fully awake. "That is a dangerous thing, is it not?"

"Yes, it's quite serious."

"Are you ill now?"

"No, but I could be after some time."

"How did you get it?" His voice rose just a little bit.

"A couple of months ago, in the theatre, I had an accidental injury with a scalpel."

"Why were we not informed about it?" he demanded.

"Oh, it was such a minor thing and I didn't want to bother you with it. The patient succumbed a few weeks later, before they could test him. But it's certain I got it from him."

"Is it dangerous to life?" he asked anxiously.

"Not immediately, Appa," Suresh reassured him.

"Are you sure there is no treatment? Something must be available somewhere," he continued hopefully.

"Not that I know of, Appa."

After a few moments, Suresh could hear him take a deep breath. "Come home then, as soon as possible."

"Don't worry, Appa, they are doing a lot of research on it," I parroted. "They will soon find out something."

"Yes. Let's hope," he said with a voice that had lost a good part of its usual vigour.

"Please tell Amma. I don't want to tell her, it will be too much for me."

"Come home, son," he repeated."

"I will be there in a few days' time, Appa. Bye."

The next day was even more difficult for me, because that is the day I told Sunithi. She was my fiancée. We thought we would get married after I finished my surgical training. Sometime in the evening, I called her hostel and told her that I wanted to see her and that we could meet in the visitor's room in ten minutes.

"I am on duty. Is it urgent?" she enquired.

"Yes, it is."

"Okay, I will give my pager to my friend and come."

She was waiting, and we sat opposite each other. Seeing my distraught and unshaven face alarmed her. She immediately took my hands in hers. She had probably never seen me this upset before.

"What happened, Suresh? What happened? Tell me," she implored. I could not say anything. "Is everyone at home fine; are you sick?"

Finally, I broke it to her. "Sunithi, you remember the small scalpel wound I had some months ago?'

"Yeah, that was nothing much."

"Yes, but I seemed to have got something with it."

"Oh! Hepatitis, is it? That is not so bad, most people get over it in time. Anyway, how did you find out?" she asked.

"I gave blood a few days ago, and the day before yesterday they told me the result. I tested positive for HIV, Sunithi."

She sat there immobile for a few seconds, as though frozen in time.

"Can't be," she whispered through trembling lips. "They must have made a mistake. Anyway, I don't think they do that test."

"Yes, they do," I said calmly. "They started doing this in the blood bank three months ago."

She slowly withdrew her hands and clapped them over her ears. She had her eyes closed before she started weeping. I reached across and took her hands in mine.

"This must be some mix-up, they will probably ring up again," she said, reassuring herself. We sat without a word for a time, while she dried her tears and got back her poise. Fortunately for us, there was no one else in the visitor's room.

"My friend must be wondering what has become of me," she said as she brushed back her hair and got up to go. Thus, we parted.

The next day, Sunithi and I went for a walk. The minute I saw her, I knew she had been grieving a lot and had lost a good bit of sleep. Her face looked tired and haggard; her eyes were swollen and red. I had never seen her without some makeup; now there was none. After we had walked a while, I was the first to speak.

"Sunithi," I said, "I don't know what my future will be, or if I have any at all. So you decide what you want to do."

"Don't talk nonsense," she declared vehemently before I could say another word. "Nothing will change between us."

"But you will have to tell your parents, won't you?" I cautioned.

"Yes, I will," she replied confidently, with her voice raised a pitch or two.

"I am sure they will have something to say about it," I countered.

"They will be okay with it," she replied confidently. "I did a little reading myself, Suresh, we will handle this together."

When we said bye that day, I felt a lot better. Whatever happened, at least Sunithi would be there by my side. But little did I know that I would never see her face again.

Late that night, I caught a train to Cochin where I would spend the next five days at home. Days that were soaked with my father's gloom and my mother's tears. The day after I arrived, I tried to ring Sunithi to get some cheer. But they said that she was not available. The story was the same the next time I tried. On the fourth day, they said her room was locked.

In desperation, I phoned my friend Ajit who rang back the same evening. He had done some asking around and found out that Sunithi's parents had come and taken her home. My father's behaviour did nothing to soothe my troubled heart. He was sullen and angry. He was even thinking of suing the college.

In another few days, I was back in Sevur. I was soon called up by Dr Madavan. He sat me down and after some small talk, said what he had for me. "You can join back whenever you want; of course, you will not be allowed to operate, but we will make sure that you complete the course and take the examination." Normally, what I heard would have been devastating, but now I was half expecting it. By this time, a layer of hardness had enveloped me on the inside. After all, I thought, the worst was behind me.

"I will join on Monday, sir," I said.

"We are looking forward to having you back, and again, if you need any help, we are there," Professor Madavan said kindly before I left.

On Sunday morning, I was informed that I had an overseas call and so I rushed down to the common telephone on the ground floor.

"Hello," I said.

"It's me, Sunithi." The voice was so feeble and tremulous, I hardly recognised it.

"I am here in Dubai with my parents. I told them. At first, they were OK but after they enquired a little, they changed. They want me to discontinue the course and they won't send me back."

"How does that help, Sunithi?" I enquired, not knowing what to expect. The sound of muted sniffling was all I heard for a time, and I knew she was crying.

"They will not listen, Suresh," she said. "They want me to break off our engagement. I don't know what to do." Then again, the sound of weeping.

"They are right, Sunithi," I said, putting up a brave front, but my shaky voice betrayed the anguish within. "I don't think we should carry on with it."

"Then what will I do!" she whispered. "Then what will I do?"

"You will be alright," I said, trying to reassure her.

"I will tell you what," she replied. "I will somehow convince them otherwise."

"Fine," I said at last. "If that is what you want to do."

"Bye," she said. "I must go." A click on the line and she was gone, and that was the last I heard from her.

In the next few months, many things changed for me. Many things I thought important, lost their shine for me. I learned a lot about life. I learned about loneliness in the midst of a crowd. I learned about stigma and prejudice, but I also learned about kindness and charity. On the whole, the people were very nice and supportive.

At first, not many knew, but in some way, the news got around. Most people gave me an extra-large smile, but there were few that avoided my gaze. Friends did a lot for me, especially Ajit Shah. I cannot forget him. Many of them took my hands and assured me that they were for me and with me. Some funny things happened. It was far from humorous, when I was going through it, but now that I think about it, I feel amused.

One incident concerned the men doctors' quarters' barber. He would come every Thursday to the common room and if anybody wanted a haircut, he would go down and have it done. He had cut my hair for years and so knew me. The first month he did it as usual. But the next time, I ran into trouble.

I entered the room and said, "Muniappan, I need a cut."

"Oh Sar," he said, getting up from where he was sitting reading his newspaper. He looked at me as though he had seen a ghost. "Sar, I have got to go now. Have something urgent to do." He hurried out, giving me a wide berth. The next time he came, I went in and found him already working on a customer. He looked at me and looked down, keeping a tight face. "I have got to go after I finish this job, Sar, come some other time."

I went the next week and the same charade was played out. By this time, my hair had grown to unsightly proportions. Finally, Ajit said he would cut it for me. Out of desperation, I let him loose on my hair. But it turned out to be a fiasco. In the end, it looked as though a pack of clumsy rats had been at it. What could we do? I covered my head with a shawl, bought a pair of scissors and headed for the outskirts of town on Ajit's motorbike. We found a crummy salon. Someone was already having his hair cut. We waited patiently and when his customer had departed, I unveiled my hair, or rather what was left of it. His eyes widened as he looked us over and asked with genuine concern, "What happened, Sar?"

"Oh," my friend said, "it was a kind of experiment."

"Experiment!" he retorted. "Even a monkey could have done a better job."

At this, Ajit's face grew red. "Yes, yes," he declared valiantly.

"Don't worry, Sar, I will make it alright," reassured the unsuspecting fellow. "Please sit down," he said.

That is when Ajit extended the new pair of scissors. "Oh, what is this?" asked the craftsman.

"My friend is very afraid of germs and things like that so please use these." And that is how I had my hair cut.

Then there was this other episode, when a senior friend of mine invited me to his house for tea. We had belonged to the same fraternity in the men's hostel. So here we were having tea, with his wife and his child sitting on the sofa nearby. The two-year-old girl was very friendly; we quickly exchanged smiles and when asked, she told me her name very cutely. Then suddenly, for some inexplicable reason, the little one suddenly got down and started coming over to me. You should have seen her mother. She lunged for the child as though she was heading towards a precipice. She grabbed and pulled her back to herself with alarm on her face. Then she made a gallant effort to regain her balance and disguise her intentions.

"Meena!" she told the bewildered child. "Don't bother Uncle." Within a few seconds, it was over and then we all went on as though nothing had happened. But you could see the atmosphere had become a little awkward.

Within me, I wanted to shout, Hey! HIV doesn't spread like that. It does not spread through touch. It's not that infective. It's okay to share utensils, live in the same house and even hold hands. I wish you knew.

But I said nothing and sat there, trying to pretend and hide my feelings as best as I could. The next day, my friend apologised for what had happened.

"Oh, Suresh, I am sorry about yesterday. She does not know. These magazines say all sorts of stories."

"It's alright," I said, brushing it aside.

In a few more months, I had cleared my exams. Before this, I had pondered hard and long about where I would work. Previously, I had been offered an opportunity to stay on and become a member of the faculty. But I was informed that this door was not open anymore. Then I heard about Dr Ravikumar, four years my senior. His good work was being talked about in institutional circles and I had no difficulty finding his address. I wrote to him and he was kind enough to reply immediately, saying I was welcome. That is how I came to be here, Usha.

Chapter 18

Life Together

The wedding was a simple affair. The conference hall was the biggest room on the campus. And this was where they chose to have it. The few chairs they had were arranged in a couple of rows closer to the entrance, along with the last row of benches at the back. They gathered all the mats they could find and carpeted the front half of the space with these. A central aisle was left free. The red oxide flooring showed through, along that strip. You could imagine that it was a carpet.

All the staff pitched in to decorate the interiors. Someone had bent a long discarded steel construction rod into an arch, with its ends sunk into large, used paint cans filled with sand. When they had finished the job, you would hardly believe they were old paint containers, so skilfully were they covered with gold and silver paper cut in artful designs. On the skeleton of steel, the archway was fabricated. Twigs of fern were wrapped around, forming a body of green, and on this, yellow, orange, white and red bougainvillea were entwined in spirals of glorious colour. A chain of jasmine flowers ran along the walls in waves. At each crest, this string of white flowers was supported by carefully concealed nails that held a bouquet of wild lilies with a background of pine leaves. In Dr Ravikumar's opinion, the simple beauty of what had been achieved with the material on hand could easily rival the city weddings he had seen with expensive orchids and professional artists.

The bride and her groom walked down the aisle hand in hand. Suresh had to bend just a little bit to manage the archway. Usha was dressed in a green silk sari and in her other hand, she held a bunch of white and crimson roses. Suresh had considered wearing a dhoti, but later chickened out, knowing that he would be constantly ill at ease wondering if the knot that held it together would come loose and the whole thing slip down. Finally, he decided to take it easy and go for peace of mind rather than tradition, choosing instead dark grey trousers and a blue Khadi kurta. Blue was his favourite colour. They looked a pretty sight; green, grey, blue, crimson and white. All this was crowned with the smile on their faces—so joyful and calm—that went beyond the splendour of outward things. Jasmine, with a pink frock, came right behind them with the other close relatives.

The ceremony itself was nothing elaborate. A song or two, and then officiated by Dr Ravikumar, Suresh tied the Thali around Usha's neck. The Thali was a tiny gold pendant, resembling a grain of rice, threaded on a yellow cotton string. The grain of rice symbolised the man's promise to provide for his bride all his life. The music from the harmonium grew louder and the rhythm of the tabla rose to a crescendo as they finally exchanged garlands. Immediately, they were showered with handfuls of rice from all sides.

Suresh's parents had come. There was no one else from his side. The few relatives that Usha had were there. After the ceremony, the chairs and benches were rearranged. A sumptuous lunch was served from desks in one corner of the room. It was a buffet meal, where each would take on to his plate what they wanted. The younger and more dexterous among them sat cross-legged on the floor. The newlyweds were seated at the high table (the bigger of the two available), with a beaming Jasmine between them.

After lunch, they went down to the registrar's office in Oddanchatram where they signed their names in fat leather-bound tomes in the presence of the officer. Now they were man and wife. This was the start of a new life.

They spent the week of their honeymoon in a little cottage that one of Suresh's rich non-resident friends had lent them. It was by the seaside, about sixty kilometres south of Sevur and the medical college where he had spent nine years. He did not want to go to Sevur, in spite of invitations from some of his classmates who had joined the faculty there. That was a part of his life he would rather not relive. In addition, Usha's meagre knowledge of English would be embarrassing to her.

Usha was quite willing to leave Jasmine with her mother, but Suresh wouldn't hear of it. So the three of them roamed about the beach. Jasmine was fascinated by the seashells and collected as many as she could carry. When hungry, they went to a little dhaba under the coconut palms. A nice old gentleman prepared their meals for them. At night they listened to some music on the cassette player—some Tamil, some English and even a few Malayalam oldies. By 10 pm, Jasmine was safely asleep in the small bed in the tiny drawing room and they had the double bed all to themselves. They talked, loved and in time, wrapped their naked bodies together and got to know each other as no one else would.

After their delightful five days at the beachside, they returned to Pachalur and fell into the routine of work. But their life was far from routine; each day was a new delight. They would go down to Leech Valley to sit on the boulders, munch on the sandwiches and frolic in the lively waters of the stream.

About a month after they were married, Suresh had a proposition for Usha.

"Shall we make our status public? This will facilitate a better understanding of the disease among the people, and will help at least some of them get over their fear, guilt and shame. By identifying ourselves with the host of innocent sufferers, I think we can give them courage and hope. After all, the disease does not define our personhood."

"What about Jasmine?" enquired Usha after some serious thought.

"Eh, I thought of that," replied Suresh. "We can't keep this a secret forever. She is bound to know sooner or later. And I would rather she hears it from us than from someone else."

That was how they found themselves telling their stories in one staff meeting. All their colleagues were very supportive and encouraging. Over the next year, they got invited to share their experiences in many places throughout the state. One magazine even had a small write-up about them and their mission to dispel the stigma around this new disease.

Late in December, three months after the wedding, they visited Suresh's parents in Cochin. They feasted on Malayali dishes and went for a boat ride along the backwaters. Their craft moved along lazily along the canals, with palm trees from the shore leaning over them. They did not go to meet any of Suresh's relatives and Suresh's parents did not insist on this either. They knew that it would only make everybody more uncomfortable. Just a smirk might have spoilt it all for Usha who was beginning to feel at home with his parents. Usha learned a fair bit of Malayalam and Aleykutty, Suresh's mother, an equal amount of Tamil so that the two could communicate quite freely. She knew she was totally accepted when, one day, Aleykutty called her 'Mol'—an endearing term for a daughter. A few days before they left, she called Usha into her bedroom, sat her down on the bed and proceeded to open her steel almirah. She took a rexine bag from it and gave it to Usha. "What is it, Amma?" asked Usha, noticing that it was quite heavy.

"It's a good share of my gold jewellery, mol, it is for you. Who else will I give it to? It's years since I have seen Suresh so happy."

"Thank you," she said with trembling lips, as Aleykutty threw her arms around her daughter-in-law. The two women wept unashamedly for a while.

"Are you sure, Amma?" asked Usha hesitantly. "After all, I am a stranger."

"Stranger!" she snapped back, almost angrily. "Never say that again, mol. You are our daughter, and always will be. Remember that if there is anything you need, I will be there for you; at least till I am alive."

The two women again shed tears, when the three of them boarded the bus to return to Pachalur. It was the same bus that Suresh had often travelled on, but this time he was not alone; he had two people who were dependent on him.

Pachalur seemed chilly to them when they got back from Kerala. Each day was exciting, with new things to do together. By this time, they had acquired a second-hand car that had run only about 40,000 kilometres, and so was still in good shape. One of their most memorable trips was one Sunday evening when they went down to the lake. They zigzagged down the bends and finally onto the flat road that skirted the lake. The water level was lower than usual, so they could hop onto a crop of rocks that had now become quite visible. They sat there, enchanted by the beauty around them.

The sun was just behind the western mountains. But it sent out pencils of light that shot out from behind the misty hills and spread out like an ethereal golden fan across the blue sky. On the eastern side, the firmament was equally wondrous and held a peach-coloured glow. Just above the horizon, an almost fully grown silvery orb was making its shy entry into that mesmerising scene. Jasmine was the first to spot it. "Moon! Moon!" she cried in glee.

"See how large it looks, Usha," said Suresh and then mused on, "You know, they really don't know why the sun and the moon look so much bigger on the horizon than they seem to be when they are up in the sky at the zenith of their journey. Maybe it's just like our lives, where the first few years and the last few years seem more prominent."

"We are such different people, I wonder how we ever met, Suresh," said Usha.

"We were meant to, Usha. It was decreed long ago. Perhaps even before time began. Certainly, before the first stars were born, which sent their beams into silent space. Before the dinosaurs roamed the earth, before the earth grew flowers and the winds blew, that made them bend to kiss each other. We are those flowers, Usha. And remember, there will always be a morning; there will always be 'a morning'. They write fairy tales, Usha, but we are the ones living it."

Jasmine enjoyed sitting on a small rock and splashing the water with her feet, while Suresh held on to her arm firmly. "Look," cried Suresh suddenly, pointing to the far shore where a majestic stag had come to drink. He spread his forefeet, cautiously bent down his neck and dipped his mouth to the water, all the time keeping one wary eye on them. In a short time, it drew up its head, turned and was gone as quickly as it came.

A flock of black cormorants rested on an outcropping of rock almost towards the centre of the lake. A gaggle of wild geese bobbed about the water near the far shore. Suddenly, one of them stirred from its place on the water. It noisily beat the dark surface of the lake and propelled itself forwards, leaving behind a white trail of wing-prints that soon faded. Only the quiet whisper of the bird's flight remained.

As the moon became brighter, the light was fading. "We better get moving," said Suresh. "Even the other day, I heard that an elephant had blocked the road." They quickly made their way to the car. By the time they took the flat stretch and the road rose up to meet the slopes, the twilight was over and the night was upon them. The headlights picked out the way for them to Pachalur and home.

So, the happy days went by. Next Sunday was the 12th of October—their first wedding anniversary. No one but they remembered. Everyone had lots of things of their own to think about, they reckoned. Anyway, they were not disappointed in the least. As far as they were concerned, it was the best year of their entire lives.

Almost every evening, Jasmine would wait for Suresh to come home. With gentle reminders from Usha, he had slowly metamorphosed from just being 'Chocolate Uncle' to becoming 'Suresh Appa'. Suresh Appa was her idol. She would follow him around the house, he would tell her stories. One of the tales was about Velitharakan. The little girl loved that story and was content to listen to it again and again in its various avatars. For each telling was a little different, but yet the same. She even told her mother about Velitharakan. As a consequence, Usha was waiting to hear it herself, and this chance came to her that very weekend.

Chapter 19

Velitharakan

Suresh was tired as he trudged up the mud road towards his home, past the hospital and then the park. Looking down, he picked his way among the stones but his mind was preoccupied with thoughts of Kuppusamy.

Kuppusamy probably had typhoid; it was four days now, but the fever was not responding to ciprofloxacin. He would have to switch him to a higher antibiotic. It would be very much more expensive. Could Kuppusamy afford it?

The antibiotic resistance in this part of the world was frightening. *Where is it going to end?* he wondered. The rich who could afford these expensive drugs would live. And the poor? They would die. *No, not all of them*, he surmised. Some would come to Dr Ravikumar, who always had a stock of these antibiotics stashed away in some corner. Where did he get them? He assiduously wheedled it out of the few medical company representatives that came around.

They would have to do something by the next day, if his temperature stayed up.

By this time, he had reached the chicken wire fence and the wicket gate that led into his small garden. He went around and approached the porch from the side He looked up just in time to see the figure of a little girl disappearing through the front door.

Jasmine was up to her customary game. She must have been playing with her friends on the veranda; for there they all were, left behind on the floor, in a circle. Dimple the baby doll. Tara the Barbie doll. And of course, her favourite—Tinto the raggedy doll. He wondered why she liked that one more. Perhaps because she thought him less fortunate than the others who were endowed with such fancy features.

Now he would have to play out the familiar role of the seeker.

"My little girl is lost, I wonder where she is," he said aloud as he went from room to room. She should not be found too soon, for then the charm would be taken out of it.

"Is she under this bed?"

He pretended to search in a few more places before he reached the storeroom; that was where she usually was. With his eyes closed, he peered behind the door. Jasmine had her eyes closed as well, as though she would somehow become less visible that way.

"She has been found," Suresh shouted. They usually opened their eyes at the same time, and then he would triumphantly carry her into the living room.

That evening over supper, suddenly Jasmine asked, "Suresh Appa, tell me more about Velitharakan."

"Who is this Velitharakan?" asked Usha as she came in with a bowl of sambhar. She sat down opposite him with a smile of curiosity on her face. "I know you have been telling Jasmine a lot of stories, but this Velitharakan seems to figure prominently in many of them."

"Oh, he was one of my forefathers," said Suresh casually. And it was left there, but not for long.

That night when the dishes were done and Jasmine had been put to bed, they sat out on the porch with their feet on the steps leading down to the garden. He leaned back against the wooden columns that supported the roof, and she leaned against him. The land dropped a little way beyond their fence on the northern side of their house, and for some time they sat there staring across the Parapalar valley and into the dark void beyond.

He crossed his legs over hers and tickled her sole with his toes. She snuggled up to him with a sigh. "I have waited long enough," she said after some time. "Tell me about Velitharakan."

"It's going to take some time," he replied.

"So what?" she countered. "We have got the whole night, tomorrow is Sunday."

He continued to gaze ahead.

How could he tell her about Velitharakan without telling her about Kottara-Ammachy, and how could he tell her about Kottara-Ammachy without telling her about Kottara—that sleepy little village in southern Kerala. For that was where she lived, in an old mid-sized tiled roof house. It had teak panelling, but only in two of the most important rooms. The grounds had had some fine cashew trees, the low-spreading branches wonderful to climb on. But these had all been cut down to make way for coconuts. So now the house was in the middle of a coconut grove. Each tree spreading out against the next, like umbrellas in a crowd when the rain came down. Palm leaf to palm leaf, they made a continuous canopy of green.

The busiest place in the village was a hundred metres down the mud lane, where four roads met. The 'four-road junction' was what it was called. It boasted a few wayside box-on-stilts kiosks, a cheap cloth outlet and even a general store. A huge banyan occupied one angle of the junction with a 'sit-around' built about its base. It stood in handsomely for a bus shelter. The buses were only about twice a day, passing through to Quilon and back.

"My grandmother, Kottara-Ammachy, it was she who told me all this stuff," Suresh began. "We visited her every May, and sometimes in December.

"Electricity had not reached this village in the early sixties and so dinners were early. By the time the short twilight faded away, lamps would be lit and we would all gather in the large middle room for prayer.

"The antlers of a few deer and the horns of a bison looked down on us—relics from Grandfather's hunting years—and the wavy flames of a large kerosene lamp sent quivering shadows on the walls behind. Grandfather's eyes were closed and his lips moved, intoning earnest prayer.

"Our eyes were supposed to be closed in prayer as well, but I opened mine a whisker and saw my cousin Reggie looking at me. We exchanged wicked grins.

A suicidal beetle flew around in dizzy circles, and then went for the flame. It seemed to fly right through it and then again in circles. At the second pass, it zigzagged onto the floor and lay there twitching, with wings half burnt and legs raised to the ceiling. I have always wondered why they do this," said Suresh.

"When prayers were done, all of us cousins would gather around Kottara-Ammachy. We would ask her, as you asked me tonight: 'Tell me about Velitharakan.'

"Before that, let me begin with some background information," said Suresh.

"The great battle-axe left Parasuraman's swarthy hands and shot into the sky like a missile; its descending trajectory saw it plunge in and hit the ocean floor. Alarmed by such a rude awakening, the seabed rose to retaliate but could never lie low again. Thus was born this green emerald strip of land—Kerala, the one they call 'God's own country'."

"You are starting off like a tourist brochure, Suresh," said Usha. "I have seen Kerala when you took me to visit your parents last year. It looks a lot like Sri Lanka."

"Oh," replied Suresh, "I guess there is a resemblance but it can't be that beautiful."

"It is too," said Usha with fervour. There was silence for some time before Usha spoke, "You have not told me about Velitharakan."

"That's exactly what I was starting to do, you know. Okay, let's forget mythology and start with some history. A few Jews and Syrians brought Christianity to Kerala about 1900 years ago and my forefathers have been Christian from those early times, centuries before the British heard about it.

"The Cheras ruled Kerala in the first many centuries. They and all the subsequent rulers allowed the Christians to live quietly, going about their business as traders, landowning farmers and apothecaries. Did I say all? No, there were times when foreign powers influenced the kings to disturb the lie of things. This is what happened to Velitharakan.

"Kottara-Ammachy's family were locals from the nearby town of Kottarakara. She died six years ago, but her image is so fresh in my mind. She had a hooked nose, kind but sharp eyes. Like the women of her times, she always wore a nondescript loosely made white top. Below, she had a white wrap-around skirt with prominent pleats at the back. This costume disappeared with her generation and is not seen these days. She wore gold earrings that made her earlobes sag an inch or two. You could put your little finger through the hole that held the earrings, each of them the size of walnuts.

"My grandfather's clan, on the other hand, came from the north. Velitharakan's was the first family to migrate south. Now, let me tell you the story, as Kottara-Ammachy told us.

"Velitharakan was your great-grandfather, five times removed, was how she would start."

He was apothecary to the king of Elumali. A kingdom probably the size of present-day Bombay with all its suburbs included. Life was good for Velitharakan. He lived in his ancestral home, a kilometre downstream from the palace estate. He had influence because he was distantly related to the king's family. He loved his church, its ancient liturgy, its simple customs and above all, the freedom it gave its flock. His land had plenty of pepper and coconut; there were servants to keep the paddy fields. One corner of his property, he had set apart for his precious herbs. These, he tended with his own hands.

In the midst of all this flowed the river Pamba. The river had finished all its youthful mischief in the eastern mountains and now flowed calm and serene like a grand old maid.

The king's palace held the whole of twelve rooms, which in those days was a lot, for a kingdom of this size. The roof was tiled with decorative cones where the ridges met on top. At its ends, it hung over and seemed to point up much like the prow of a boat. It had spacious courtyards with wooden latticework. The thick laterite walls held up huge teak beams that supported the floor above. Ornately carved dark rosewood furniture decorated every room.

It was an impressive affair but it would not 'do for a boot' compared to the grand palace of the Samutiri in Cochin. Velitharakan had seen it just once. It had an impressive twelve-foot granite outer wall. The central complex alone had 24 rooms, including the magnificent throne room. Around this, the rest of the palace sprouted out in different directions. There were different sections for women, separate from the central complex, sometimes connected by covered corridors. At the back were the kitchens. In addition, there were stables, guard room, etc.

The red brick walls sported weapons, paintings and European mirrors. Some rooms had huge mat fans that hung down from the ceiling. Ropes attached to their frames passed cleverly through pulleys high in the wall and over to the next room; there, servants would pull to make the fans oscillate to and fro. A few rooms even had beds that looked like giant swings suspended from the ceiling with iron chains.

The Samutiri held reign over much of central Kerala in the 1500s. Nine kings were their vassals, including Vasudev Moopen, the ruler of Elumali. Their influence extended from the river Achenkovil in the south, up to some distance north beyond the river Pamba. Above this was the territory of Kunhali Marakkar, the Muslim king who ruled from Kottakal.

Things changed with the arrival of the Portuguese. They befriended the Samutiri with trinkets and promises. Alfonzo de Albuquerque, Viceroy of the Portuguese possessions from Gujarat to Kanyakumari, made a treaty with the Samutiri in

1513, allowing the Portuguese to control the ports in return for revenue to the royal treasury. The Samutiri even had a few Portuguese officers in their service, to teach their men the latest secrets in the art of war. The northern Muslims were excellent seafarers, and it was the Portuguese design to break their hold over the sea lanes. This they did by inducing the Samutiri to attack their northern neighbours. None of these affairs made a difference to Velitharakan or his native Eastern Orthodox church, but there were things that did.

One day, two white men arrived in the palace at Elumali. One was a stern rugged soldier fully armed with dagger and sword; he even had one of those new-fangled flame spitters. The other was a Jesuit priest, equally stern in face and manners, but different only in the garb he wore. They had come with gifts for the king and a letter from the Samutiri. Vasudev Moopen was happy with his gifts, but the parchment and what was written on it spread a cloud over his face. The two Europeans had come to fulfil Portugal's hidden agenda; which was to annex the native Syrian churches into the Church of Rome.

They visited the churches in Elumali. They spoke of the glories of Rome and the superiority of the Latin liturgy. They promised them special status when Portugal would finally rule the world. Few were persuaded, but none opposed them as fiercely as Velitharakan. Friends had advised him to lie low, but he would have none of it. How could he stand by, when the freedom of his church was at stake?

Months went by. The European friar was achieving a few cures of his own among the palace community, but the clout that the Portuguese pair wielded became apparent only when Velitharakan was suddenly informed, one day, that his services were no longer required in the palace. From that time on, he knew he was a marked man. He also knew that they would not let it lie there.

On the same night they made their decision, Velitharakan called his wife Thoyamma into his room. She sat on his bed and he sat on a chair opposite her. Suddenly, he got up and made for the door.

"It's alright, dear," said Thoyamma, calling him back. "I have had Hari check the grounds outside the window."

He came back to his chair but the grave expression on his face remained.

"I know what you are going to say, Tharakan, and I am not for it."

She can read me like a book, Tharakan thought to himself. (Tharakan was his name. The title Veli, which means big or chief, was only added on later in his old age and stayed with him and beyond into the legends that followed.)

"Come on, Thoyamma, be sensible. It's me they are after. You and the kids will be quite safe here with the servants. The jungle is not a safe place."

"Wherever you go, we will go and where you stay, I will stay, and there I will remain," said his wife with jaws set in firm resolve.

"Well then, get prepared. You know how to carry the jewellery. Don't forget to take the parchments."

The next few days were quite something like the calm before a storm. None of the usual visitors dropped in, the neighbourhood must have been enjoying a remarkable period of health, for not even patients came.

On the fourth evening, a trusted servant from the palace ran through the gate with a note scratched on palm leaf:

Dear Son,

If and when you get this letter, please understand that tomorrow, they plan to arrest you on trumped-up charges. Farewell.

Rohini Chedathy.

Rohini Chedathy lived in the palace. She was the king's grand-aunt by marriage and Thoyamma's grandfather's cousin. But for many reasons, she was closer to the Tharakans than blood could decree.

Quietly, the household fell to feverish activity. Tharakan had noticed that a few extra guards were posted on the main road leading west. The boats in the vicinity were commandeered by the palace on some pretext. By one in the morning, everything was ready.

The boathouse guards turned to see where the sound and lights were coming from. Soon, all the guards in the palace heard the commotion—running feet and then the flames. By the time they converged on the scene, people were already trying to put out the fire that had started in a haystack behind a cattle shed.

Unknown to them, a dark silent figure swam up the river towards the boathouse. With the last few powerful strokes, Hari was beside the nearest boat. An ordinary goods carrier, about five feet in breadth and four times that in length. He reached for the side, pulled himself out of the water and slid over the edge and onto the floor. He crawled back, found the knife in his waistband, drew it out and, with one neat stroke, cut the coir rope that moored the boat to the quay. He scrambled forwards, found the oars and dug gently into the water, struggling to get the boat alongside the shore. A few feet upstream, strong arms reached out, secured the bow and pulled it ashore.

Velitharakan and his family were waiting with the little baggage they could carry. A wooden box with brass beadings, a few leather bags, a cloth bag with dried beaten rice and jaggery. The precious metal they carried on themselves. Thoyamma had her jewellery sewed to the inside of her petticoat. The gold coins were strapped across Tharakan's chest, the silver coins stashed away in a small leather purse in his belt, alongside his old trusted dagger.

They clambered aboard. It was only a few weeks after the monsoons. The swollen river flowed briskly along its middle, but the waters near the shore flowed slower. It would have been easiest to go downstream but that was not their purpose. They had to get across the river to Kesavan Nair's place. Normally, they would have just punted straight across. Hari would stand on one end. Using long poles dug in against the floor of the river, his legs would push back on the boat and as the boat moved beneath him, he would start walking in place. As he pulled up his pole, another would start the whole process from the starboard side.

Today, they headed the boat upstream with difficulty. They slowly made their way for some six hundred feet and then made for the opposite shore. The force of the water took them over in a tangent, bringing them against the shore 150 feet downstream. But this was sufficiently away from the boathouse and the guards. Hari jumped out, waded to the shore and looped the rope about a bamboo stump. Soon, the boat was beached. They had to walk up to Kesavan Nair's house, about half a kilometre inland and east of the place where they landed. Tharakan had treated many of Kesavan Nair's family. Kesavan was especially grateful to him for the life of his son, Vasudevan, whom he had cured of a bad attack of jaundice.

Kesavan Nair had a living fence of betelnut palms around his property and as the group came up to it, dogs barked. At length, a servant approached them with a lighted palm-frond torch. The eerie shadows around him shortening and then lengthening as he passed. The yellow light fell on Tharakan and his compatriots. As he recognised Tharakan, the beginning of a smile crossed his face, but it quickly became an anxious mask. Without a word, he turned around and led them back towards the house with the dogs in tow. After a little commotion from the house, Kesavan Nair came out to greet them. His smooth face was creased with worried lines as he asked Tharakan, "What is the matter, Tharakan?"

Tharakan did not say a word as they were herded into the house. Once inside, they went to a corner by themselves and spoke in whispers for a few minutes, and then the household burst into action. A swift horse cart was harnessed, a strong small team assembled, with spare horses. They set out swiftly along the dirt road that reached eastwards into the mountains. To keep up the fearsome pace, horses were changed every ten kilometres. Dawn was breaking when they came to the last village on the edge of the forest. They stopped well outside the village, goodbyes were said and the cart and horsemen returned down the road they had just travelled. They were on their own now, as they plodded past the village and on to the small trail that led into the forest. His 21-year-old son, Thoman, led the way; Thoyamma and their 18-year-old daughter, Annamma, followed; Tharakan brought up the rear. No one gave them more than a casual glance as they passed by the village and on to the small path that made its way into the forest beyond.

An ordinary family on a pilgrimage to the Kola Devi forest shrine, they thought. This sacred temple lay some 15 kilometres up into the mountains. The trail was well worn by other feet that passed that way every day.

"Where are we going, Appa?" asked Thoman.

"You will see," said Tharakan enigmatically.

"If one of Kesavan Nair's servants squeals on us, it won't be safe for us to go to Kola Devi shrine, Appa."

"No one knows where we are going, son, and it's not to the Kola Devi shrine."

The morning was well on its way out and vertical shafts of sun came through directly above them as they climbed higher.

"Can't we rest a little, Tharakan?" pleaded Thoyamma. Even with frequent small stops, Thoyamma was winded.

"No dear, we will not be safe until we are off this path," said Tharakan as he urged them on. By mid-afternoon, perhaps 10 kilometres into the forest, they reached a huge tree by the right side of the path. About fifteen feet from the ground, its cylindrical trunk broadened as it came down and spread out on to the forest floor with massive wedge-shaped buttresses on every side. One of these had been partly chipped down flush to the floor where it crossed the path. Five people, with their arms stretched around, would have found it difficult to encircle it. From this foundation, it shot up a full seventy feet where its leafy branches towered above its neighbours'. On the right, there seemed to be a thinning of the undergrowth.

You would have thought that there might have been a long forgotten footpath there. Then again, it might be nothing; perhaps the wake of a herd of bison or wild boar. It was through this that Tharakan led them. Soon, they realised it was indeed a track, but one that nobody had used in a long time. Here, a thick vine bore machete marks where it had been cut;

there, a few stones were arranged to make a few crude steps. But the jungle was already surging in to erase these blemishes. Cobwebs stretched from side to side, and fresh branches grew across their path.

They trudged on for another half an hour and came upon a clearing where Thoyamma collapsed onto a patch of grass. She could go no further. The men put down their loads and found stones to sit on.

"Where will we rest for the night, Appa?" asked Thoman.

"Another 7 kilometres away, there is an ancient temple. I have been there more than once on my hunting trips. Once a year, for two whole days, it's crowded with worshippers, rites are performed and a feast is kept. For the rest of the year, it is left in the care of the rain, wind and forest."

After a good while, they set out southwards with renewed vigour. The path seemed to wind up and down, but generally took them higher, where the air around them grew crisp and cool. Soon, it was time to rest again.

This time, Tharakan found an outcropping of rock that he climbed. He found a comfortable spot and sat down facing the setting sun. He could see for miles around. Far away, he imagined he could almost see the faint coastline.

From where he sat, a sea of misty green rolled down and away into the west. In the distance to his right, he saw the Pamba River with the glint of the sun on its waters. It lay like a thin thread of molten silver and on its banks—the land they had called their own. God knew, he might never see it again.

He was awakened out of his reverie by Thoman calling him, telling him that everyone was adequately rested. He climbed down and resumed his trek, a few feet ahead of the rest; this time, his son came last. They spoke little; each one immersed in their own world of thought. After about an hour, all of them, and especially Thoyamma, felt they could not go much further. The light was also failing them.

"We are almost there now," encouraged Tharakan, as if he knew for sure. But it kept them going.

They came around a ridge and then they saw it in the distance. From where they were in the dark forest, it seemed bathed in a nest of amber light, as the last rays of the setting sun lit up the clearing where it stood. As they came nearer, they saw the twelve granite pillars that held up the stone roof. The dark sanctum was chiselled out of the rock beyond this. A banyan tree reached down protectively with thick roots as big as a man's thigh; one embraced a pillar, another ran around the granite roof. A stream ran on the bank above the temple on its southern side. Somebody had cut out a conduit on the rocks, which brought a tiny stream of water right up to the steps of the temple where it dribbled over a rocky spout, like a tap left open perpetually.

They had just enough light to help them gather twigs, dry leaves and bigger chunks of wood for fires they needed. Without this, they had no defence against the wilds. It was lucky, thought Tharakan, that the beasts respected fire, if not Man—the fire maker. Thoman climbed up to the roof of the temple, which would be their home for the night. They hoped it would not rain; nevertheless, they kept some dry firewood inside the courtyard of the temple. Tharakan helped the ladies up onto the roof, and they soon had a small fire in the furthest corner of the roof. The iron pot they had over the flames held just enough rice for the four of them. With flint iron and a little of their precious tinder, they made another fire in the western end, adjacent to the rock, before they settled down.

Thoman was supposed to keep guard as long as he could before waking up Tharakan. He sat awake, alone, after the others slept. He thought he heard noises in the woods above them. He wondered what they were. In time, fear gave way to weariness and he sank down and was soon lost in sleep. Below the rocks, the fire in the corner had gone out completely. The night was past its zenith when something woke Tharakan from his sleep. Perhaps it was the cold that swept in unchallenged by the dying embers. Or perhaps it was a presence that he felt. What he saw made him freeze. A pair of eyes was watching them. Tharakan knew that all it needed was one effortless leap to bridge the gap to the edge of the roof. He sat still for a moment, as he studied what was left of the fire next to them. Then, in one fluid movement, he grabbed a branch whose other end still held an angry glow and threw it at the creature. The eyes darted away and disappeared into the dark. From the amount of sound the creature made as it retreated, it must have been a big animal. Tharakan set about rekindling the fires on either side. He set on more wood and once satisfied, he lay down to sleep again.

Morning came with dim shades of black and white and the chattering of birds. The family ate rice flakes and jaggery that Thoyamma handed around. Tharakan set out for them the task that lay ahead for the day. They were to set out south through the forest until they crossed two small tributaries of the Pamba. These lay within five miles from where they were. Then would come a long and gruelling trek. At all times, they were to have the mountain peaks on their left. Tharakan and Thoman would take turns at leading the way and, using the only machete they had between them, clearing the undergrowth whenever necessary. This would bring them to one of the tributaries of the Achenkovil River by the end of the day.

Once they crossed over, they would be in the territory of the king of Pandalam. The king of Pandalam was vassal to the Kula Anandhana kings that ruled the great Venad realm from the river Achenkovil, all the way south to the tip of the subcontinent. They would be beyond the reach of the Samutiri of Cochin and the Portuguese. After that, they would feel safe to climb downwards from the ghats to meet whatever civilisation that came their way.

Things did not go quite as planned. They crossed the first two streams easily enough, but then the jungle seemed to go on and on. Leeches clung to their legs and thorns scratched and stung their arms. The day was all but over before they came to that welcome sight. The swift rivulet was deep in places and would have been difficult to cross on a moonless night, such as it was going to be. The short tropical twilight gave them just enough light to find a safe place to wade across. It was already dark when they flopped down on the other side.

After some discussion, they decided that it would be too dangerous to go on at night. They made a crude torch out of sticks, dry grass and leaves dipped in a little oil. With its light, they went up and down the shore. About fifty feet upstream, they found an overhanging granite cliff with huge boulders that blocked it from one side. It would have to do for the night.

They gathered their belongings into the deepest part of their shelter and set about the task of making a fire at the entrance. After they had eaten a meal of rice and mango pickle, they lay down to sleep with the ladies occupying the inside and the men lying across the entrance with their feet near the fire.

The next morning, they got their things together and followed the stream down from the mountain. At certain places, the drop was so precipitous they had to take long detours, but they managed to get back to the water. They heard a little commotion, but saw nothing. As they neared what they thought to be a village, dark figures suddenly rose from the bushes on either side of the path. They had their arrows loaded on their bows and these they pointed menacingly at the intruders. The only clothes they wore was a piece around their loins.

Tharakan spoke to them slowly and they seemed to relax. Presently, they lowered their weapons and motioned with their hands to follow them. They came to a big hut. Outside on a stool sat their headman-chief who, like them, was scantily clad, but his cool eyes held an openness that Tharakan guessed was in their favour. He spoke in a language similar to the Malayalam that Tharakan knew a little.

"Where do you come from? And what is your business here?" asked the chief.

"We have escaped from the king of Elumali, and we are going to Pandalam," said Tharakan respectfully.

At this, the old man smiled and the tension in the air seemed to ebb away. "We are their enemies too. They come on horses, make raids on us. You are safe with us."

Tharakan reached down, rummaged in his bag and came out with a knife he presented handle first to the chief. He also gave him two silver coins.

"You will stay with us today, and tomorrow, we will send you on your way." So saying, he gave orders. People picked up their luggage and escorted them to a nearby hut. That day, they feasted sumptuously on pork and millet gruel. Their legs got the rest they longed for and that night, their minds rested in secure sleep. Something they had not known for the last four days.

The next morning, they set off down the hillside, but this time in style. Their luggage was carried for them. They were led by men in front and a few brought up the rear guard behind them. By late afternoon, they reached the main road that would lead them to Pandalam. The tribals bid them farewell and headed back into the forest. The four of them watched them go and stood staring after them even after they were lost from sight.

"What nice people," said Tharakan, breaking the silence. The four of them were once more by themselves with their burdens. These they heaved onto their shoulders and walked down the road that led southwards to Pandalam.

Their first few days were spent at the common inn, until Tharakan could gain an audience with the king. The king patiently heard him out, but what made the difference was an old parchment—a certificate of apprenticeship with the famous Velankara Vaidyan. The king arranged for them to rent a house at the edge of town. Thoman, on his part, did a good job scouting around town and finding an Achen (padre) who welcomed them into his church.

Life slowly fell into a different but regular rhythm. They had to make new acquaintances. Now they had no servants at their beck and call. Tharakan walked to the palace court every morning, where the other apothecaries kept their distance and viewed him with suspicion and distaste. After a year or so, he slowly gained their grudging respect and even the friendship of a few. In the evenings, he would see a few patients that came to him.

His big chance came three years after they arrived in Pandalam. One of the king's trusted soldiers chanced upon a bison on a hunting trip with the king. The animal gored him severely in his chest and the man lay dying in his quarters. The other physicians had done all they could for him, and they reluctantly sent for Tharakan. He found the soldier in a sorry state. He was toxic and ran a high fever. His chest wound was small, ragged and unhealthy, discharging loads of pus and the wind burped out of it every time he exhaled.

"Not a good situation. It would be touch and go," Tharakan told the king, who urged him to try. Tharakan called for the things he needed. He had his trusted instruments cleaned and dried in the sun, and then gave the sufferer a strong dose of drink. Cautiously, Tharakan trimmed away all the unhealthy tissue, making the wound bigger. He heard again in his mind what his mentor had taught him decades ago: 'Don't be afraid to cut dead and unhealthy tissue.' That was what Velankara Vaidyan had said. 'Remember, good drainage is the key.'

He irrigated the wound and the large cavity it led into with copious amounts of vinegar. Turning the man towards the side of the wound, he allowed the fluid to drain out. The attendants were instructed to feed him well and nurse him in this position, changing his dressing at least thrice a day, after irrigation with vinegar. On the third day, the patient began to take a turn for the better. The wound cavity healed slowly from within, and in four months' time, the man was back in the king's service.

Five months from this time, the king called him into his throne room one day. "Tell me, Tharakan, you are living in a rented house."

"Yes, your majesty," said Tharakan respectfully, standing, bent a little at the waist and hands held in front of him.

"Would you like to have to your own piece of land?"

"At your pleasure, your majesty."

"There is a hilly region about thirty miles southwest of Pandalam," the king said. "I could give you a hundred acres there for a small sum paid into the treasury. Meet the secretary

Kunjalen tomorrow, and he will make out the deed and have some officials come with you to measure it over to you. There are some servants on the land who will be of help to you. There is one condition, Tharakan."

"Yes, your majesty," said Tharakan.

"Your services are to be available to the court at all times," said the monarch.

And that is where we are now, children. That is how Kottara began. Much is gone out of our hands, but we and our relatives still own a good part of it.

Kottara-Ammachy made as though to stop. And as though on cue, we children would demand loudly: "What happened to Hari, Ammachy?"

"You know it, you rascals," said Ammachy in a tone of false annoyance, for we knew she loved telling it as much we loved listening.

"We forgot, Ammachy," we fibbed.

"Very well, you will hear it again."

"Many years later, Tharakan heard that some new drugs were available with some Arab traders in Cochin. So he decided to make a trip to the port city. They were in comfortable circumstances now. Tharakan had already decided in his mind that he would try and find Hari if possible. That is how, on a clear cloudless night, someone came calling at Hari's gate. Hari went out to the servant that Tharakan had sent, who bent down, cupped his hands and whispered in his ear:

'Velitharakan is here and he would like a word with you.'

At the mention of the name, Hari's face froze and became pale, his palms instinctively came together below his chin.

After he had taken in what he heard, he went into the house and came back wearing a shirt.

His wife called out after him, "Who is that? What does he want? And where are you going at this time of the night?"

"I will be back soon," he said as he walked away briskly with the stranger. Tharakan was waiting by the river's edge. With the moon resting on the palm leaves above them, the two friends threw their arms around each other.

"The years have been kind to you, sir, you look much the same," gushed Hari.

"You look much older, Hari. How are you?" asked Velitharakan.

"Oh, Tharakan sir, we suffered much after you left," said Hari as they sat down on some stone steps.

"You should have seen that Portuguese priest's face, when they came the next morning and found the house empty. It went all tempestuous and red. And then his friend brought some of the guards. They tied me up around a tree and threatened to cut off my fingers if I did not tell them where you had gone. I told them the truth when I told them I did not know, and yet they beat me for it. They only let me go when my wife and children came and fell at their feet. For many days, I could not get up.

The children...they are grown now. The eldest started as a stable boy, but he is so good with the animals that now he is the caretaker of the horse farm. Somehow, we have managed to get by. After we left you that night at Kesavan Nair's place, we took the boat back across the river and then let it drift downstream. Next afternoon, they found the boat five miles downstream at Thoracad. They thought you might have escaped that way and sent soldiers to Thoracad and beyond, all the way to the coast. They never thought that you would go east into the dangerous mountains. They gave up in a few days, and then we were left alone. And somehow, we have managed to get by, sir. And often, we have wondered and worried about what became of you and the children."

"We have done well, Hari," said Velitharakan. "We have quite a bit of land down south; why you don't consider moving with your family? We will look after you well."

"No, sir," said Hari without hesitation. "We are comfortable here with people whom we know. Thank you for thinking about us."

"Very well; in that case, accept this that I have been keeping for you." So saying, he reached into his satchel and brought out a small pouch, which he handed over to Hari, who stared at him in disbelief.

"There are 10 sovereigns and 27 silver coins in it."

"Oh, now I can get my youngest daughter married," said Hari with trembling lips and eyelids that fought to contain tears.

"Oh, Hari!" said Velitharakan. "Is she that big? She was only knee high when we left."

After exchanging more news and then a hug, Velitharakan and his servants rode away into the night. And Hari was left all alone, holding the bag of coins close to his chest. He lived many years after this; long enough to dandle his grandchildren upon his knees. And that's what happened to Hari.

"And now, off to bed with the lot of you," Kottara-Ammachy said finally, as she finished the saga. But this command was lost on the younger cousins who were already fast asleep. They had to be carried onto the mats, where we

children slept on the floor, packed one against the other like pencils in a box.

"There are other stories, Usha," continued Suresh. "Stories about the struggle of the native Syrian church against attempts to assimilate them into the foreign Church of Rome and its Pope. But by and large, they stayed true to the Eastern Orthodox Church and never bowed to the dictates of Rome."

As Suresh thus finished Velitharakan's story, Usha let out a long sigh.

"You must be proud of your heritage, Suresh," said Usha as she rubbed his chest with her fingers.

"I used to be at one time, but now what's the use of it? Does it matter?" Suresh tightened his grip around her waist. "These things don't matter to me now, as much as you do, Usha," he declared as they snuggled close.

They knew it was well past ten o'clock, when they heard the last bus moaning and groaning its way up to Pachalur. The mist had cleared and beyond, in the valley, a few farm lights flickered faintly in the distance. An owl flapped its way over the eaves and reached up for the lowest branch of the giant pine tree. Then there was silence and as she lay her head upon his chest, the only sound that Usha heard was the thud of his heartbeat.

Chapter 20

The Last Sunset

The trouble started about two months after their first anniversary. Suresh developed a hacking disturbing cough that would not go away. One day, it became so bad that it kept him awake at night. Usha woke up hearing his cough go on and on. She brought him some cough syrup, rubbed his back and chest with Vicks. She even made him a cup of hot tea with lime and ginger in it. Whether it was this last concoction or the cumulative effect of everything, she did not know, but mercifully, he slept reasonably well after that.

The next day, she told Dr Ravikumar, who ordered a chest X-ray and some blood tests. The X-ray was normal and except for an ESR, which at 60mm/hr, was on the higher side, there was nothing in the results to cause alarm. Antibiotics were instituted and he was better in a few days. The respite lasted about ten days, after which it insidiously came back upon him. This time, he developed profuse sweating in the evenings that lasted into the night; so much so that even the sheet he lay on would become wet. Usha also noticed that he was not eating as heartily as he used to. People began to comment on how thin he had become.

This time, the X-ray revealed a little fuzziness in the apex of his left lung. But it would take more than that to prove he had tuberculosis. He was not putting out much sputum, so a gastric juice AFB (Acid Fast Bacilli) had to be done. Even for those patients who did not have much sputum, the little that they swallowed would stay in the stomach and since the bacilli were acid-resistant, a good number of them were often recovered from the gastric aspirate.

This was what they did. Sure enough, the slide showed the bright pink rod-like bacteria that stood out against the pale blue background. Dr Ravikumar himself went down to the lab to have a look. Everyone was relieved; at least now they knew what they were up against. Anti-TB treatment was initiated and gradually, he improved. However, since his breath could have bacilli, Suresh took some precautions at home. He wore a mask around the house, especially when talking to Jasmine. The little girl could hardly comprehend what was happening.

"What is wrong with Suresh Appa?" she would ask.

"Some bad germs have gotten into his lung," her mother told her.

"Can't Dr Ravikumar drive them out?" she would reply indignantly. "Can you see them, Amma?" she enquired.

"No, Thangam. They are so small you cannot see them with your eyes."

"If I could see them, I would chase them with my broom," Jasmine said resolutely.

"He will be better soon, Thangam," her mother reassured her.

Suresh decided to sleep in a separate room, just to be safe. Often, Usha would creep in beside him and at this, Suresh would reach for his mask. But before long, Usha would grab the mask and despite his protest, take it off and kiss him full on the mouth. "Usha, you should not be doing this," Suresh chided.

"What is there?" she replied defiantly. "I don't care if I get the disease, if that is the price I have to pay to be close to you."

"Think of Jasmine," he reminded her.

This seemed to make her ponder for a while. "She will be alright," she said, "there are people to look after her."

All this was difficult, but what vexed him the most was not being able to talk freely with Jasmine. In about a month's time, things changed. The mask was gone, his appetite increased and he put back most of his weight. Life was back to how it had been. Often, they would succumb to the call of Leech Valley. What lovely times they had there. They once went down to the lake and spend an idyllic evening by its waters. They did not see a stag that day, but the magic of the sunset and the hills around them made it a wondrous few hours. With the diagnosis of tuberculosis, Dr Ravikumar had started Suresh on antiretroviral therapy, the first that had become available. Even though all these drugs often made him sick, he plodded on with them.

A few weeks afterwards, late one evening, after Jasmine had gone to sleep, Suresh told Usha, "I discussed some matters with my parents the other day, especially since I started this disease before you did. I was happy for them to give the property in Kerala to my brother; anyway, you would not have been able to manage it, Usha. Some money they had in fixed deposits for me, I am transferring to our local bank here. I am putting my bank account and those deposits in both our names with an 'either or survivor' advice on it. You have to sign some papers for these things tomorrow. I have registered Dr Ravikumar as the nominee. In case anything should happen to both of us, then he will make sure the money goes to Jasmine."

"Don't say all those things, Suresh," said Usha at length. "It makes me feel sad. I don't want any money, I want you. Please don't give up," she pleaded.

Taking her in his arms, he gently caressed her forehead and scalp. "What makes you think I am giving up? I am just as much a 'prisoner of hope', as you are. But some of these money matters have to be dealt with, Usha, even if we were a normal couple."

Five months after its remission, the disease again raised its ugly head. The nagging cough and low-grade fever returned. This time, the chest X-ray was unambiguous. The infection had eaten away a good part of the left lung, and now the apex of the other lung was beginning to corrode. This in spite of the multidrug regimen he was on. After discussion, it was decided that Dr Ravikumar would contact one of his seniors, who was a professor of medicine at Sevur medical college. After a discussion over the phone, Dr Ravikumar told Suresh, "Professor Sheshadiri wants you to go over to Sevur, to do some investigations that are not available elsewhere."

It was decided that they would drive down; but they had to get a driver because Suresh was not well enough to drive. They drove down the hills and beside the lake. Usha gazed at its shining surface and found Suresh doing the same. He even craned his head back to get one last look, before the car took them beyond sight. They looked at each other and smiled knowingly. "We will soon be back," Usha assured him. It was a tiring journey that took almost 9 hours, and they were glad that they had left Jasmine behind with her grandparents.

Suresh had a classmate who was on the faculty, from whom he had had a casual invitation. However, they preferred not to disturb him and so stayed at a hotel just outside the campus. Usha was at first overwhelmed by the tall buildings and all the technology, but she soon was oblivious to these, as she saw to Suresh's every need. She smiled weakly at the few acquaintances that Suresh introduced her to.

Dr Sheshadiri saw him the very next day. The sputum was positive for AFB (Acid Fast Bacilli) and so they decided to do a sputum AFB culture. Since the tubercle bacilli multiplied almost twenty-five times slower than ordinary organisms, the result of this study would be available only after two months. In a few days, all the tests were over and Suresh was started on the second line of drugs. They then set out on their arduous journey back. Nightfall robbed them of a chance to have a good look at their beloved lake once more.

In a few weeks, Suresh felt better. The cough had retreated, and he was eating a little better. But then the improvement seemed to plateau out. The final culture report came a few weeks before their second wedding anniversary. It showed that the bacterium was resistant to all drugs, except one that he was already on. Even though the cough was almost gone, he was not his usual self. Dr Sheshadiri wanted to see him again, so they made the trip back to Sevur.

This time, they took more cultures; they found a few nodes, and so took a biopsy, hoping it would be something else that they could treat. Finally, they were told to wait for the results and unless they found something very different, there was nothing else that could be done. Suresh was silent for much of the journey back. Usha tried to lift his spirits. "They might find some new drugs soon, Suresh. It will be alright." This time, they had started early and so, they could see the lake, and even stopped a while on their way up. This brought back the cheer to his face.

Suresh saw patients at the hospital for a few weeks after they returned. After this, it became too much for him. He moved around the house with difficulty and he lost even more weight. But somehow, he had weathered the blues and was much more cheerful. He was not able to carry Jasmine any longer. She would sit by his side and he would tell her tales through his mask. He would tickle her and she would giggle with reckless abandon until she became breathless. His time with Jasmine was restricted, but it became the highlight of his day and he waited for her. It was not long before Suresh became tired quickly. He could not tell her stories any longer. He would lie back with a smile, which was all he could offer.

Over time, Suresh's appearance changed bit by bit. He became pathetically thin; his skin that had become much darker, clung to his bones with nothing much in-between. His cheeks had hollowed out. His eyes seemed larger than life, as they looked out from the depths of their sockets. Every so often, a violent spasmodic cough would convulse his whole body. The child did not seem to mind all these frightful changes that were coming over her Suresh Appa. At their daily appointments, she was there for him, and he for her.

Music was one thing Suresh still enjoyed. On many a day, Usha would come home to find him with his eyes closed, the old Panasonic cassette player by his side and his favourite song wafting out from his room and spreading gently through the house.

Soft as the voice of an angel, breathing a lesson unheard

Hope with a gentle persuasion, whispers a comforting word

Wait till the darkness is over, wait till the tempest is done

Hope for the sunshine tomorrow; after the darkness is gone.

Weeping may tarry for the night, but joy comes in the morning.

Dr Ravikumar visited Suresh almost every day; every few days, he would frantically ring up Dr Sheshadiri to find out if there was something new by way of treatment. The results had not found anything that would make a change for Suresh. It was two months since his last visit to Sevur. By now, Suresh could hardly walk and lay inertly in bed. Each laboured breath was an effort. A cylinder of oxygen was moved from the hospital and this seemed to make it a little easier for him. A few days before the end, he somehow found the strength for a short excursion. With Usha and another friend supporting him, and another bringing along the oxygen tank, he dragged himself, mask and all, to the veranda that overlooked the Parapalar valley. Here he sat on a chair for a few minutes, looking at the clouds, the twittering birds and the green vale below them, with the distant lake at its furthest end. The body of water looked so small, but its blue shining surface stood out like a magnificent brooch on a dull carpet of green. Suresh looked up at Usha and a faltering but courageous smile lit up his face. Then he indicated with his hands that he wanted to go back inside. By this time, he could not get up. Fortunately, yet another friend had also dropped by and between the four of them, they carried his light body to his bed. "Thank you, thank you," he whispered in a voice that could hardly be heard.

Usha was on leave for the last ten days to look after Suresh and was by his side most of the time. It happened one evening. It was almost eight o'clock. His face was a mask and each arduous breath came with increasing difficulty. Someone sent word for Dr Ravikumar. However, just after he entered the house, he was called away for a delivery. As he walked back to the hospital, the doctor thought to himself about the vagaries of life. Soon, he would deliver a baby and a new life would make its start; and yet, a few metres behind him, Suresh lay dying.

One journey would be beginning, while another would find its end.

Meanwhile, Usha climbed onto Suresh's bed and held him in her arms. Her left hand went around his shoulders and he lay half upon her chest, with his head resting on her shoulders. Her right hand held his left hand, palm to palm, and Usha felt an almost imperceptible squeeze from his hand. Thus they stayed until it was all over. Each breath became shallower as the candle of life burned down to its end. Then the flame rose with one last laboured heave and went out altogether. The long silence that followed was gradually intruded upon by Usha's subdued sobs that seemed to have no ending.

Usha's parents and a few of the staff stood around the bed, and soon Dr Ravikumar joined them. About a month earlier, when Suresh had known that the end was inevitable, he had convinced Usha and Dr Ravikumar to make the funeral as plain and quiet as possible. He had even given it in writing. He did not want a coffin, for he felt it was a waste. He wanted his body to be wrapped in a large reed mat, fastened by ropes and lowered into the ground. His parents had offered to take him home a few months earlier. But he had refused. This was where he belonged and this was where he would be. They had been informed earlier that day and were on their way. They would arrive in time for the funeral the next morning.

They buried him early the next morning, soon after his parents arrived and before the work in the hospital began; that was how he had wanted it. When the body was in the house, a few staff and some patients had brought garlands that they had put around his neck.

Finally, after his parents had come and just before they took him out, they removed the garlands and wrapped the body in the mat and tied it firmly. The body was taken to the eucalyptus grove across the road from the children's park. After they had sung a song, the mat with its contents were slowly lowered into the grave. Between sobs, Usha threw in the first fistfuls of sod. Then she turned around and leaned into the arms of Suresh's mother who was by her side. The two women hung to each other for many minutes, each one drenching the other's shoulders with the waters of grief that fell freely from their eyes. The workers shovelled in the earth and a simple concrete slab was placed over the top of the grave.

The first few days after Suresh's death were not easy for Usha, and Jasmine suffered with her. The little girl went with her on her visits to the grave every day, for a whole week.

Ravikumar and Malathi were a constant support. At the end of the week, they called her home one evening and they sat talking until nightfall.

"Usha," said Ravikumar during the course of the visit, "I don't think you need to go to the grave every day. I don't think it's good for you, or for Jasmine. You know that Suresh is not there. He is in a much better place. He would not have wanted it. If you think we are going to forget him, be assured that this will not be the case. We are planning a marble tombstone for him, something simple."

"Thank you," Usha mumbled gratefully. From that day, Usha stopped her daily visits to the site. There were many who called to comfort her, brought her food and helped in myriad ways.

The thing that made the most difference was her trip to Leech Valley. Jasmine had been badgering her for days and finally, about three weeks from the funeral, she gave into the child's repeated requests—but she had gone reluctantly and sullenly. But then, it had made a difference and become one more giant step towards her recovery. A week from that time, Usha was back at work.

Chapter 21

Return to Leech Valley

It was a Saturday afternoon in February; many months had gone by. That morning, Dr Ravikumar had brought up the matter regarding Usha's further study, and her going for a post-certificate bachelor's degree in nursing at Sevur. She said she would think about it. Now she had Suresh's letter in her hand.

She had taken it out again, not to cry over it like in the first few months since his departure, but this time to get the assurance and guidance that she needed. She had not read it in more than a month. Smudged with many tears, the foolscap page already looked old, but today, she would be brave and not add to these stains.

My dearest Usha,

If Ravikumar has given you this letter and you are reading these words, it means that I am well on my way.

Look after Jasmine. Every day, give her a kiss from me, a kiss from 'Suresh Appa'. And if she asks you where I am, tell her I have gone to a better land where there are no mosquitoes, and butterflies live forever. Tell her that it will be a happy ending after all. And as for you, Usha, don't grieve or think too much about me. I am doing just fine. Usha, there has to be a better place, where cruelty and evil have no entrance. There has to be a better place, where the world is kind to our mistakes and true love gives life immortality. I will be there.

Get on with living, Usha. Join the post-certificate bachelor's nursing course and even a masters. Remember, our love will never end; it's big enough for time and eternity. We will meet again soon. Until then, goodbye, my love.

Your own Suresh. Still and always with you—a prisoner of hope.

By the time she finished the letter, her resolutions had given way and the tears started to flow, but she made a quick recovery and sat there for some time, thinking about how she would cope in Sevur. She felt intimidated when she remembered the hectic, bustling pace of life she had witnessed there. But this was what Suresh would have wanted her to do, as she finally made up her mind.

Just then, Jasmine walked into the room, rubbing her sleepy eyes. "Let's go to Leech Valley, Amma," she begged. This time, Usha gladly agreed. *Suresh would have wanted them to do just that*, she thought, *he would have wanted to see them happy, or perhaps he was watching them at this very time.*

So the two set out, crossed the village and its dirty streets, then up and over the top of the ridge on the other side.

They strolled through the cottonwood glade, waded through the tall grass and onto the wide meadow, which was as mystical as ever. The rocks, wet with a late morning's shower, glistened in the bright sun. As usual, the place seemed to always have some butterflies for Jasmine to chase. Then down they went into the forest and soon found the steps cut into the rock. The bright blue over them gradually turned to brilliant emerald green. Soon, they forgot about the outside world as the place wove its magic around them. Jasmine went for the stream and found her usual niche in her favourite child-sized waterfall. When she had had enough of a dip, she played around trying to catch a few minnows darting here and there in a small pool among the boulders. Then she tickled a crab with a twig until it retreated into its den.

"Amma, how do these stick insects float on water?" she asked her mother who was lying back against a rock with her feet in the water. She had brought Suresh's Walkman along with her and had its headphones over her ears so she didn't hear her daughter the first time. "Amma, are you listening?" the child asked again, louder this time. "How do these stick insects float on water?"

"It's because they are so light, dear," her mother replied. The child seemed to be satisfied with this explanation and went back to her play. She had soon collected a small mound of pebbles with which she was trying to make some sort of structure that looked like an altar. In time, Usha brought out the packet of chocolate chip cookies, which was Jasmine's favourite. Together, they munched on the square-shaped delicacies, until it was all gone. Then Jasmine returned to the water and resumed playing with the pebbles she had collected, and Usha went back to her music.

Being February, the evening came on them early.

"It's time to go, Thangam," she called out to her daughter. Jasmine quickly got out of the water and her mother towelled her dry and soon got her into dry clothes. They collected their belongings and climbed from the water's edge onto the sand and up a steep slope that soon took them to the steps cut into the granite. They climbed hand in hand. Behind them, Leech Valley lay silent, except for the brook that churned on, laughing its way over the boulders and into the dark woods below.

Postscript

A few years after Suresh's demise, new antiretroviral drugs with fewer side effects became available. Dr Ravikumar made sure that Usha was one of the first to receive them. She went on to do her bachelors, and then her masters' degree. She became a prominent resource person for the national AIDS control organisation.

At the turn of the century, a special international amnesty, granted to Sri Lankan refugees in India, gave them permission to visit the island nation that once had been their home. Murali and she made the trip back and met some of their relatives. Things had changed. Their house was still standing but it had been made a store for a government-owned enterprise.

Usha lived many years after that. Long enough to see Jasmine married. Suresh was never far from her thoughts during the day, and at night, in her dreams, they walked side by side.